FOREVER DEFEND

FOREVER DEFEND

THE KURTHERIAN GAMBIT™ BOOK 17

MICHAEL ANDERLE

DISRUPTIVE IMAGINATION®

DON'T MISS OUR NEW RELEASES

Join the LMBPN email list to be notified of new releases and special promotions (which happen often) by following this link:

http://lmbpn.com/email/

LMBPN Publishing
PMB 196, 2540 South Maryland Pkwy
Las Vegas, NV 89109

Version 2.02, March 2023
eBook ISBN: 978-1-64971-584-5
Print ISBN: 978-1-64202-059-5

FOREVER DEFEND TEAM

Beta Editor / Readers

Bree Buras (Aussie Awesomeness)
Timothy Cox (The Myth) - working on it ;-)
Tom Dickerson (The man)
S Forbes (oh yeah!)
Dorene Johnson (US Navy (Ret) & DD)
Dorothy Lloyd (Teach you to ask...Teacher!)
Diane Velasquez (Chinchilla lady & DD)

JIT Beta Readers

Alex Wilson
Erika Daly
Melissa OHanlon
Kimberly Boyer
Brent Bakken
John Findlay
John Raisor

Paul Westman

Joshua Ahles

Keith Verret

Thomas Ogden

Peter Manis

Sherry Foster

Kelly ODonnell

Micky Cocker

Thanks to our JIT Readers for this Version

Dave Hicks

Veronica Stephan-Miller

Deb Mader

Diane L. Smith

Rachel Beckford

James Caplan

Peter Manis

Kerry Mortimer

Dorothy Lloyd

Timothy Cox (the myth)

If I missed anyone, please let me know!

Original Editors
Stephen Russell
Lynne Stiegler

This version edited by
Lynne Stiegler

Thank you to the following Special Consultants
for FOREVER DEFEND

Jeff Morris - US Army - Asst Professor Cyber-Warfare, Nuclear Munitions (Active)

To Family, Friends and
Those Who Love
To Read.
May We All Enjoy Grace
To Live The Life We Are
Called.

PROLOGUE

They say that history is written by the victors, and they are right. The reason is completely logical. Those that lost aren't around to write anything.

As the dead can't write from beyond the grave.

The latest and most impressive ship built in the Yollin's new military shipyards slowly and smoothly slid from its moorings as hundreds who watched from nearby ships raised their hands in salute.

The Empress stared in silence as the massive new ship slid into place next to her official royal in-system Transport Pod. The doors opened to allow the Empress' transport to enter the ship's cavernous bay.

It wasn't long before those in the Transport Pod disembarked and made their way to the bridge, which was built in the center of the massive vessel.

Bethany Anne stopped outside of the bridge to look at the dark, six-foot-wide, gray stone monument that had so many names chiseled into it. She reached up and rubbed her hand across a few. Turning, she wiped a tear from her cheek as she took the last few steps to the bridge, the doors opening automatically for her.

She nodded to those standing around waiting for her arrival. The

1

MICHAEL ANDERLE

Yollin head of the shipyard, those that worked to make this ship useable by both humans and Yollins, and those who had been employed on the massive electronic infrastructure.

Necessary to house the new Intelligence.

She walked straight to the captain's chair, turned, and sat down. The Shipyard Master looked over to the Minister of Defense, who winked back at him.

"This is Empress Bethany Anne of the Etheric Empire. Show yourself." She commanded.

A face, a replica of the Empress herself, slowly brightened into view on the front screens, her eyes flaring red. Some of those on the bridge were shocked to see the face of the Empress on the screens.

Their Empress, however, smiled in satisfaction. "Hello, ArchAngel. It's damned good to have you back."

The face on the screen looked around at everyone standing on her bridge. Then, she looked at the woman seated in the captain's chair and smiled.

"Hello, Mother."

There was a second where no one even breathed, as the AI continued, "This is the Leviathan-class Superdreadnought ArchAngel II. I have been commanded to protect the Etheric Empire by Empress Bethany Anne. All lockdown protocols on this ship have not yet been implemented. Does the Empress command I enact lockdown protocols?"

"No, I do not," Bethany Anne replied.

"Lockdown protocols are not activated. Leviathan-class Superdreadnought ArchAngel II is now fully operational and will fight all who attack the Etheric Empire until Victorious...or dead."

Bethany Anne smiled, her eyes red in memory of those whose names graced the stone outside the bridge. "Good, it's time you kick some more ass, ArchAngel."

Yollin System, Ten Years After Straiphus Rebellion

It had been ten years since the battle that had seen the original

2

ArchAngel reduced to so much scrap in another system. The Etheric Empire had grown in influence, power, and prestige. Unfortunately, what they *hadn't* grown in was knowledge of where Kurtherians might be hiding.

In the intervening time, those who were aware of the rumors of the human Empress discounted them. While she was very commanding in person, most didn't believe the stories the humans told in the bars, cities, and outer reaches.

Or the few videos she still permitted to float around.

That was about to change.

CHAPTER ONE

Pirate Ship _F'zeer_

The vessel on his screen was neither sleek nor svelte. In fact, if you looked closely at it, you might have called it a large bathtub in space.

It was ugly, but it wasn't small. The potential value of its contents was significant enough that even a small piece of them would be worth a couple weeks of gluttony on one of the pirate worlds.

Or on some of the seedier space stations that existed in most systems.

Brell, the captain of the pirate ship _F'zeer_, stayed the course as he watched the passive viewing instrumentation's data. For the last five years, those damned humans had made his job more and more difficult in the outer reaches of the Eubos, Straiphus, and Gorn systems.

First, he had been forced to give up his minor slave-trading efforts in Eubos. Then black-marketeering had largely become unprofitable in Straiphus. Now the rumor was that just a bit over thirty days ago, a set of news torps had shot into the Gorn

System, warning that the Etheric Empress' Rangers would be extending their damned reach into that locality.

For the good of all citizens.

Well, Brell thought, *it wasn't for the good of his clan. So apparently, the Etheric Empire didn't consider his kind citizens. Which was fine.*

He didn't want to be a part of their special clique anyway.

"Captain?" First Officer Wig turned to look at him from his seat a step lower on the bridge. "Permission to engage?"

Brell hadn't found any ships following the massive commercial vessel, and he had his team try, and try hard. His ship had placed large emitters on the other side of the trajectory the ship was expected to fly. If there had been a cloaked vessel lying in wait, they would have known about it.

"Go," he commanded finally and reached for his logbook. They might be pirates, but that didn't mean they ran a loose ship.

If you weren't a good businessman, being a pirate could be an excellent way to lose your life.

Commercial Transport *Kleen II* Out of Yollin Territory, Heading Toward Gorn Station 2215

The bridge of the ship was calm, the Yollins reviewing their consoles glanced up from time to time, but everything had been calm so far.

"Captain, we just got hit by active sensors!" Radar Operator D'ber yelled.

"Dammit." Captain M'rin clicked his mandibles and locked his four legs to his couch. "I had hoped the memos would do the trick."

"You were hoping the memos would do the trick because you lost a hundred credits to me," the steward commented as he placed a drink and a stim pill next to the captain.

Captain M'rin turned to look at his steward, who had a small

6

gleam in his eye. "Well, it might be that, or it might be those idiots." He pointed toward the main screen on the bridge, which was now plotting the location of the suspected pirate vessel. "Might just blow some holes in us instead of boarding."

Steward A'nick sniffed and shrugged his shoulders, a completely human movement. "We all have a time to die, Captain."

"Well," M'rin turned toward the screen as he waited for the next step in this dance, "if it is all the same to you, I don't intend to do that anytime soon."

A'nick nodded. "I doubt our passengers wish to perish either."

Captain M'rin punched a button. "This is the captain speaking. We have a possible pirate heading in our direction. All secondary personnel, go to your safety zones and remain there until we sound the all-clear or call you for support services. Please be aware that decompression might occur. Take all necessary precautions."

He clicked off the call button and blew out a breath of air. "Okay, patch me into Section Two-Two-One."

Section Two-Two-One, Mid-Spine, Commercial Transport
K'leen II

Ryu held his hands straight out, palms down. His face was a study in composure, eyes unblinking. If you didn't know any better, you might think him a 3D-printed statue.

The set of hands beneath his barely flinched, but the change was enough for him to pull on the Etheric and move his hands out of the way. The female's hands sliced through the air where his had been a microsecond before.

"DAMMIT!" Tabitha hissed as she missed Ryu's hands. She had decided that he would use a straight-back exit strategy for this game of slaps, but the little bastard had pulled his hands in two separate directions.

"That is officially seven misses in a row, Kemosabe," the Japanese man told the Hispanic woman. "You now owe me seventy pushups."

"*Gott Verdammt!*" Tabitha eyed him. While she technically outranked him, he was still one of her two mentors and counselors. She had learned a lot in the last few years, but she would never catch up to the knowledge Ryu had acquired in the hundreds of years he'd been alive.

"Double or nothing?" she asked, smiling at Ryu in an attempt to sell it better.

He raised an eyebrow but shook his head. "No."

"Double-dammit!" Tabitha groaned as she dropped to the floor. "This is *so* fucking embarrassing."

"You need the exercise anyway, Tabitha," Ryu consoled her. "Why is it that doing the exercises is a problem?"

"It's exercise," she grumped as she started doing her reps of forty pushups. "That's all I should have to say. Hell, it's not chocolate or sex, so why would you even have to ask?"

The speaker came on. "This is the captain speaking. We have acquired suspected pirate activity. What is your command, Ranger Tabitha?"

Tabitha spoke up as she kept pushing up, dropping down, and then pushing back up. "Mind your Ps and Qs, Captain M'rin, and tell me where the fucking exit on this ship is. Or at least where they are going to come aboard."

Pirate Ship *F'zeer*

Captain Brell nodded to his communications specialist. "Put me on tight-beam to the *K'leen II*."

Brell was hoping that he... Yes! As he was waiting for the communication video link to connect and steady, he heard that the captain of the other ship was a male Yollin. He wondered if he could get the captain to defect from the Etheric Empire and bring his ship along for the ride. "This is Captain Brell of the *F'zeer*. Who am I addressing?"

The video didn't show. "This is the captain of the *K'leen II* out of the Yollin System, part of the Etheric Empire. To what do I owe this honor?"

Captain Brell released the transmit button so his voice wouldn't travel back to the Yollin ship.

"Honor?" He looked around his bridge and heard the chuckles he had anticipated. He pushed the button to talk. "*K'leen II*," he started, leaning into the mic, "you will slow down, and we will board your ship. We are going to review your manifests and decide on the most valuable tribute to take for allowing you to continue on your way."

Brell exhaled dramatically. "And unfortunately, Captain, you and your command staff will be offered the opportunity to join us here on the *F'zeer* as our short-term guests. And by guests, I really mean slaves. Now, if you don't like this choice, I would like to offer you the chance to join our navy. With such a handsome ship as the *K'Leen*, you and your command staff would be celebrated upon your arrival."

Brell muted the mic once more to talk with his own people. "Of course," Brell continued, winking to his First Officer, "everyone else on the ship will be either sold into slavery or spaced. Probably half his command staff will also be sold or spaced." Brell shrugged his shoulders. "But what he doesn't know probably won't affect this next decision, anyway."

The *K'leen II*'s captain's voice came back over the speaker, his annoyance evident. "*F'zeer*, you can kiss my Yollin ass. There is no way I will give up my ship to you useless Skaine bastards."

SKAINE

ART BY ERIC QUIGLEY

Brell punched the button. "Why are you suggesting we are Skaines, Captain?" He released the button and continued speaking to those on his bridge, "Not that you are wrong. I'm just curious."

The answer didn't make him any happier. "Because," the *K'leen II's* captain replied, "the Etheric Empire has scan data on many of the Skaine ships, and we have a ninety-eight-point-seven percent match to your ship, real name *Kurket*. This information has already been sent to our home office, and from there, it will be sent to Central Defense Command."

Section Two-Two-One, Mid-Spine, Commercial Transport *K'leen II*

"*Gott Verdammt!*" Tabitha hissed as she listened in on the conversation. "He's going to fuck up my opportunity here."

Ryu shook his head. "The goal, Kemosabe, is to protect the transport and the assets and reduce piracy. Not to kill every Skaine in existence."

Tabitha looked at her Tonto. "Well, those might be the written commands, but I received a memo." Tabitha's focus went distant, her memory still haunted by the fateful death of one of her own at the hands of the Skaines.

"Yes?" Ryu looked sideways at his boss. Memos had become digital voodoo with Tabitha. The more outrageous they were, the more believable it was that they were real. How she alone received them in foreign systems so she could point to them when she needed to, he wasn't sure.

Ryu and Hirotoshi had tried questioning Achronyx, only to have him tell them he didn't have the information they sought.

Both knew Tabitha had enough programming prowess to accomplish such sneakiness as the memos but had figured she would have engaged Achronyx's assistance in any such endeavor.

So far, they had gotten nowhere.

"Yes, the memo stated that the Skaines would be dealt with 'in a manner commensurate with their previous behavior.'" She focused on him once more. "Their previous behavior was murder, piracy, and slavery, all punishable by death sentences in the Etheric Empire."

Her voice dropped down a little as she flashed him a smile and shrugged her shoulders. "Sucks to be them."

QBBS *Meredith Reynolds*, Yollin System

The main meeting room, also called the 'throne room' when Bethany Anne wasn't around, was filling with dignitaries from three different alien groups.

The Ixtalis had come back. After their first attempts had gone fantastically wrong—using spy technologies to capture information about the humans and/or trying to get them to trade for their gems—they had sent a second trade mission.

The second mission had never even made it onto the *Meredith Reynolds*. They had held one video meeting with Bethany Anne during which the Ixtali legate had demanded that the Etheric Empire engage in trade. Bethany Anne had simply looked at the legate on the screen, then turned her head to speak to someone off-screen. "Tell ArchAngel I wish her to remove a ship from my presence."

The Ixtali legate's ship had made it back through the commercial Gate damned quickly when the Leviathan-class super-dreadnought on their sensors had started moving in their direction.

The Yollin ships waiting in the third ring to go through the Gate had snickered as the Ixtalis negotiated with a freighter captain to exchange places in the queue to facilitate their departure.

This third time, the Ixtalis had sent a bigger delegation, complete with two high-ranking officers. Surprisingly, they had asked politely for a chance to speak with Bethany Anne. No trade required, no technological efforts to subvert anything.

No one on the *Meredith Reynolds* had believed them, but so far, the Ixtalis had acted in good faith.

Her first meeting with them would be held this morning.

Her second meeting of the day was with a group of tall blue bipedal beings that reminded her of light blue basketball players. Well, ones with non-human noses, anyway.

Her final meeting looked to be the most interesting. This group, the Yaree, was an alien version of Earth Gypsies who searched the stars. The nicest thing you could call them were archeologists. The worst? Possibly grave robbers.

Either way, this delegation supposedly wanted to pay tribute to the new Yollin Royalty. Bethany Anne had a bet on the side with TOM over what they really wanted. ADAM was holding the money and would decide who had won the bet.

The large Yaree ship, a sphere with a large pyramidal-looking structure jutting from the back, held off from the QBBS *Meredith Reynolds* at the coordinates provided by the humans.

Inside, Delegate Tomthum reached up to his right eyestalk and scratched it halfway down. He had three eyestalks, all of them able to turn in different directions. Presently, he was looking at the screens ahead of them.

"Do not," he told the other three on the bridge with him, "move us from this location."

The shallow eyestalk-bobs he received from the captain and crew provided the Delegate with comfort. This was the opportunity his people had waited on for generations.

YAREE

ART BY ERIC QUIGLEY

Most aliens did not know the true history of the Yaree. Considered nothing more than wandering hucksters or thieves in better quality space ships, they were scorned and reviled in bars all over the systems.

No one had been tasked with sharing the true story of their people with an outsider for over two generations.

This small group had been tagged at the last Festival of Assembly to seek out a meeting with the leader or leaders of the people who had taken out the rumored Kurtherian leader of the Yollins.

They were directed to divulge the true story to this alien Empress.

Or kill her to keep the truth hidden until another race might show themselves to be trustworthy.

Most doubted they had the time to find another to help them if this group failed.

City of Bouk, Planet Straiphus, Straiphus System

The bar wasn't dingy, not as bars in Bouk went. The large Yollin ex-mercenary wiped down his drinking establishment's tables and kicked over one of the few couches that seated the four-legged Yollin elite who would occasionally come into the bar.

Many of the owner's patrons enjoyed using the long couch. If it hadn't been such an expensive proposition and a waste of good floor space, R'yhek would have just purchased couches and replaced all his normal chairs with the more expensive furniture.

That would have shown he didn't have an issue with the new rules, elite seating for everyone!

He stood up from cleaning a table and reached back to shove his carapace into place. The damned thing had been blasted out of position in a different life, and it would occasionally slip when he bent over to clean.

By Yoll, it *hurt* when it did that.

He rubbed his mandibles in thought and eyed the space. He rarely, if ever, was full-up in here. He looked around.

Maybe if he took out a third of his tables to give him extra floor space, he could upgrade all the chairs?

The door to his bar opened, and he turned to see who was

entering this early in the afternoon. It was usually someone who had pulled a double shift and was just getting off work.

His eyes widened in surprise when he had to look down, and then down some more, to see who had entered.

The alien seemed tiny.

And it was human.

QBBS *Meredith Reynolds*, Yollin System

Bethany Anne looked at John, who was blocking the exit from her rooms. "You have *got* to be shitting me!" she fumed, trying her best to shoot lasers at him from her eyes.

TOM chose that moment to pay attention to what she was doing.

That's not going to work

Why the hell not? I can throw fire-fucking-balls!

You have also figured out eighteen other neat tricks. But attenuating light at the intensity of a laser isn't going to do your eyeballs any good. You will spend all your time in pain while you heal them.

Bethany Anne huffed. *You're a damned party-pooper.*

"Nope," John returned simply. He held out the large case with one arm. She knew it was heavy as shit, and she considered standing there until he either had to use two hands or let it drop.

Then she could make a break for it and run around him on the right, bouncing off the wall to get through the door. Or she could just walk through the Etheric and bypass him.

But that wasn't how these games were played.

"You can stand there," John told her, "and make me hold this all afternoon." He smirked when her eyes told him he had guessed her thoughts. "But let me inform you that this box isn't very heavy, and I recently had Jean add a new feature to my armor."

Bethany Anne raised an eyebrow and bent at her waist to peer under his outstretched arm. "Sonofabitch," she murmured. She took a step forward and reached out to feel along his side and underarm before confirming with the man who was staring down at her with a grin on his face. "Your arms lock?"

He nodded.

She looked closer at the geometric designs in the armor. "What is this fucking design?" She traced it with her index finger to figure it out. The armor plates linked, and yet each seemed to slide beneath the next.

"It's something TOM came up with." She gazed back up at John, who winked as he told her, "It involved *lots* of math. I just zoned out."

"That figures," Bethany Anne grumped as she reached for the case. John released it before she got a hand on it, but she snagged the handle before it could fall six inches. She pivoted and turned back to her quarters, asking over her shoulder, "What color?"

John lowered his arm. "Why, your favorite, of course!"

"Hey!" she protested as she turned to close the door to her bedroom, holding the box. "No one can see me bleed wearing this color!"

The door closed, and John grinned. "Well, yours or anyone else's blood, anyway." He looked around the personal meeting room for the Empress of the Etheric Empire and raised an eyebrow, then walked the fifteen paces to the cooling unit and opened it.

There were at least four types of beer, including a couple of Yollin beverages, in the top third of the unit.

The bottom two-thirds was filled with red bottles with a completely (mostly) legal swoosh along the side. Bethany Anne had said she doubted the Coca-Cola company could bring her to court in another galaxy for trademark infringement, and besides, it helped her remember what home was like.

She had her Cokes in the lower part of the fridge because cold air was heavier than warm air and she liked her Coke just this side of frozen.

He didn't find one Pepsi in the bunch. He closed the door and smiled. Ecaterina must not have been in here lately.

A moment later, his Empress came out of her room decked in a blood-red suit of armor that gripped her body like latex. He was surprised to see that her boots had two-inch heels. "What is that shit?" he murmured.

When he looked up, she winked at him. "I told Jean if she didn't figure out how to give me heels, she could keep the next suit of armor. Apparently," she looked down at her feet, "this armor can be manipulated to be flat for fighting or have heels."

She started toward the door. "What else can it do?" she asked as John Grimes, her friend, guard, and presently amused guy shook his head and followed her out of the suite.

CHAPTER TWO

Pirate Ship _F'zeer_

Captain Brell examined the two officers responsible for the boarding action. He pointed to the Skaine on his left. "Officer Strill, you are responsible for making sure the bridge is under our control. Shoot one of the bridge crew as an example. Be certain you point out something he has done wrong before you blast his head off."

"What if they haven't done anything wrong, sir?" Strill asked. "I know we are supposed to find something, but…"

Brell wanted to slap his officer. Unfortunately, Strill was the most competent to accomplish this operation he had available. His previous boarding officer had died in a poorly-executed bridge encounter. "Skaines always find someone to kill. It keeps the sheep docile."

There was a moment of silence as Strill thought about Brell's comment. That was Skaines 101, but until his people had to do it, they rarely thought about the _why_.

Strill finally worked it out in his head. "I understand, sir." This time, Brell thought there was something new in his voice. A moment later, the captain smiled. It was the sound of a backbone growing.

About damn time.

"Make it happen, both of you." Brell looked at them. "I want them to show respect for Skaines, and I want this to be the *F'zeer's* life-changing haul, got that?" His stern visage made the impression he was looking for. Given that the *F'zeer* had supposedly been recognized and its information sent back to the misbegotten Etheric Empire—and that bitch of an Empress—was it too much of a risk to seize the *K'leen II*, or should they just blow it?

Brell's eyes narrowed as he turned his head to his right. "Officer Mobik, I want you to see what type of engines they are using and if they are in perfect working order before you lock them down."

Mobik replied, "Sir, engines are *never* in perfect working order."

Brell smiled, his eyes alight considering the result of a poorly working engine. "*Precisely!*"

The captain's voice came over the speaker. "Pirate ship coming alongside External Sector One-One-Five, Ranger."

"Seven hundred and seventy-fucking-five!" Tabitha spat out and then jumped up, pointing to Hirotoshi. "Ha!" She turned her face toward the speaker. "Thank you, Captain. We will be there in a moment."

"That would be appreciated. The Skaines are known for their aggressive methods of keeping a ship's crew in line."

"Yeah." Ranger Tabitha grimaced as she locked her tools around her body. She couldn't bring her favorite coat on this trip. "The Skaines didn't get that memo."

"Or," Ryu set his headgear in place and spoke through his

subvocal connection to Tabitha, "they might not see it until Achronyx bypasses their security and places it in their queue."

Hirotoshi, Katsu, and Kouki stopped at the door before they deployed to protect the ship from the inside. Hirotoshi winked to Katsu but spoke to Tabitha and Ryu. "Then he back-dates the memo to show they always had it." He paused a second. "That's not very Rangerly."

Tabitha smiled but stayed quiet. As the three went down the hall, Katsu's voice traveled back to her, "But it *is* very Tabitha."

"Have I told you," Tabitha commented conversationally, as she and Ryu paused in the doorway of the small, specially-built exit from their hidden section of the ship's hold, "that I am starting to like these zero-gee trips?"

Ryu looked around at the brightness of space. The ship they were about to leave had slowed to almost stationary. The pirates had caught them at a logical and tenuous location. They didn't have enough velocity to escape, and the ship was turned the wrong way, anyhow. These large commercial ships were useless for any sort of maneuvers. "That is because we have the flight suits."

"Well, perhaps," Tabitha admitted as their suits pushed them away from the *K'leen II* toward the *F'zeer*. "Huh, would you look at that?" Tabitha pointed toward the location where the ship's name was supposed to be painted on the outside. "Seems like the captain's database was accurate."

Ryu looked in the direction her arm was pointing and had to admit that the poorly-erased name gave the lie to the *F'zeer* designation. Tabitha toggled the HUD command to enable her helmet-cam to take pictures.

"You know they will probably try to sabotage the ship, right?" Ryu asked. After all these years with Tabitha, he still couldn't figure how strategically aware she would be in any given situation. Usually, she was intelligent enough to overcome the advantages his age difference and accumulated wisdom gave him.

Other times she would step off the top of a building, forgetting it was three stories down.

It was always a toss-up which Tabitha he would get.

As the two of them drifted down the length of the *K'leen II*, Tabitha unclipped two pucks from her belt. Both were about three inches in diameter. She casually tossed them toward the back of the F'zeer and ignored where they were headed. "Achronyx, make sure those pucks end up someplace that will cause massive problems with their engines."

Her EI's voice came over her implant, "Engines always have problems with them, I understand."

"Yes, they do, you know?" Tabitha mused as the two of them engaged their suits' cloaking abilities. While a sharp alien might still be able to see them if one should be looking, there wasn't a technology known that would be able to locate the two humans as they broke away from the protection of the commercial transport and headed for the pirate vessel.

"Are you into their computers yet?" Tabitha asked her electronic companion.

Achronyx came back, his voice modified to sound offended. "Katsu could have broken their security blindfolded."

"Yes," Tabitha mused, "but you didn't answer my question. Are *you* in their systems?" She chuckled.

"Is that supposed to be a joke?" the EI asked. "Please clarify, because I am working to alleviate your concerns where my communications have caused friction in our relationship."

"Uh..." Tabitha came back after a couple of seconds. "The hell, Achronyx? When did you start caring?"

"I notice you didn't answer the question," the EI responded. Tabitha couldn't tell if his voice sounded smug or curious. Before, she would have assumed smug.

"I'm off my damned game," Tabitha muttered. This time her comment wasn't passed through to her EI.

QBBS Meredith Reynolds, Yollin System

A couple of jump Gates away, inside the most powerful woman in the galaxy, an AI was...chuckling.

If only to himself.

Bethany Anne put a hand up to stop General Lance Reynolds from making a comment. He had barely raised an eyebrow when she went inside herself to have a conversation.

Why are you laughing, ADAM?

>> ADAM isn't here right now, please leave a message after the beep.<<

>>Beep.<<

Cut that shit out. Who are you fucking with?

>> Wait, why would you think I am presently messing with anyone?<<

You live inside my head. Perhaps, just perhaps, I've learned a trick or two over the years. Now, who is it?

He paused long enough for Bethany Anne to register his hesitation before he answered.

>>Tabitha.<<

Bethany Anne mentally chewed on that answer for a small part of a second, looking at the different ways ADAM could interact with her Ranger, and why he would.

Are you messing with Achronyx?

>>Well,<< he gave her the mental equivalent of a sniff, >>she keeps complaining about Achronyx, so I thought I would modify his code. With his permission, of course.<<

Make sure it doesn't affect an operation. She was just about to return to the conversation with her dad when she added, *and keep me in the loop.*

The General's eyebrow was still raised in curiosity, as he had waited less than a couple of seconds before she came back to him.

Pirate Ship *F'zeer*

The pirate ship's hatch unlocked and allowed Tabitha and Ryu to enter. Its warning systems had been hacked to prohibit notification of anyone inside. Both humans deactivated the protective shield that had facilitated their short spaceflight. The shield had kept radiation and other nasty things away from them, and heat, oxygen, and pressure near them so they didn't die while in space. Tabitha wrinkled her nose and whispered, "Why do Skaine ships always smell so nasty?"

Ryu nodded in agreement. "It would be nice if they would sanitize a little more before we came over to kill them."

"No shit," Tabitha agreed as she checked her weapons. She unsnapped a couple of secondary weapons, making sure they were loose and available.

Captain Brell turned in his chair. "Notify Command of our location. Send them all of our information. If we are going to get busted, we need to make this a haul worth talking about."

Communications Mate Yuhig smiled at his captain and sent a very short message.

It was time the Skaines brought in the big guns. No more being careful with the Etheric Empire.

City of Bouk, Planet Straiphus, Straiphus System

R'yhek looked down at the human.

He was pretty damned large for a Yollin. Many figured his mercenary years had made him a fighter, but while he could hum the tune quite well, his preference was to make money by trading. When he left the teams, he had bought himself a halfway-profitable bar away from the main planet and bullshitted with other Yollins and the occasional alien in exchange for some cash.

R'yhek scratched one of his mandibles in consternation. "Are you even old enough to drink, human?"

The young woman smiled, then winked one eye at the Yollin. "Depends on whether my parents are around, Barkeep." Her Yollin was fluent, which surprised R'yhek.

His eyes narrowed in concentration. "Table or bar?"

The young woman nodded toward the bar. "Bar, if you got time to talk?"

R'yhek shrugged. "Bar it is." He took a couple of steps, then twitched and grunted, grabbing at his back. "Stupid-ass weather."

"You having a problem with the carapace, Barkeep?" the little human asked from behind him.

R'yhek turned to look down at her. "What do you know about Yollin physiology?"

She shrugged. "Quite a bit, actually. Usually, when a Yollin is holding his back like you are, we need to break off some chiton so your back plates can move easier."

"Oh?" He clicked his mandibles twice. "How do you do that?" He paused for a moment. "And I didn't get your name."

"That's because I didn't offer it, barkeep," she told him, then smiled. "But I'll share it with you."

She leaned toward the larger Yollin a little, a glint in her eyes. "My name is *Christina*."

Pirate Ship *F'zeer*

"The battleship should arrive in…" the crewman's voice faded a moment as the captain swiveled to look at his communications personnel, "…about a twentieth of a turn, sir."

Captain Brell turned to First Officer Wig and shrugged. "I wonder where the hell they're going that they were so close?"

The First Officer pursed his lips. "I'm thinking they were lying hidden somewhere nearby and staying dark. We should have known they were around otherwise."

Captain Brell nodded. "That *is* puzzling. We had intel on this ship we didn't share, and yet one of our battleships was that close by accident when we called out for help?"

Brell stood and looked around. "Ask them to send us the verification sequence." He put his hand on the all-call button.

"Sir, they aren't replying!" Communications came back, his eyes wide with concern.

"Well, how the hell am I supposed to know what the verification sequence is?" Tabitha hissed to Achronyx. "It's not like I'm the one inside their computers right now!"

"That information," her EI came back, "is not in any area I'm capable of accessing. There is no way for me to confirm that I'm the ship they want to see at the moment."

"Well, that tears it," Tabitha huffed as she pulled a pistol. Ryu raised an eyebrow and unclipped his own gun. "Make sure Barnabas knows the score, as well as our guys on the ship. We should be fine, but the jig is up now. We need you here."

The EI responded. "Yes, Ranger Tabitha."

There was a moment of silence as Tabitha cracked the door to peek into the hallway outside the small room the two of them had been hiding in. Achronyx came back online.

"Ranger Tabitha, Barnabas has been notified, and now we have a more serious problem."

"What's that?" she asked as she pointed Ryu toward the engines. He rolled his eyes and took off.

"We really do have a Skaine battleship arriving about the same time as I am."

Tabitha headed toward the bridge. "Well, that's just fucking fine. More Skaines to line up for Justice."

Back on their ship, Achronyx sent the update Barnabas had requested as he pushed his engines into the red. His was a capable ship, but even he couldn't duke it out with a battleship and win.

If he couldn't get there in time and Ryu couldn't convince Tabitha to leave, there was going to be a problem.

Tabitha had already promised to never run from a fight with Skaines.

City of Bouk, Planet Straiphus, Straiphus System

"Huh." R'yhek reached down to slap her outstretched hand. "You know a few of our customs."

Christina twirled her hand in a circle. "Turn around. I'll deal with your back problem."

"What, just like that?" R'yhek asked. "Don't you need some medical equipment?"

"Well," she shrugged, "that would certainly help, but if you can handle a little pain, one of my uncles showed me how to do a field-expedient fix for the issue."

"What are you going to do?" he asked.

"I'm going to slam my open palm," she told him, opening her mid-sized hand and gently pushing it forward while pulling her other arm back, the fist closed on that hand. "Right between the two plates, pushing the middle one out."

R'yhek blinked a couple of times, then shrugged. *How hard could this little human hit, anyway?*

He turned around. "Okay, I'm game." He clicked his mandibles in humor. "What the hell, how much can this hurt?"

"Well," she told him, "my uncle says it hurts like a sonofabitch."

"What's that?"

"It's the son of a female dog, but I know a few dogs, and I've no clue why he says that."

"Who's your uncle?" R'yhek asked.

"This one's name is Kiel," she told him. "Now hold still for two seconds…"

CHAPTER THREE

City of Bouk, Planet Straiphus, Straiphus System
The slap to his back, when it came, was nothing like R'yhek had expected. It was everything her uncle had said it was.

And twice as painful as he would ever have believed possible.

He let out a roar of agony as he staggered three steps before falling into a table, bouncing off, twisting in the air, and landing on his back on the floor.

"Oooowww," he groaned as he heard footsteps come closer to where he was dying in pain. Or living, yeah, he guessed he was living in pain since he still felt it.

"So Uncle Kiel was right, huh?" someone asked.

R'yhek looked for the person who belonged to the voice. His eyes finally focused on the young human again. "What did you hit me with?" he moaned. "I feel like I've been run over by a bistok."

"My palm," she answered, lifting her hand. From where he was lying on the ground, it looked inflamed. Just as if she had used it to hit him.

"How?" he whimpered.

"My aunt says if you are going to hit something, do it hard, fast, and continuously."

"Another Yollin?" he asked.

She shook her head. "No."

"Who is your uncle?"

"Uncle Kiel is the Leader of the Empress' Yollin Mercenary group."

R'yhek followed what she said, but then his brain caught up. "WHO?"

"Uncle Kiel." She shrugged.

"Not that who." R'yhek had just realized who she was talking about, though. No Yollin who paid any attention to politics in the Etheric Empire was unaware of the Empress' Yollin Mercenary team or their leader. Kiel.

"Oh, my aunt?" she asked him, holding her hand out.

He reached up, not thinking about how much he weighed versus her. It wasn't until she helped pull him up that he realized she was damned strong.

Really damned strong.

He reached around and grabbed his back. He gingerly twisted to his left, then right, and finally bent back further than he had recently dared.

He *was* pain-free. "I'll be dropped in bistok shit," he murmured. She made a face of disgust. "What, have you been around bistok shit before?"

"Too many times," she agreed. "The Bitches like to go play with them. It's just *gross.*"

Her casual use of an Etheric human term twigged R'yhek once more. "Who did you say your other relative was?"

"I didn't." She grinned. "But I can tell you I'm named after her."

"Christina?" he asked. "I don't recognize that name."

"No?" She smiled. "My whole name, good sir, is Christina *Bethany Anne* Lowell."

R'yhek's eyes opened wide. He knew exactly who this human was. There were whispers about her all over the place, and he looked around in concern. Wherever she was, her parents were bound to be close. Those three couldn't come into an area without all kinds of whispers happening.

You absolutely didn't fuck with the girl. But if you did, you had best make sure Mom didn't find out, or you would get your kneecap shattered by a bullet.

And for bistok's sake, you didn't *ever* want to get her father pissed off.

"Oh, they will be here shortly," she told him. "But don't worry. We aren't here to screw you over," Christina told him as she moved toward the bar and slid onto a stool.

R'yhek slid behind the bar and walked over to the human. When he reached under the bar, he noticed her tense and drop an arm to her side. He knew she had something in a pouch, but he hadn't realized it was a weapon until he grasped just who she was.

He slowed his movements. "Just liquor." When he brought out a clear bottle with a deep amber liquid inside.

She winked. "Sorry. I can never be too careful." He noticed she kept her arm lowered.

"That's damned smart," R'yhek agreed, grabbing two small glasses from behind him. He put them halfway between the two of them and poured each about a third full. "This is from the Eubos system. In general, the stuff they distill could be used to clean engine parts." He closed the bottle. "But they have a station—"

"Seven-Seven-Two," she interrupted. "I recognize T'ller's mark on the side of the bottle."

R'yhek blinked a couple of times at the human and turned the bottle to see. She was right. He looked back at her. "How do you know T'ller?"

"Um, my," she scrunched her face, "I'd say aunt again, but Aunt Tabitha says to call her my BFF because calling her 'aunt' makes her feel too old."

"Tabitha?" R'yhek felt a little cold at this revelation. Given the crowd she was running around with, there was probably only one human named Tabitha she might know. "You mean Ranger Tabitha? Ranger Two. *That* Tabitha?"

"Sure." She grabbed the two glasses and handed R'yhek the one in her left hand. When he held it, she clinked her glass against it and took a large swallow, then shook herself quickly. "Damn!" she got out before taking a smaller sip. "That first shot fucks a person up."

R'yhek eyed the human as he slid the bottle back under the bar. She had just taken a shot of T'ller's best, and strongest, alcohol. Most Yollins in this town would have had to spend a day working to earn enough money to buy that swallow.

He eyed his own glass and mimicked her shrug. He took his first swallow and grinned at the blaze of fire as his body seemed to come alive. He wasn't sure what it did to a human, but from her flushed face, it was certain she was feeling something.

"And your aunt?" he asked, leaning on the bar with his left arm and manipulating his glass with his right.

"Tabitha?"

"No, the one... Oh..." R'yhek closed his eyes. "Your name." He took another large swallow of his drink and let the fire hit him a second time before he asked, "Would someone like me call her 'Empress?'"

When she smiled and nodded her head, all R'yhek could wonder was...

What did he do to have the who's who of the Empire walk into his bar?

It was at that moment that his doors opened again, and R'yhek looked up to see two more humans come in.

Her parents.

R'yhek sighed. He was well and truly fucked; he just didn't know how—yet.

. . .

QBBS _Meredith Reynolds_, Yollin System

Bethany Anne had followed a plan for the last five years: set up meetings, go to meetings, find out shit at meetings.

And mostly be bored to tears at meetings.

Everything had been new and exciting for the first couple of years. With TOM to give her insights, she could make a difference. But at this point, her teams had acquired almost as much information as TOM possessed, and it was certainly more recent information. Her need to be in these meetings had ceased a long time ago.

Except for this one.

The Ixtalis are going to fuck up, guaranteed.

>>So far they have followed all protocols, and we haven't found any evidence of double-dealing.<<

Just because we haven't found it doesn't mean it hasn't occurred. It's like knowing that if you grab a scorpion, it's going to sting you. That's what they do.

Are you suggesting that they can't learn a lesson?

I'm not suggesting it, TOM. I'm flat-out telling you they can't learn a lesson.

I'd say you are too cynical, but I actually side with you on this one.

>>I thought we had an agreement, TOM.<<

We had an agreement to be open-minded. Open-minded does not mean you choose the most illogical solution and call it open-minded. That's just being stupid and wrapping it up in beautiful, stupid paper. Unwrap it, and you realize you have been an idiot.

That's... Wow, that's impressive, TOM. I didn't think I could turn you so conservative.

You haven't. I'm still an alien of this galaxy. I'm just not naive.

Bethany Anne had continued walking toward the chair at the

top of the dais while they held their conversation. She fucking *hated* this setup, but apparently, this bullshit was expected by both her own people and those she met with.

Not that the aliens had a specific understanding of what the platform and chair meant. However, the humans knew it meant something. The reverence, the pomp and circumstance, of her having a throne on a raised dais helped the aliens recognize the sense of power.

Bethany Anne had thought they should meet around some sort of executive table instead.

Even her father had shot that idea down.

So here she was, ascending the twelve steps to her throne. She had tossed on a robe to cover her armor before coming in here. Once she was sitting on her throne, Eric came up the other side and offered her the Empress' crown. She nodded, and he set the crown on her head.

"How is Gabrielle?" she whispered. "Still pregnant?"

"Like you wouldn't know if she had already popped?" Eric commented, smiling. "TOM and ADAM are keeping tabs on her every damned minute because of the Pod-doc sessions, so I know you are aware if she so much as sneezes."

Bethany Anne smiled. "You know Stephen is planning on pampering the shit out of those twins, right?"

"Don't remind me." Eric winced. "Gabrielle says something is a no-go that he wants to do, and Stephen just lets it slide right off him. He's slicker than Teflon."

"Wow!" Bethany Anne glanced around for a second. Everyone in the throne room knew that whatever she was talking about with one of her Own must be important.

No one bugged them.

"I haven't heard that term in a loooong time." She looked at Eric, who had stood up. "Been waiting to lay that one on me?"

"No, just slipped out," he told her, a glint of humor in his eyes.

"Uh-huh," she replied. "So, who are we meeting first today?"

"Still the Ixtalis, boss lady," Eric replied, "nothing's changed in the two minutes since you looked it up before you left your room."

"Damn, just one small break would have been nice." Bethany Anne faced the room as Eric took up his customary protective stance. She raised her voice. "Okay, let's get this shit over with."

Ixtali Legate Addix looked around the throne room of the Etheric Empress and considered her options. For probably the first time—well, the first time that any high-level Ixtali official would admit to—she was here without any technological support.

Meaning, she didn't even wear consumer-grade hearing amplifiers that would have let her know what the Empress and her soldier were saying up on the podium.

It was obvious from his movements that he was a warrior. When he stepped behind her and took up a position of protection, her observation was proven correct.

When the Empress spoke, her choice of words gave Addix to understand that the Empress considered the meeting as something that was going to be painful, and she wished it to be over.

Quickly.

Unfortunately for the Empress, that wasn't Addix's goal. She needed help, and the Etheric Empire was probably the best choice.

If they would consider her request.

Pirate Ship *F'zeer*

"What do you mean, we've been boarded?" First Officer Wig was busy getting information from a screaming Skaine down in the engine room. Wig slapped the alarm a second later and pointed toward two bridge guards. "Lock us in!" A moment later, he ordered Inner Engineering to isolate themselves from Outer Engineering.

The bridge guard on the right had already started entering the code when he figured out what was going on with Wig, and a second later the blast door slid across the opening.

Wig turned toward his screens. They showed two ship contacts heading in their direction, and tracking said they would arrive at nearly the same time. In fact, they would cross paths before they arrived.

While the Skaine battleship *Shllet* was impressive, the other was one of those damned Etheric ships. He wouldn't want to be on the *Shllet* right now.

Then again, he had his own troubles; he wasn't sure who the hell they had aboard. Since they were attacking an Etheric Empire ship, he guessed it was that damned Ranger group.

Wig swallowed.

"Captain?" He turned, catching the captain's attention between orders. "I think we have Ranger Two on board."

Wig had to give Captain Brell the credit he deserved. The captain just nodded and calmly continued issuing orders.

As if the Skaine equivalent to a boogeyman weren't on their ship at this very moment.

City of Bouk, Planet Straiphus, Straiphus System

Christina watched the Yollin realize who her parents were. She had wondered what he would do and had placed a small wager with ADAM—which she had now lost.

Looking resigned wasn't one of her choices. She surreptitiously removed her hand from the region of her hidden weapon and placed it on the bar.

. . .

Etheric Empire Ship _ArchAngel II_

Barnabas looked at the message and pressed his lips together, then leaned back in his chair and considered his options.

The only sound in his office was his fingers tapping. It wasn't a coincidence he was here when Tabitha's team was working this operation. He had four offices in total. Two on the _Meredith Reynolds_, one here, and one on a new ship that hadn't been commissioned.

Yet.

"That woman..." he mouthed as he continued tapping. He leaned over and punched a button. "ArchAngel, I need to speak with the Empress, and I believe you need to be in on this conversation."

Within moments, Bethany Anne dropped into the conversation. "What's up, B?"

Barnabas grimaced. He wasn't sure if he was pleased or annoyed. He decided to opt for pleased, reserving the option to switch to annoyed. "My Empress," he started.

"Uh-oh," Bethany Anne murmured, then her voice came back in a monotone. "This is Empress Bethany Anne. I'm out at the moment dealing with some annoying Ixtalis. Please—"

Barnabas ignored her and cut in, "I need to request that _Arch-Angel II_ take me to an obscure sector near Gorn Station 2215."

"For?" she replied immediately.

"Seems Tabitha is a little stuck," Barnabas temporized.

"Barnabas, you always allow her to get her shit unstuck. She has a good team. If you're asking to go, this isn't a small situation. Level with me."

Barnabas paused. "The Skaines somehow sandbagged us and have a battleship heading toward a Ranger effort in an unaligned area of space. Their people are attacking the Yollin ship _K'leen II_."

"Stop right there!" Bethany Anne's voice dropped an octave. "To be clear, I don't give a _shit_ where one of our ships is. If someone attacks them, they better understand they'll get an unannounced visit from my people."

ArchAngel spoke up. "So I can go?"

"No, I didn't say that, exactly," Bethany Anne told the two of them.

"This is what I want to happen..."

CHAPTER FOUR

QBBS *Meredith Reynolds*, Yollin System

IXTALI
ADDIX

C 2017 MICHAEL ANDERLE
KURTHERIAN GAMBIT

ART BY ERIC QUIGLEY

Ixtali Legate Addix was actually *Senior Principal Trade* Legate Addix. But, for some reason, the High Council had decided to send her with a more humble title.

As if that would make everything all right between her people and the Etheric Empire.

For what felt like forever, the Ixtalis had been able to use the same playbook with all races it had encountered, and it had worked out well. Until the Etheric Empire.

The first group they sent had, in her opinion, done an admirable job. They had to deal with what was an unimaginable challenge at the time. A new group of aliens, who not only didn't need their services but had their own. The response to their mission? The Etheric Empress had tossed their first legate out on her ass, dared them to challenge her, and for a finale, had blown up a Yollin super-dreadnought to prove her point.

Hiring a mercenary force had proved to be too damned expensive after that little episode. Even their clips of the beam that had destroyed the fleet were not that valuable. Too many other ships had been nearby and provided excellent coverage, so their vids were, at best, of slightly higher quality.

But not by much.

Their second effort had been beyond a catastrophe. They'd sent in that pompous hothead X'tellek, and he hadn't even made it inside their base before they threatened to blast his useless ass out of space. That episode required her people to convene the High Council to vote on attacking the Etheric Empire.

The council had fifteen heads. Twelve had voted to leave the Etheric Empire alone, and three to attack at once.

Then there had been twelve votes to toss the three dissenters out on their asses. So, in order to preserve an odd number of votes on the High Council, Addix had been selected to join as "most likely to keep her wits about her." She had immediately been loaded onto a ship and gated over to speak with the human Empress.

Who was looking particularly pissed at the moment. Legate Addix leaned over to X'Bock on her left and whispered, "When was the last time her face glowed red in public like this?"

Without missing a beat, X'Bock replied in a soft voice, "Well over three years ago, in this room at least. We have rumors of two other occasions involving Yollins that our bugs picked up. However, those were not verified."

"Why not?"

"Because," X'Bock turned to look at her, "we can't seem to locate suitable leverage to induce the Yollins to speak about the subject." His voice fell flat. "Apparently they love her too much." He sniffed in irritation.

Addix looked at the Empress as her face dimmed. "X'Bock."

He continued staring at her. "Yes, Legate?"

Addix, her voice displeased, continued, "Do not make one more derogatory comment about the Empress. Or, I will personally ... "

Bethany Anne was mouthing words, but nothing was coming out of her mouth. Instead, she was listening to the Ixtalis' conversation; the legate was ripping the male next to her a new asshole.

"...I will personally eject you into space if she tosses us out of here because you said something impolite."

Bethany Anne barely kept her face composed. She wanted to snort but wasn't sure if Ixtalis understood human expressions, both facial and auditory, well enough.

Well, except for her glowing red face denoting anger. *That was kind of a gimme*, she mused.

"Allow the Ixtali legate," she turned to look at John, "and *ONLY* the legate, to approach please." John nodded and spoke into the microphone on his collar. They had agreed to keep the communication capabilities inside their heads secret when in public.

So far, the fact that all of Bethany Anne's personal people were wired was still a secret. At least, they hoped so.

A moment later, two Etheric Empire Guardians, both of whom towered over the Ixtalis, walked up to the legate. One of them directed her toward the massive dark red carpet that radiated some twenty-five feet out from Bethany Anne's throne. If you set foot on that carpet without permission, your life became incredibly painful in less time than it took to move three steps.

Not only were the Empress' Guardians on the outside and the Queen's Bitches on the inside, but military EI Reynolds continuously watched and had multiple types of weapons inside the throne room to take out attackers.

Surreptitiously placed, of course.

Addix nodded. Bethany Anne could hear her four feet clicking on the rock floor as she approached the carpet. While Bethany Anne had never personally seen an Ixtali without the robes they wore, she understood they had four legs, rather like a cross between spider legs and crab legs, underneath those robes.

That visual rather grossed her out.

Legate Addix nodded her understanding to the Queen's Guardians that she would approach alone. X'Bock had taken a breath to make some comment that would have caused her to have to kill his useless ass right here in front of everyone.

And the humans would know that she had killed him. When the first trade mission had come back, their people had obviously been very upset about the kill switches that had been installed in each of them. Those damned humans had been a pain in their ass since the beginning.

Then the humans did something that confused the High Council even more.

They told no one.

As far as the Ixtalis could figure, the humans hadn't announced it to any of their people, or any other alien group. That had allowed the High Council to be lenient with the three and broker a deal with the trade mission that wouldn't include immediate implementation of the suicide solution.

The three would be pulled from legation duties and their kill switches deactivated. Should it ever come out that any of the three had spoken about it, they would be hunted down and killed for divulging state secrets.

Now Addix was walking into the den of the monster. She hoped she would make it out alive.

Tell me we have a fix for their kill switches. Bethany Anne spoke to the two platonic friends she slept with every night.

>> **We do. Why?** <<

You believe someone here is setting her up?

What do you think? Bethany Anne asked, watching the legate approach and start across the carpet. Sure enough, Bethany Anne could tell when the revelation hit the legate. She noticed how the Ixtali's eyes seemed to dart every which way.

The cone of silence, as the guys liked to call it, always screwed with those who approached her.

>> **Command?**<<

If you can, shut the kill command down and knock her out if someone pushes her button. It would be all I needed to have the most recent Ixtali Legate killed right in front of me. Stupid fuckers.

>> **I understand.** <<

John?

Yes.

Make sure if the Legate falls, we capture whoever tries to kill her.

Not you?

I'm wearing some of Jean's finest. No one is fucking with me today.

What makes you so sure? John asked, risking a quick glance at his friend.

Because I look too damned good to blow up today. Bethany Anne moved in her seat, and John had to give props to Jean.

She made the best armor.

As Addix stepped onto the red carpet, two sensations hit her at once. The first was expected. The carpet was luxurious; she felt like she was walking on the soft land of her birth planet. The second was unexpected.

She could hear nothing except for those inside the throne area.

Addix wanted desperately to stop and look around, and possibly stick her head back outside the noise attenuation field. She'd really like to see how this group had implemented the field. While the capability to reduce sound wasn't unknown, these aliens had taken it to a new level.

The Ixtalis should know. They had been able to insert two spies with minor equipment, stuff that wouldn't get them in trouble if discovered, and they had not been able to overhear any audience with the Empress unless she spoke to everyone in the whole room.

The council had presumed it was a sound barrier, of course. However, perhaps not one so effective as what she was experiencing. Then again, these humans had annoyed them too many times to worry about it at the moment.

A tall blue male delegate watched the Ixtali legate, face impassive. Keeping his thoughts to himself, Cannock looked around the large room, considered his current conversation, and decided to toss it.

This Empress was beautiful. Estarians, by and large, were

only attracted to their own kind. Other aliens rarely captured their attention.

Cannock had to admit, however, this one had something that wasn't physical. He lifted his arm and rested his chin on his hand, narrowing his eyes.

What was it about her that was intriguing him?

"Hello, Legate Addix." Bethany Anne nodded to the Ixtali. She appeared relaxed, arms on the throne's armrests, legs crossed. "I don't hold much to protocol, so let's figure out what the hell has brought your people back to talk. And this time, try to avoid shoving your importance down our throats?"

Legate Addix bowed slightly in Bethany Anne's direction. She had stopped where the carpet ended and the stone dais with its twelve steps began. It seemed prudent not to get closer to the two men staring at her from the Empress' sides.

The legate lifted her arms as she tried to explain. "I cannot apologize for the Ixtalis being ourselves," she admitted. She was working hard to speak the Yollin language properly, as the human tongue had been too difficult to learn. "However, there are times when the universe finds an imbalance, and it will act to rectify the issue, one way or another."

Bethany Anne pursed her lips. "Are you suggesting that the Ixtalis' ongoing hubris has run unchecked for too long? Because if you are, I'm going to find this to be an interesting conversation. Maybe more interesting than I had originally thought."

Addix rocked her hands in the fashion Ixtali intelligence had determined was a human gesture for indicating a qualified false and true at the same time.

"Our efforts are intended to protect the Ixtalis as a people, which, from what I understand, is not something that would upset your...ethics," Addix admitted. "However, there are those in positions of power who believe that domination over others is the path we should take. At this time, we have a group that wishes to continue striving to increase the feeling of self-importance within our own peoples in order to become more confrontational with others."

"We call that heightened nationalism," Bethany Anne replied. "Sometimes it is very useful, but when it runs amok, it can cause many problems." Bethany Anne stood up and casually paced down the stairs. Addix looked to the left and right, then slowly backed up as the Empress came closer.

Bethany Anne stopped two steps from the bottom and cocked her head. "Why move back, Legate?"

Addix stopped and her four major mandibles closed. Her top and bottom minor mandibles were indicating agitation. She pressed her hands against her teal and gold robes. "Empress, you must know you are a puzzle to my people. You speak, and have previously spoken, very aggressively. Your people do not seem very interested in negotiation at times. You, yourself, upon rare occasions, display glowing embers for eyes," Addix waved her odd hands across her face, "and fiery lines of power radiate across your face."

John snorted from behind Bethany Ann. "Rare?"

Bethany Anne looked up, then up further, since John was not only taller than her but had stopped two steps above her. "*Et tu,* Mr. Grimes?"

"What?" John answered, "Just because it isn't in public..."

Addix filed the language away for future clarification. One of the tools inside each intelligence asset unit was a memory of what was seen and heard. She would clarify their communication later.

Bethany Anne turned back to the legate and returned to speaking Yollin. "Well, that makes it easy to know when I am upset, right?"

Addix agreed by separating her major mandibles, then

touching the top two together. The Empress seemed perplexed for just a moment, then realization dawned on her face. "So, since I am not radiating anger at the moment," Bethany Anne continued, "perhaps you don't need to step back?"

Legate Addix touched her two top mandibles together once again. This time, there was no hesitation in the Empress' understanding of her mannerism.

Cannock heard a phrase he was not expecting, and in his own tongue.

"Greetings of the day to you, Senior Delegate Cannock."

Cannock turned and looked down. Staring up at him was a human female, and she was causing a similar feeling to Bethany Anne's. He was starting to worry.

Who were these humans that they were causing him strange feelings?

"My name is Gabrielle, and I've been asked to speak with you separately. If you would be so kind as to come with me?"

Cannock turned to look at the Empress as the lady spoke again. "Delegate Cannock, I promise you a meeting with the Empress, but we can get some of what you wish to accomplish done before our final meeting, which will be held in *private*."

Cannock was surprised when the Empress put a hand up to halt the Ixtali, then looked him in the eyes and nodded before returning to the conversation.

Seemed like he would be going with this new human. Cannock nodded to the under-minister, who turned to follow them out of the throne room.

X'bock watched with some humor as the Senior Legate stepped back when the alien stood and started down the stairs to approach her.

While he couldn't hear anything, Addix's retreat proved she wasn't worthy of the council seat she held.

That was especially true since three of his own had been ejected from the council for their forward thinking and unwillingness to bow before aliens such as these.

Three patriots for the Ixtali people had been stripped of their honor, when in fact they had been the only ones thinking of what would be best for their people.

Their own future.

Their own *accomplishments*.

The humans had slowed the Ixtalis' rise significantly. Too many other races were now asking why the humans didn't need to trade with the Ixtalis for their gems or for the Ixtalis' information. In short, if the humans didn't need a relationship with the Ixtalis...

Maybe they didn't either.

It was time to regain their former respect and power, and X'Bock had been provided the key to start the effort.

He was just waiting for the perfect moment.

Commercial Transport *Kleen II*

Captain M'rin watched as the pirates boarded his ship. He was relieved when he saw the fragmented images of Ranger Two's men racing through his ship.

By the time the pirates approached the bridge, the pair of Yollin guards had been removed and in their places stood a single human.

Captain M'rin could tell that this human was the one named Hirotoshi, the leader of what the Ranger had called the Tontos.

He was the one who had always seemed to be very, very quiet.

M'rin had watched as the video showed a blur, then the sudden arrival of the human. He had pointed to each of the guards and then pointed toward the bridge.

So much for Captain's Prerogative when it came to the Ranger and the Tontos. They were here to accomplish a job, and his people were theirs to command.

He nodded to his guards and directed them toward the seats for visitors to use while on his bridge. A moment later, the blast doors to the bridge sealed, leaving the human outside standing between him and the pirates.

M'rin had spoken with one captain who had watched the Rangers work on his ship for half a year. That conversation had been enough for M'rin to decide not to complain about how they usurped his authority. They were polite, the other captain had told him, until the pirates came.

"Then," he continued, "watch and feel sorry."

"For the Rangers?" M'rin asked him, taking a sip from his amber drink.

The other captain had shaken his head, mandibles rubbing together, "Hell, no! Feel sorry for the pirates. They are already dead. They just don't know it yet." The captain had picked up his red drink, but stopped before taking a swallow and looked M'rin in the eyes.

His voice was quiet but firm. "Whatever you do, stay out of their way." He thought a moment before adding, "And be ready to clean up the mess."

Pirate Ship *F'zeer*

"I've got two Etheric Empire agents running around my *ship*!" Captain Brell yelled at the captain of the battleship. "So how about you stop saving your damned precious fuel and get over here a little faster?" Brell looked at the status of his men on the *K'leen II*. "Not to mention, my people are getting cut to pieces over on the Yollin ship!"

"That might be," Captain Theoth replied, "because you have very poor discipline on your ship, and now you have no ability to take down the people who have boarded you."

"I cannot get through this new door design," Ryu told Tabitha over their personal communications. "It seems even Achronyx cannot hack a manual lock."

"*Gott Verdammt* Skaines," Tabitha grumbled back. "I've got the same shit here." Tabitha looked for handles; something, *anything* that would allow her to get through the shield.

"Well," she started feeling about her body before reaching around to her back, "fuck, yeah!" She ripped a small pouch off her back and pulled it around to unzip it.

"What is that Ranger doing?" Brell asked no one in particular. "She seems to be active now, where before our blast doors were giving her trouble." His eyes narrowed as he leaned toward the video displaying the hallway where she was located.

"This," he tapped the screen, "can't be good."

"You have activity on your six, Tabitha."

Ryu's voice penetrated her concentration, and she listened a moment before rolling her eyes.

Dammit to hell! She reached around and yanked off another device. This one was seven inches long, three inches in both width and height, and damned heavy for something so small. She knelt and placed it at a ninety-degree angle to the walls, and activated the device.

All she saw was a blue light.

She looked up in time to see a group of Skaines coming around the corner. "Hope this fucker works," she spat, and then the shooting started.

CHAPTER FIVE

City of Bouk, Planet Straiphus, Straiphus System

R'yhek looked at the male and then the female human, and started a slow walk down toward the other end of the bar. "Be right with you two." He motioned. "Just sit by Christina, and I'll get your drinks for you."

Nathan could feel Ecaterina staring at him, so he shrugged. "Beats me what he's doing." He then slid onto the stool to Christina's right, between where R'yhek had to pass him before reaching his family. Nathan felt he was a good judge of character, even Yollin character, so he wasn't worried about the barkeep burning them.

But he hadn't lived this long by taking chances.

Ecaterina wasn't so casual. "This pistol," she began in her heaviest accent as she pulled it from a holster on her side, "is a pain in my ass at times." She laid it down on the bar.

A Jean Dukes imprint showed on the red wooden handle.

Christina eyed the gun. "When am I getting my JDs, Mom?" The young woman didn't bother picking up her mother's pistol since she couldn't fire it.

"You know the rules," Ecaterina answered. If this was the first time, then it was easily the fiftieth, she had answered this question. "Jean Dukes can only be delivered with the Empress' direct approval. You have to talk with your Aunt."

Christina made a face as R'yhek walked back toward the three humans. He ignored the pistol until he saw the insignia. No one who cared about weapons was ignorant of the famous Jean Dukes.

In certain quarters, *she* would be the one they clamored to meet. The Empress would receive respect, but she did not have the same fame. Many people over the years had wondered if Jean Dukes was married.

When they found out she was mating with one of the Empress' personal Guards, they were annoyed. When they found out which Guard it actually was, they would often make the sign of protection.

Even if they didn't believe in gods.

Everyone had seen at least one, if not many, of the videos of John Grimes and how he took care of the Empress' problems.

Permanently.

The first video had been shot relatively soon after the Etheric Empire had conquered Yoll. It had gone viral in six nearby systems.

The second video hadn't been as professionally filmed, so it wasn't as well viewed. The third video, in contrast, *had* been well recorded, and the scenes of the carnage done to those who had decided to rebel in one last spectacular effort had been the final nail in the coffin (many coffins) of the Kolin and Chloret caste rebellion.

That time, John Grimes had arrived with two more of the Queen's Bitches, but they hadn't fought the rebels inside the large stone defensive building. No, the two extra Bitches had simply walked through the crowd and pushed back some of the bystanders.

They told them they might want to be outside the blast zone for their own protection.

The death and destruction John Grimes rained down on the building had completely leveled it and taken out the hundred and seventy-two elitists who had been inside.

"This is your one warning," the video showed John Grimes yelling to those inside, "before I bomb the shit out of this building and make it your final resting place."

Then he counted down slowly from ten. He had been fired on well over fifty times during that countdown, but none of the shots had done any damage. Twice he had destroyed rockets that had been shot toward him, and once he dodged a rocket that screamed in from the side.

He shot the two rebels who had fired the rockets through the hearts as he spun into the air to dodge the final projectile.

It had exploded against a building two blocks down the street.

His countdown had reached three when that occurred. He quickly finished, "Two, one, NONE, you sonsabitches!" Then he put both hands up and pushed down.

The building had started collapsing from the top, and copious amounts of debris exploded out the windows. Pundits had pointed toward the cause being weapons stationed above the building. Almost immediately, the whole area was engulfed in a sandstorm, and the ability to see John Grimes had been lost.

Minutes later, the crowds watched as the dust and sand slowly settled to the ground and a lone human wearing red armor came out of the cloud.

The three humans had then entered a Pod that was waiting for them, and it took them back into space.

The next day the air had cleared. There was nothing left of the building except rubble. However, a picture of a fanged female had been painted on a section of brick, underneath which were the Yollin words, "May this warning help the next generation learn not to become caste in their thoughts. There are no Kolin, Chloret, Mont, Shuk, or Kiene. Yoll is for Yollins. Everyone deserves a chance to spread their talents toward the stars - *The Queen Bitch.*"

The reporters had learned over time that while the Empress showed a different persona, her Queen Bitch side was very undiplomatic.

R'yhek was looking at a pistol that guaranteed he was speaking with people in the Queen Bitch's inner circle. He placed a bottle in front of the man, then the woman. "It is the Pepsi drink. Rumor has it you like it."

Nathan smiled and twisted the top. The gas expelled, and he sniffed.

The drink even had the right ingredients.

"I cannot believe," Ecaterina commented as she twisted the top off her drink, "that Bethany Anne still allows you to find pockets of this stuff to drink."

"She doesn't do it for me," Nathan replied as he took a sip of his drink. "Damn, R'yhek." He winked toward the barkeep. "This is good stuff." Nathan turned the bottle around, looking for a maker's mark.

There wasn't one.

"I make it," R'yhek admitted. "I was waiting for your evaluation before admitting that," he told Nathan as his mandibles clicked in humor.

"How is your back?" Ecaterina asked, "Did Christina fix it?"

R'yhek reached around. "Yes. Yes, she did." He nodded his head toward the young human. "I would have paid you good money to do that." He rubbed a mandible. "Of course, I would have first had to believe it could be done before I agreed to pay you."

"Easy-peasy." Christina waved a hand. "I'd have done it for free, with the agreement that if it worked, you would pay me."

"And if I lied and didn't pay?" R'yhek asked her.

Christina shrugged, "I would have tossed in a video camera to watch you for thirty days, then ADAM would have let me know if you had lied. If you had lied, I would have come back."

R'yhek blinked a couple of times before asking, "And done what?"

"Demanded my payment, on pain," she answered.

"On pain of what?" R'yhek asked. When she looked confused, he clarified. "Usually, adults will say 'on pain of death' or something similar."

"Oh, I would have just kept causing pain until you paid, I guess," she answered, shrugging. "I haven't had anyone refuse to pay me long enough to worry about it."

R'yhek turned to her father. "Is she bistok shitting me?"

Nathan snorted. "No, and before you ask, she gets that from her mother."

R'yhek had to turn to his other side when the mother in question yelled, "WHAT?" As the lady leaned forward, the girl took her drink and leaned back out of the way of her parents. "You think Christina gets this from me?" She was pointing to herself.

R'yhek saw him raise an eyebrow, point to her, and nod.

"That is Bethany Anne, not me!" she argued. R'yhek noticed she called the Empress by her given name, not her title.

"No, that is you, Mom," Christina pointed out. "Dad gets you to prove the point every time because you explode in anger, and then no one believes you when you try to pin it on Auntie Bethany Anne."

"Ooohhhh," she fumed.

There's that name again. R'yhek sighed.

"I'm Nathan." The man reached out his hand. "You've met Christina, and El Diablo there to my left is my mate, Ecaterina."

"I'll El Diablo the shit out of you next time on the mat, Nathan Lowell!" Ecaterina grabbed her drink and took a large swallow, her eyes pinning Nathan to the mat in her mind. Moments later, she turned toward the bottle in surprise, then pulled it over and looked at it as she smacked her lips in appreciation. "Hey, R'yhek, this is good!"

R'yhek grabbed Nathan's hand and shook it. "I'd say I'm glad to meet you, but I have to admit that I'm concerned about having the elite of the Empress' friends come into my out-of-the-way bar." He reached up and scratched his neck, then, looking puzzled, leaned to the side to stare between the two females. "And I'm just noticing how I've no more customers today. Which is odd."

"Not so odd." Christina shrugged. "I put up a warning sign that this place was under watch for contagious sexual diseases."

R'yhek spat out his drink. "You did WHAT?" he asked loudly, staring at the girl.

"Yeah." Christina jerked her thumb over her shoulder. "I found the sign on a building three blocks down."

R'yhek thought a moment...*three blocks down?* He rolled his eyes and stared at her again. "From the prostitution house? Purple, with green doors? That location?"

"Yeah, that's the one." She nodded.

His mandibles twitched in agitation. "I'm not going to live this down, you know," R'yhek told her, his voice dry.

"See, that's the great part." Nathan leaned forward. "You won't have to, R'yhek, because I've got a job for you."

R'yhek turned to see the human smiling. Then he caught the other two out of the corner of his eye and looked at them. They were smiling as well.

Truly, he thought, *fucked.*

Pirate Ship *F'zeer*

Her shield popped into place and was soon peppered by slugs and plasma fire. It was holding, but Tabitha had never been a fan of being shot at.

It was something she never believed she would get used to. "Achronyx."

"Yes?"

"Do you have enough focus to help me with some pucks?"

"I'm trying to outrace a battleship. Doesn't use too much processor power, Ranger."

Snarky-assed PITA. "Great, because you need to pull my sensor feeds and locate the pirates sending all sorts of dangerous shit my way." She allowed the tiniest of pauses. "You got them yet?"

"Yes."

"Good, take them out."

"With what?" Achronyx started to ask when he caught the incoming details from the puck: its location in space related to Tabitha, the shield's height, the hallway, bulkhead, walls, pirates.

A moment later, the puck zipped off toward the pirates in the hallway. Tabitha grimaced when the first body exploded.

Achronyx might be snarky, but she had to appreciate the efficiency of his puck placement. "You done?" she asked when no more bullets, plasma, or screams came in her direction.

"Yes."

"Good." She scrambled up. "Now take out the bridge's blast door without causing decompression!" As she spoke, she threw her body over the shield to protect herself from the backblast. "Or hitting me!" she added as she felt the puck whizz by her.

The loud *bang* crumpled the center of the blast door, pushing the sides out and allowing Captain Brell to see light from the outer hallway stream around the door. "Prepare for attackers!" he barked, pulling his sidearm and sliding off his chair.

Those doors were supposed to be impenetrable.

"What the hell, Achronyx?" Tabitha asked. The loud concussion from the puck hitting the blast door hurt her eardrums. "For all that noise, you can't even perform?"

"You said without causing decompression," the EI reminded her.

"Well, yeah," she agreed. "I just thought Skaine doors would be easy." She watched the puck wobble back past her, moving slowly enough that she could track it with her eyes. "That puck is looking a little worn out."

"It is barely holding together," Achronyx replied. "This is the last shot for this puck."

Tabitha eyed it. "Give me a second before you try anything!" She reached out and switched off the shield, grabbed the small metal box, and headed toward the other end of the hallway, "God, this is gross!" She carefully walked around the remains. She put her helmet on and activated the internal air. "I refuse to smell that." She caught her reflection on a shiny surface not covered in blood. "We need better-looking helmets."

"May I?" Achronyx asked as she stepped around the corner.

"Yes, yes." She watched the puck as she poked her head around the edge far enough to see what was happening, keeping her hand on her pistol.

The puck jerked ahead but flew down at the floor some five paces from the door. It ricocheted off the floor, angling up to punch into the door near the upper right-hand corner. The door broke out of its frame and went flying into the bridge. The screams and crunching sounds caused Tabitha to wince. "Wow, you suck at flying pucks," she commented. "Weren't you supposed to hit the door, not the floor?"

"Who says I missed? If you look at the door, the calculation—"

Tabitha tuned Achronyx out for a moment. In times like this, the EI could make her wish to become a celibate nun.

Well, perhaps a nun. Damn, nuns were celibate by default, right? She couldn't remember. Okay, not a nun then.

The first shots were fired from the bridge, striking the wall on the other side of the hallway.

"Well, hell," she muttered and tossed the shield device back down the hallway. "Same shit, different direction."

She turned her head towards the bridge area. *"ARE YOU COMING OUT WITH YOUR HANDS UP, OR ARE YOU GOING TO MAKE ME COME GET YOU?"* she screamed to the bridge.

"You Ranger Bitch!" a male yelled back. "Skaines don't surrender!"

"That's bullshit," Tabitha smiled. "I've had you titty-suckers surrender before." She reached down and reduced the pistol to level three. That ensured she wouldn't puncture a hole through the ship's walls out into space. Not that she had used a Skaine ship to test that theory before.

No, actually she *had* totally done that and sent the video out to all the known Skaine hangouts. They got so worked up when you destroyed one of their ships. It had truly been a wonderful experience.

"What's a titty-sucker?" the captain yelled back. She recognized that he spoke her epithet in his version of human speech.

She cross-referenced human to Skaine and called back, *"Coh'vichee laile!"*

She had to back around the corner and wait out the hail of shots that thundered out of the bridge.

Apparently, Skaines hated that term.

Tabitha smirked as the wall that could be hit from the bridge got torn up by the impacts. Pieces blew off in big chunks and crashed to the floor.

This raid wasn't going to be useless after all. Provided that big-ass battleship didn't blow them into infinitesimally small atomic bits, she now knew an expression that pissed Skaines off.

CHAPTER SIX

X'Bock turned to the delegation's Communications Director and asked discreetly, "Is her video relaying to the ship?"

"Of course." He sniffed. "We continually record everything from the team and external as well."

X'Bock turned back. That little tidbit was annoying, but he doubted it would matter when he was finished with his operation.

He sent the kill command.

Bethany Anne walked down the last of the stairs and took two steps toward Legate Addix.

>>**We have Ixtali communication.**<<

Bethany Anne ramped up her speed.

Gott Verdammt! Bethany Anne's eyes looked beyond the Legate. _**From Dickhead Maximus over there?**_

>>**Yes.**<<

Make sure you have disabled the Legate's kill switch and, if possible, knock her out.

>>**There is a twelve percent chance she will die.**<<

Fucking aliens brought their fucking internal problems to me, Bethany Anne fumed. *It's a chance she took. Make it happen.*

In front of her, the Ixtali legate's eyes seemed to glaze over, and she started to collapse. Not the most enjoyable sight, an alien with all four black eyes staring at you. "Eric!" Bethany Anne shouted, catching the legate as she fell. The Empress twisted around, tossing the body as gently as possible to him. She continued her turn. "Meredith!" she yelled, her eyes going red. "DROP MY DAMNED SHIELD!"

"Oh fuck," John yanked his pistol. "Turn on her suit, Reynolds!"

Delegate Tomthum had been watching the different groups attending the meeting area with interest. He had noticed all delegate groups here in the throne room were provided with the same amenities. There were no size differences, and the only difference in rank was indicated by which group met with the Empress first.

The Ixtalis were across the room and to the right of the throne from where the Yaree delegation had their area. Between them and the throne were a group of Estarians.

He didn't mind Estarians, but they were rather bland as a race. They were very 'Greetings to you and also to you' emotionally nice aliens.

Formal, at times. Even their underground people were polite. As far as he was concerned, a boring people. He was surprised when a human met with the Estarian group. A few moments later, the Estarians followed her out of their waiting area through a door in the back.

Fortunately, that meant nothing was blocking Tomthum's view when the action started.

Bethany Anne saw that the male Ixtali's eyes showed surprise when she turned and started heading in his direction. He had subconsciously reached for a weapon, and that was enough of a guilty plea for her.

She formed a ball of electrical energy and threw it across the intervening forty paces. His body was still convulsing when she took her last step and ended up right in the middle of the five Ixtalis. She backhanded the Ixtali who was convulsing.

And he disappeared.

Bethany Anne looked at the remaining Ixtalis, her eyes pinning each one. "Any of you dickless wonders working with the same group as that asshole?" she asked, seeking any clues that might help her.

"Fuck it." She spread her arms wide, and the lines on her face glowed brightly as she broadcast electrical energy. All four spasmed and dropped to the floor.

She looked down at them. "Lock them down for questioning. I'll be right back," she told John, then sidestepped and disappeared.

Delegate Tomthum stood there in shock. His eyestalks were all blinking at the same time, and his brain was trying to catch up with what he had just witnessed. This was the alien of the stories, the one who was whispered about. His people had heard the tales and failed to believe.

This was the Queen Bitch.

He waited, trying to slow his breathing as he noticed her

Guards and Guardians quickly restraining the Ixtalis after the Empress disappeared.

Neither of her personal Guards seemed worried. One continued holding the female Ixtali legate in his arms.

Bethany Anne stepped into the Etheric and reached up to remove her crown and unclip her hair, letting it fall naturally around her face. Her eyes were still glowing like embers, and her hair started rising as she continued to pull Etheric energy.

X'Bock looked up in shock at the Empress, who was only a few feet from him in—he struggled to look around—he had no idea where. He couldn't move easily, but his eyes were under his control, and what he saw made him second-guess the belief that this alien was all bluster.

An alien who could blast him with energy and move him into what looked like another dimension wasn't powerless and full of boasts.

"You have no idea what you tried to do," Bethany Anne spat out to him. "You wanted to pull the Etheric Empire—MY Empire —away from our efforts to find and get rid of the Kurtherian menace, and for what? Your personal *EGOS!*"

X'Bock's four major mandibles opened, but she pulled a red ball of energy and threw it next to his right side. It exploded, burning him in the process.

"I didn't say you could talk!" she spat. "The only option you have is to die right here."

X'Bock gritted his mandibles and sent the command to execute himself and trigger the explosive device in his pack, to hopefully hurt this alien as well.

Nothing happened.

"What?" Bethany Anne asked him when he looked surprised. "You don't think humans have had self-sacrificing sorry sacks of selfish camel dicks trying to use themselves as bombs before?"

She spat to the side, "You Ixtalis think because you have gems, you own the ability to trade? That your ability to trade in secrets and stay neutral somehow makes you superior?"

X'Bock looked her in the eyes, realizing that his group had seriously underestimated the alien Empress.

"I'm through being 'nice Empress,'" she told him. "Trying to play the political game and smooth over the fucking waters. Well, the Etheric Empire is me, and I am officially beyond pissed off!"

She reached down and grabbed the Ixtali by his robe. "Time to go back, fuckwad." Bethany Anne threw X'Bock to her right, then took a step in the same direction and disappeared.

Delegate Tomthum was shocked a second time when the vanished Ixtali appeared in the middle of the throne room and flew some twenty paces before he hit the ground, rolling over several times before he smashed into the wall to Tomthum's right. Next, he saw the Empress, hair flying on waves of energy, step out of nowhere and continue walking toward the Ixtali.

"Try to blame me for killing your legate!" She hissed as she walked toward the Ixtali. "Plan on using it to create problems for the Etheric Empire!" She spoke louder as she reached for the Ixtali, who was attempting to stand up. As the Empress grabbed him and turned around, he tripped and fell. She dragged him back toward the one named Eric.

"MEREDITH!" the Empress yelled.

Tomthum was surprised when the AI, another alien construct the Yaree were not too familiar with, answered.

"Yes, Empress?"

"Wake up the legate!"

Tomthum noticed that the Ixtali being dragged seemed very agitated.

Addix's mind was fuzzy when she received the jolt. All four of her eyes opened, and her brain tried to remember what was going on.

That was when she realized she was being held in someone's arms. She looked up to see a human gazing down at her.

"Oh..." she mumbled.

"Are you all right to stand, Legate?" the Guard asked her. She was about to agree when she heard the Empress' voice from her side.

"She better be okay to fucking stand up," the Empress ground out. "She needs to be part of this."

Addix saw the Empress walking toward them. As she was being assisted to a standing position, she noticed the rest of her party in restraints on the ground. "What has happened?" she asked. She saw X'Bock dropped to the ground, and she ground her mandibles together.

"If you so much as *flinch* more than I want you to," Bethany Anne told the Ixtali she had dropped, "I will send so much energy into you that you will twitch until next week. You understand the Yollin I'm speaking to you?"

X'Bock had been giving her his full attention. He nodded.

"Good," she replied. He observed the arcs of electrical energy jumping between the fingers of her hands as she stood above him.

Bethany Anne snapped her fingers to get Addix's attention. "Your number-two guy here sent a kill command to your internal suicide switch. We intercepted and stopped the command."

Addix subconsciously reached behind her head as her mandibles, both major and minor, started moving erratically.

"How is that even possible?" She took a step toward him. "You are not privy to those commands!"

She stopped. "You were given them by the ousted." Addix seemed to calm down. "It will not matter which one. They have all signed their death warrants." She sighed. "And now you have reduced me to—"

"Oh no, he hasn't," the rough voice of the Empress interrupted her. "He already tried to implement his own suicide switch when we spoke a moment ago. Plus, he was trying to trigger the bomb in his pack as well."

Addix looked at the Empress, shock on her face.

"X'Bock," Bethany Anne, her voice primal, "you are hereby condemned by the Etheric Empire for seeking to attack us. Your life is forfeit." She reached down to pick up the Ixtali. "Meredith?"

"Yes, Empress?"

"Set his internal systems to work again in fifteen seconds."

"Done, Empress."

"Good," she looked at the Ixtali, "Have a nice life, however little of it is left," she told him and pushed him into the Etheric once more.

Bethany Anne turned back to Addix. The legate, mandibles open, body in shock, stared as she took in Bethany Anne's ability to cause people to disappear.

"You should always," Bethany Anne told the legate, "be careful whom you ask for help."

Some forty or so steps away, the Yaree Delegate licked his lips.

It seemed like she was talking directly to him.

City of Bouk, Planet Straiphus, Straiphus System

R'yhek looked at the human, his mandibles tapping very gently. "I was really afraid you would say that."

Nathan waved at the barkeeper and took another two swallows from his drink. "This is really good," he admitted. "Hell, I would have picked you just for your ability to make this stuff."

"It takes more science than I would have thought," R'yhek admitted. "But you are only trying to get me to feel good instead of agitated."

"We want you to join our team," Christina jumped in. Nathan turned to look at his daughter in consternation when he noticed she was using her juju on the older Yollin Master At Arms.

And he was falling for it.

"Why?" R'yhek looked at her. "I'm old, I'm beat up, and even with you fixing me, I don't have that many years left."

"Maybe," she replied. "But what years you have, do you want to finish them here?" She waved at the bar. "It's not a bad place, but we can fill your years with fun, and…" she pointed to herself and then her parents, "with family."

"Family?" R'yhek looked at the three humans. "You *have* noticed we don't look alike, right?"

"Silly!" Christina grinned at him. "Family is what we make it, and who has your back. Besides, who has had your back lately except me?"

Just then, the door to the bar opened and three toughs came in. The humans all turned to see what was going on as R'yhek sighed. "One moment. These three believe they can intimidate an old Yollin mercenary." He started walking toward the end of the bar to get around and speak to the new entrants.

"Seriously?" Nathan muttered. "Those guys can't lift their legs to piss in the right direction, much less…."

Ecaterina eyed the three toughs, "Okay, Christina, you took over the negotiations from your father. You had better close this deal."

"Yes, Mom. I got this." The younger woman turned and slid off her stool, then reached down and unlocked her pistol. She cricked her neck left and right as she followed R'yhek.

"What are you doing?" R'yhek asked the young female as she came closer.

She looked up at him and winked. "Showing you how I know you have my back." She jerked her head toward the three waiting for them. "I'll call us square." Christina casually reached out, grabbed one of the heavier chairs, and tossed it up in the air. High enough that R'yhek caught it and realized she had tossed the heavy chair up...

One-handed.

"Hey, spineless shit brains," she called. The three toughs looked down at the young girl. "That was three names, by the way." She pointed to each one. "You are Spineless, you are Shit, and that leaves you," she told the last Yollin, "to be Brains." She looked him up and down. "So, do you have any?"

"What?" the third Yollin asked, clearly confused.

"Brains." She shook her head. "Well, that was a bad call on my part," Christina admitted as she pointed to R'yhek. "He and I are in the middle of a discussion, and you have about as long as it takes me to toss your asses out the door to understand you aren't wanted here."

"You and what army?" Spineless asked the short human.

"God, I was hoping you would say that," Christina answered, her eyes flaring yellow.

"What the hell?" N'nook looked at the bullshit poster on R'yhek's front door and ripped it off. "Stupid kids playing practical jokes. This came from the prostitute house," he muttered, surreptitiously scratching his genitals.

"I should know," he grumped quietly.

He took the two steps necessary to throw the sign away in a public trashcan. There was no reason to let R'yhek know about it; he would just worry about shit he couldn't control and what people would think about him.

He was a worrier that way. It's why N'nook liked the old mercenary so much. Until he could make enough money to buy his own bar, he would get his drinks here because of R'yhek. N'nook turned back around in time to see the door to R'yhek's bar explode outward as a Yollin tough emerged at high speed to roll in the street.

N'nook's eyes widened even further in surprise when another tough back-peddled out of the bar. His face was bleeding, and he was using his arms to try to protect himself from a small...human?

On him.

She perched on his shoulders, swiping her clawed hands at his eyes, then twisted down, her upper body sliding under his head to pull him off balance. She dropped to the ground as the bruiser tumbled into the street.

N'nook saw a third run out of the bar as the young female reacted to a call. A large piece of wood flew out of the bar but missed the third Yollin.

Bad aim, that.

N'nook realized his mistake when she caught the wood and swung it at the unsuspecting thug, catching him on his shins.

He went down as well.

Then R'yhek himself came out of the bar, walking like he was not in any pain, and she tossed the wood back to him. R'yhek caught it, so he now had the complete pair again. R'yhek wielded each with deadly efficiency as he beat the ever-loving shit out of the two remaining toughs. Finally, R'yhek allowed their cries for mercy to stop him.

N'nook noticed the young human's claws and hands had returned to what he thought was normal for the race. The three thugs crawled together and helped each other up, then stumbled away down the street. The female looked up at the old barkeeper and smiled.

N'nook shook his head when the two clapped hands in the old way.

Warrior to warrior.

At that point, the two of them noticed him standing there with a look of surprise on his face.

"Hey N'nook," R'yhek smiled, his mandibles showing happiness. "You think you could find the money to fix up a bar?"

N'nook looked around and shrugged, "Sure, why?"

"Because no one should own it but you." R'yhek looked down at the human. "I've got a few years of adventure still left in me." The little human laughed and started pulling on R'yhek's arm to get him to follow her back into the bar.

"Mom, Dad, I closed the deal!" she yelled to someone inside the establishment.

N'nook followed the two as they entered, to figure out what the hell he had just witnessed.

And did he really own a bar now?

CHAPTER SEVEN

Pirate Ship *F'zeer*

Ryu's voice seemed calm compared to the fire Tabitha was taking from the bridge crew. "Are you in a bind, Ranger?"

Tabitha pulled a small wand from a side pocket, twisted one end, and pushed it around the corner. The view from the tip came up on the HUD in her goggles. "Not yet, thank you very much." Tabitha continued observing, evaluating her options. "How are things going in the engine room?"

"Not quite as well as you, I'm afraid," Ryu answered. Just then, there was a small explosion accompanied by a large shower of sparks, and a chunk of the ceiling came down to shatter on the floor not five feet from Tabitha.

"You call this progress?" Tabitha asked, knowing that Ryu could monitor her HUD.

"They built the interior door very well." Ryu replied. "Obviously they don't want us getting inside."

Tabitha thought about it for a moment. "Okay, new plan. Achronyx?"

"Yes?"

"Is there any way to piss off that battleship and draw it away from here?"

"I can micro-jump to you, grab everyone, send out a few missiles and race for the safety zone. But the micro-jump will cause a small issue with recharging. We will be within their fire zone for approximately three minutes, assuming everyone gets on board in record time."

"What about this ship, Kemosabe?" Ryu asked.

"This ship won't be a problem," she told him and broke the connection for a moment. "Hirotoshi?"

"Hai?"

"Status."

"We are searching for one last Skaine. Never mind, last pirate has been found and neutralized," he replied.

"Okay, let Captain M'rin of the *K'leen II* know we are going to be leaving and trying to pull that big-ass battleship out of here with us."

"We are going to be bait?" Hirotoshi thought about that. "I'm not sure we are bigger bait than the commercial transport."

"We are going to be such a PITA they will want to kill us first."

"Okay," he replied.

"Good, see you back in our hold in five," she told Hirotoshi. "You got all of that, Ryu?"

"Hai."

"Good. Meet you back at the exit point. I'm going to leave a gift for my friends."

"And the engines?"

"I already have two gifts for them. Achronyx has enough of their systems under his control to disengage, which he is going to do in…" Tabitha yanked a small, heavy device off her suit.

She flipped the top and pressed a red button, holding it for two seconds. "Present for you!" She threw the small device, then amped up her vampiric skills and dashed down the hall, pressure doors slamming shut behind her as Achronyx shut down what he could.

When Tabitha neared the location where they came onboard, the explosion from the front of the ship tossed her against a wall. She bounced off two walls, but kept her footing and ran the last fifteen steps.

Ryu was waiting for her.

They dogged their helmets. "Get your ass over here, Achronyx!"

The decompression happened quickly, and they felt another vibration as the ship disengaged from the massive transport. The two of them pushed off the *F'zeer* and ramped up their antigrav propulsion to jet over to the *K'leen II* as the *F'zeer* started to bank away. Once they had handholds, Tabitha turned to look for the *F'zeer*.

She dialed up the magnification to see it more clearly. "Puck those fuckers."

The explosions started in the aft engines. Small at first, then two medium and one large final explosion as the ship blew into too many parts to count.

"I guess they did have problems in their engines, after all," she commented as they drifted to the Rangers' entrance and made their way into the ship.

Tabitha found Hirotoshi inside cleaning his blade and the other two packing. "I think we have worn out our welcome," she told her team as she walked toward her own baggage. "But their using a battleship against the *Achronyx* is a bit much, don't you think?"

Ryu grabbed Tabitha's bag and tossed it to her as he stepped toward his bedding area. Kneeling, he rolled up his mat and worked to slide everything back into place. He cleaned his blade and locked it down. Moments later, Ranger Two's team was opening the door back into the ship and heading toward the pickup point for the *Achronyx*.

"Captain M'rin?" She called him over the comm.

"Here, Ranger."

"Sorry, but we aren't going to have a celebration dinner tonight. It seems we have a plus-one that wasn't invited."

"I see it," he answered. "Are you sure you should have blown up the Skaine ship? They are going to want your blood now."

"Better ours than yours," she replied. "*Achronyx* is coming here to grab us, and then we are going to work on pissing them off some more."

There was a pause before the captain came back on. "May the stars light your ways, Ranger." His voice sounded subdued.

"What the hell, Captain?" Tabitha chuckled. "This is just one more awesome story about how the Empress' Rangers kicked more Skaine ass. Don't be going all maudlin on me. Keep those Yollin mandibles clean. I've got more Skaines to deliver justice to. You worry about getting your cargo to port. Let us worry about that big-ass battleship."

"You can take it out?" he asked.

"Absolutely," is what Tabitha answered over the intercom. Then she shut it off. "In another world, perhaps."

"You do know," Achronyx came on the line, "that the chance we can survive a skirmish with a Skaine battleship is less than five percent?"

"Never tell me the odds, Achronyx."

"Noted. I'm ready for you to come across," he told them.

Tabitha hit the button to get them onto their ship.

Sixty seconds later, the Ranger Ship *Achronyx* disconnected from the Commercial Transport *K'leen II*.

But instead of heading away, it headed toward the large battleship.

"I hope she knows what she is doing," Steward A'nick fretted as he stood by the captain on the bridge.

Captain M'rin rubbed a mandible, his eyes thoughtful. They flicked to his sensors for a microsecond, then back.

"Sensors!" he barked. "Make sure we are capturing this for posterity!"

Skaine Battleship *Shllet*

"That Ranger is mentally unstable," Prime Weapons Officer Ure commented as those on the bridge watched the ship disengage from the transport and head in their direction.

"Yes, possibly," Captain Bok replied. "But this is Ranger Two, the one they call Tabitha. She has been a problem for way too long."

"Do you believe she has something up her sleeve?" Ure asked.

"Of course she does," Bok answered. "The only question is *what*."

QBS *Achronyx*

Tabitha opened her eyes and glanced around the bridge. "Okay, we have new orders." She looked at her display. "Take us to location 223.7 by 12."

"That is nowhere," Achronyx replied, but the ship turned to head to the new location anyway.

"No, it is going to be the end of the *Shllet*," she answered when Achronyx calculated their ability to reach that point before the *Shllet* took them out.

The chance of safely reaching that point outside of the guns of the *Shllet* was...bad.

"Patch me into the Skaines," she told Achronyx.

Skaine Battleship *Shllet*

Tabitha's face filled the forward screen on the battleship's bridge. She looked around as if she could see everyone in the room. To those on the bridge, it was disconcerting.

Could the human see their bridge? No, certainly not.

Right?

"You *Coh'vichee laile* have the option of shutting down all weapons and surrendering or dying." Tabitha smiled, "Please choose dying since that would make my day fantastically awesome."

"You and what navy, Ranger?" Captain Bok asked her calmly. "We Skaines have fought the *Mighty Achronyx* many times and are well aware of the ship's abilities."

QBS *Achronyx*

Tabitha received a personal ping in her ear. "I'm the mighty *Achronyx*?"

Oh, God! Tabitha rolled her eyes. *This is going to take years to undo.*

"Well, if we are about to die in battle, at least I can go out knowing I've made a name for myself," the EI added.

Tabitha thought about that for a second and smiled. "Hell yeah, you have. Let's keep the story going."

"Yes, let's," the EI agreed.

"Who needs a navy, Captain?" Tabitha sent a few commands to Achronyx. "The mighty *Achronyx* is going to kick your ass and make you beg us to take you prisoner."

The Skaine captain narrowed his eyes. "You have been an admirable nuisance to the slavers and the raiders, Ranger. However, we are the Skaine *navy*. We know which end the lasers come out of."

"You know," Tabitha grinned, "that's the same shit I get from the raiders and the slavers. None of you guys respect each other." Tabitha looked up and hit two switches, physically giving permission to override the failsafes. She looked at the screen again. "Prepare for attack, Captain."

"Just curious." The captain nodded to someone off-screen

before returning to the conversation. "What does the rest of your crew think about this suicide run?"

The captain was surprised when four new faces joined Tabitha's in the display. The men's eyes were also red.

"We say, *Banzai!*" Hirotoshi replied.

Then a fifth face joined the group, and Tabitha inhaled. This face would have been called a Guy Fawkes mask back on Earth. Completely white, it was adorned with a black mustache.

"Prepare for the Mighty *Achronyx*, Skaine!" the mask told them, then the communication signal stopped.

Achronyx disappeared.

Skaine Battleship *Shllet*

"They ran!" Prime Weapons Officer Ure looked at all of the sensors, double-checking everything.

"They have not run, Ure." Captain Bok thought about the next step and adjusted his robes.

"Why do you say that?" Ure asked. He turned and asked a question of two others near him before turning back to the captain. "We have nothing."

"Do you see the Yollin Transport *K'leen II*?" Bok asked, pointing to the ship on the main screens.

"Yes, of course," Ure agreed.

"Then they are still here." was his answer when the Ranger ship reappeared *inside* their shields.

QBS *Achronyx*

"FEAR ANONYMOUS!" Achronyx announced, his mask on screen as the large guns on the top of the Ranger's ship fired almost point-blank into the sides of the *Shllet* as the massive battleship slid by them.

"Seriously? Not 'Fear Achronyx?'" Tabitha yelled as she realized the front-facing video wasn't using magnification. They really *were* close enough for Tabitha to spot the very small text by the hatch they just flew past.

"The hell, Achronyx?" She pushed back in her chair, expecting to bounce off the battleship. "I said to get us close enough to kick their ass, not kiss it!"

"Only way for a mosquito to bite the big bad battleship," Achronyx answered as parts of the battleship's armor exploded into space.

For all the damage they were causing, it was just a pinprick to the massive ship.

"Good, now get us the fuck out of here!" she told the EI, and the ship disappeared once more.

Skaine Battleship *Shllet*

"The Achronyx is a bit dangerous," Captain Bok agreed. "Why have we not hit it yet?"

"Did not expect the human ship to be able to get inside our shields, Captain," Ure admitted as warning alarms shrieked outside the bridge.

"I'm losing patience, Ure," Bok announced, as he looked at his damage reports. No serious damage was accomplished, but they shouldn't have taken any damage.

"They have skipped again. *Got them!*" Ure slapped the desk next to him, causing the communications specialist to jump. "And...they are drifting, Captain!"

Bok smiled. "Bring us about, Helm." Bok looked at the new information Ure provided. "Take us to location 223.7 by *12.*"

QBS *Achronyx*

"Well," Achronyx announced through the speakers, "this is particularly embarrassing." The Ranger ship was mostly powered down. They only had life support and minimal propulsion.

Very minimal.

"Yeah, kinda shot our load, didn't we?" Tabitha admitted, looking at the time. "How long before that big bad-ass battleship arrives?"

"It will take them approximately three and a half minutes to turn in our direction. Then it depends on whether they just shoot us out of space or slow down and take potshots."

"I vote for a slowdown and fill us full of lead," Tabitha answered, then thought about what she had said. "That's a euphemism for blowing us apart. No lead really included."

"I understand," Achronyx answered. "I don't suppose there is any particular reason we chose this specific location?"

"Oh, sure there is," Tabitha answered as she unhooked, stood up from the captain's chair, and stretched. "Hey, do we have enough power to fix some popcorn?"

The EI ran two queries. One to figure out if she could run the food warmer. That answer was 'easily.' The second was why she would want popcorn when it was her own ship that was going down?

Tabitha walked down the hallway and made a couple of turns to reach the galley. Hirotoshi came in a moment later. "Popcorn?" she asked him as she pulled out one of the bags specially made for her team. The Yollins had a vegetable somewhat similar to corn from Earth. When you added a touch of salt and something from a beast Tabitha really didn't like to think about, it tasted pretty good.

"Sure," he answered and reached into the bag to grab a handful. "Kemosabe, I must admit you are very calm and composed with the *Shllet* coming at us."

Tabitha cocked her head to one side. "I am, aren't I?" she agreed. "Why don't you come watch this with me on the bridge?"

Hirotoshi followed his Ranger back to the bridge, and they sat at the two stations in front of the captain's chair. She put the bag between them. On the large screen, they could see the *Shllet* had finished its turn and was heading in their direction.

Tabitha took a couple of kernels and tossed them into her mouth. "You know," she spoke aloud, "if I had been at a different set of servers when Bethany Anne came to save those people in Miami, I would have been killed."

Hirotoshi turned to look at her, raising an eyebrow. "Truly?"

Tabitha nodded. "Oh yeah, she's admitted it before. She wasn't sure of her strength back then and hit the first hacker too hard. She crushed his skull or something like that."

"And this relates, how," Hirotoshi waved a piece of popcorn toward the screen, "to that ship exactly?"

Tabitha thought about it a moment and shrugged. "I guess it is a stupid feeling, but I've always thought that if everything went to hell, you guys always had my back. Then, if everything went in the shitter for all of us, Bethany Anne would have our backs."

While the *Shllet* was still too far away for laser fire, they could see that she was ejecting missiles.

"I'm impressed," Achronyx announced to the two humans. "A full spread of twelve missiles."

"Is that going to do the job?" Tabitha asked.

"He is spending too many on us," Achronyx admitted. "Even fully powered, I couldn't shrug off even six of those missiles. So, by sending twelve, he either believes I have more capability than what they know—"

"Or he is saluting us in his own way," Hirotoshi finished.

"Well, that *fuckwit*." Tabitha spat. "God, there is one decent fucking Skaine in their whole race, and he has to be the captain of the damned battleship?" She huffed. "This is *so* going to hurt."

Achronyx came back over the speakers. "Seventy-two seconds to missile impact, and the *Shllet* is not slowing down. They will be here one minute after the missiles." The two of them ate popcorn for a few more seconds, watching the missiles grow larger on the video.

Suddenly, the missiles started exploding as the massive bulk of a ship that dwarfed the *Shllet* passed over the *Achronyx*, heading straight for the Skaine battleship.

"Connect me to the *Shllet*, Achronyx." Tabitha commanded.

"Connected."

Tabitha's face filled the screen on the Skaine battleship. "*Shllet*, this is Ranger Two. On behalf of Ranger One, the crew of the *ArchAngel II*, and a fuck-ton more support, one last chance. Do you wish to surrender to me, or face the *ArchAngel II*?"

There was a pause before a resigned Skaine captain came back on, his lips pressed together. "Ranger Two, this is Captain Bok of the Battleship *Shllet*. We surrender."

Tabitha had just thrown a couple more pieces of popcorn into her mouth when another voice, one she recognized, came over the comm.

"Ranger Two, this is One." Barnabas' face appeared on the screen. He looked down to see his Ranger and her Number One sitting in the front seats. His eyes narrowed.

"Is that a bag of popcorn?" he asked.

Tabitha picked it up and lifted it toward the screen as her face relaxed in relief. "Sure is, want some?"

"Yes," Barnabas agreed, "but not that cold stuff. Now, why do our sensors show you don't have power?"

"Well, about that," Tabitha started before Achronyx jumped in.

"We forgot where we were and jumped off a three-story building, sir," the EI answered.

Barnabas stared at his people as Tabitha offered Hirotoshi the bag. He shrugged and reached in to pull out some more popcorn for himself. Ranger One raised an eyebrow. "Just how," Barnabas asked, "did you get an EI to tell that fabricated story?"

"Well, it isn't exactly lying," Achronyx answered. "It's more like creating a metaphor for how we ended up here, without power."

Barnabas shook his head and smiled. "Enough with the bullshit, Tabitha. I'm proud of you. Well done to you and your Tontos." There was a pause, then Barnabas made one last comment before he cut the connection.

"And you too, Achronyx."

CHAPTER EIGHT

<u>Space, Heading to the Yollin System</u>

Nathan came down from the bridge to join Ecaterina and Christina as they exchanged stories with R'yhek in the galley of the new ship.

The *Prometheus*.

"Now that you are here, Nathan," Ecaterina commented as the ship left Straiphus behind them, "R'yhek has asked us questions. I think we need to answer together."

"Okay." Nathan slid into the chair next to his mate and their daughter. He reached over, grabbing a chip and popping it into his mouth.

"Who would think," R'yhek asked as he grabbed a chip for himself, ignoring the bigger questions for the moment, "that the useless collin root could be so delicious?"

"We humans have learned that just about *everything* is better deep-fried," Nathan admitted. "That, and we add salt."

"But," R'yhek argued as he chewed, "the collin root is a plant we have thrown out for centuries. The root is poisonous to us."

"It's not after about three hundred degrees of hot oil," Nathan pointed out as he grabbed another couple chips. "Besides, Bad

Company is now the sole exporter from Straiphus for all collin plants and products."

"We are?" Ecaterina asked, raising her eyebrows.

"Sure," Nathan admitted. "What do you think I was doing while you and Christina concocted the operation to meet R'yhek?"

"Mom says you got lost, and that's why you two were late getting back," Christina commented as she got up from the table, which would have held eight easily, and walked to the cooler. When she opened it, her eyes went wide. She turned to the three at the table. "How did we get all these new bottles?"

R'yhek turned to look in her direction. "Oh, your father negotiated the purchase of all my remaining Pepsi as a condition of my joining the group."

Ecaterina turned to face Nathan. "You did not!"

Nathan returned her look and winked. "He's not telling the whole story."

Ecaterina turned in the Yollin's direction. "Spill it, R'yhek."

"Well," R'yhek shrugged, "to be fair, the condition was a bonus paid immediately for all Pepsi I brought with me."

Ecaterina's eyes narrowed. "I thought we were waiting for important pieces from your home."

"We were," Nathan answered, then clarified, "Mostly."

"I'm a mercenary," R'yhek added. "I have weapons we had to pull out of special locations. Nathan agreed to let me bring the armor and weapons even if you can provide better, as a way for me to connect with my past while we create a new future."

"And how long," Ecaterina asked as she looked between the two men, "did we sit at the starport waiting for the weapons versus waiting for the Pepsi?"

"Honey, have you tasted the Pepsi?" Nathan turned to Christina and put up two fingers.

"What does this mean?" R'yhek asked. "Are you telling her to bring you two bottles?"

"Yes," Ecaterina replied. "Christina, you'd better make it four."

"Yes, Mom," she replied, and the three adults heard the clinking of glass as she grabbed the drinks and shut the door to the cooler.

"We actually had to wait five minutes for the weapons after the Pepsi was onboard," Nathan answered.

"Hmmph." Ecaterina accepted a bottle from Christina with a nod of thanks. She removed the top and drank a bit. She smiled before reaching out to pat Nathan's arm. "I'm sorry. I forgot how good it was between the bar and the starport. It is lucky that one can't marry Pepsi, isn't it?"

"Well, I wouldn't go that far," Nathan protested, eyeing his wife with a smile.

"Who says I was talking about you doing the marrying?" Ecaterina asked as she winked at R'yhek.

Nathan's eyes narrowed at his mate. "Nice, sweetheart." He turned to R'yhek and asked, "So you want to know, why you?"

"Well, I assume you had a reason, but yes, I'm curious," R'yhek admitted.

"I didn't fill you in on the whole story because we had to know you were in," Nathan admitted. "Sorry about that."

"I wanted a bar, I got a bar." R'yhek took a moment to drink before putting down the bottle. "What I didn't get was adventure anymore." He played with his bottle, turning it slightly in a circle. "The occasional drunk to toss out, but since my back was messed up, I had to hire one of my regular's kids to bounce. At least, before he went to seek fame and fortune last year." He looked at Nathan. "It was a bit embarrassing."

"I understand," Nathan told him. "You know that you have signed up for a rather unique," Nathan looked around, "uh…"

"I've signed up to do something for the Empress' personal friends," R'yhek told him. "I'm sure it is something that isn't forthright because you don't do forthright." He nodded to the three of them. "Nathan Lowell and family."

R'yhek turned to Ecaterina. "The stories tell of the mate, who has her man's back and can pick up a Yollin and throw him when she is pissed. Or shoot them between the eyes at distances that boggle the mind."

He looked at Christina. "Or their offspring, who is part of the group. Whispers say you don't want to fight with her, that she is deadly and laughs like a child as she hurts others."

"That's not fair!" Christina argued. "I don't laugh because I'm hurting others, I laugh because I enjoy a good fight. And for once, *I'm* the one kicking ass, instead of everybody else kicking *my* ass." She dropped her bottle an inch to the table, providing an exclamation point to her comment.

R'yhek looked at her a moment, puzzled. "Who is it you fight against?"

"Well," Christina lifted a hand, "there's Eric, and Scott, Darryl, of course Uncle John, and Tabitha. That isn't counting Stephen and Auntie BA." Christina looked up at R'yhek and stopped when she noticed his mandibles were hanging open. "What did I say?"

"Didn't you just name the Empress, the four Empress' Bitches, one of her mysterious friends, and a Ranger?"

Christina shrugged. "Yeah, okay?" she answered, then added, "Oh, and Gabrielle, although she tends to teach more than just beat me up."

R'yhek shook his head and reached over to ruffle Christina's hair. "No wonder you are a terror on the ground, little one."

"Well, yeah," she shot back. "But I never get to *beat* them."

"You would have them cheat to placate your ego?" R'yhek asked her.

Christina's lips pressed together. "No. Well, yeah, kinda. But I get your point. I might look pretty old, but that's because my physiology is advanced due to the nature of the nanocytes within my body. Sometimes my ego is still rather young."

"Sometimes that is true," Ecaterina told their daughter. "But trust me, sometimes that is true whether you are young or an adult. We are not all mature all the time."

Nathan snorted next to her. "Or with Team BMW, any of the damned time."

"They are mature, they just choose to hide it," Ecaterina countered.

"Team BMW?" R'yhek asked. "I don't know this group."

"That's because they aren't necessarily talked about much outside of the circle," Nathan explained. "B is for Bobcat, M is for Marcus, and W is for—"

"William," R'yhek interrupted. "Yes, I know of them for their beer and their bar." His voice sounded like he approved of the group. "They are famous across many systems to all of us who appreciate alcohol. That window into space on the second deck is a window of *legend.*"

"Yeah." Nathan's focus was lost for a moment before it came back and he nodded. "Well, those three are responsible for so much more than just booze and their bar."

"Will I get to meet them?" the large Yollin asked.

"Don't know why not," Ecaterina replied. "We should see them in about a week."

"That will be good. I wish to—" R'yhek stopped and looked around. "Do I have room on this ship to set up distillation equipment?"

"I never showed you the whole thing, R'yhek," Nathan told him. "We are currently in only a small portion of the Prometheus."

"We are?"

"Oh, yes," Nathan answered and stood up. "It's time to show you the rest of our little company's assets."

"What is our company name again?" R'yhek stood up, reaching around to his back out of habit. "By the way, that was a wonder, what you did to my back, Christina."

Christina winked. "Wait till you get the next fix for your back,

R'yhek." She grinned and grabbed his hand to pull him up from his chair.

QBBS *Meredith Reynolds*, Yollin System

Bethany Anne pursed her lips as she focused on the female Ixtali. "Legate Addix, I was aware you were having trouble with him before you approached me." She started walking toward her throne once more, pointing a finger toward the Yaree delegation. "I've not forgotten you, I'll get to you in a few."

Legate Addix noticed the Yaree delegate seemed more anxious than relieved that he had not been forgotten.

Addix walked through the sound field once more, the technology now of little importance considering the abilities the Empress had casually displayed in her presence. Just who—or *what*—had she been sent to negotiate with?

Bethany Anne turned around before ascending the stairs. "Now, you can take this any way you wish, Addix," Bethany Anne told her. "But here are your options. You may submit to a questioning where nothing is held back, and by that I mean I will know your secrets. All of them. Or you may grab your people, depart, and figure out how to deal with this rot yourselves."

Bethany Anne raised a hand and stuck up one finger. "Option one will mean I know more than you want me to know." Then she stuck up a second finger next to the first. "The second option will absolutely end up, I believe, with the Etheric Empire kicking Ixtali ass sometime in the future if you don't implode from killing each other before then."

"You are not offering a third, less ugly option?" Addix asked, trying to lighten the mood.

"Sure, Ixtalis decide that peace and prosperity among all aliens is their new focus as a people and—"

Addix waved a hand. "I get it, you don't see a likely third option. The challenge, as you are well aware, is the kill switch that precludes me from speaking too many secrets before it triggers and kills me."

Bethany Anne nodded. "We suspected as much." She tapped a finger to her lips. "So long as you don't speak the secrets, you are safe?"

"Yes," Addix admitted, not sure where this was going.

Bethany Anne shrugged. "Okay. You need to give me your final answer, Addix. Is this going to be what is behind Door Number One," she put her first finger back up, "or Door Number Two, labeled 'kick Ixtali ass'?"

Legate Addix's four major mandibles seemed locked. Finally, her narrow shoulders dropped. "Whether I live or not, I trust you. I fear the result if our people fight yours." She looked at the Empress' two guards, then back to Bethany Anne.

"I choose the first."

Third Outer Ring, Yollin System Space Control

First Shift First Class Double-Starred Ship's Controller Yri-Keva tapped the command response. "Turrell?"

"Yes, shift leader?" Her friend looked over at her. "More *Arch-Angel II* stuff?" he asked when he noticed the color of the screen she was looking at.

"Yes. Make sure there is nothing in her quadrants."

Turrell turned to his screens. The locations the *ArchAngel II* used rarely had to deal with any sorts of troublemakers. The ship was massive, easily the largest the Yollins had ever built. It also included a significant number of upgrades and enhancements the humans built into the ship after it came from the yard.

To just about everyone, it was both mysterious and deadly.

By now, everyone who paid any attention to the Etheric Empire's ships knew the story of the original *ArchAngel* and her crew. How they had gone into battle against two fully-crewed Yollin super-dreadnoughts.

And defeated them both. The names of those lost in the engagement, about a third of her crew, were chiseled into the stone you passed on entering the bridge of the current incarnation.

The ability of the ship wasn't what scared most away. It was *who* the ship was.

It was the reincarnation of the Empress herself as a ship of war. Those who communicated with the ship saw the Empress' face on displays. Those who would annoy her found the face of the Empress, with her red eyes, enough incentive to toe the line. The ship never hesitated to take the power of the Empress anywhere she was directed to go. She and four other Yollin/Etheric Empire battleships and seven destroyers had recently left on a mission. Now she was coming back.

For Yri-Keva and Turrel, it had been an amazing sight to see. The Etheric Empire's *ArchAngel II* and the Yollin Navy had powered up, and within fifteen minutes, they had all disappeared.

Without using a standard Gate.

It was proof, yet again, that the Etheric Empire wasn't constrained by permanent Gates, and that the *ArchAngel II* must have power beyond comprehension to take that many ships through a Gate she created.

And no one who saw the ships come together and leave ever doubted it was the *ArchAngel II* that created the Gate.

Now they were returning. What would Systems Control see when they did? Had they been in battle? Just what was coming back to Etheric Empire space?

They would soon find out.

"All *ArchAngel II* areas are very clear," Turrel told his leader. "But I sent a warning message."

Yri-Keva clicked her mandibles in humor. "You know that just means everyone is going to be looking for their arrival."

"Of course," Turrel agreed.

· · ·

Skaine Battleship *Shllet*

Tabitha sat in the captain's chair, with Captain Bok next to her. He was watching the Ranger doing something to her nails.

"May I ask what you are doing?" he inquired, nodding toward her hands when she looked at him.

"I'm filing my nails down a little. I don't like them long. They get in the way when I have to go into a firefight," she answered. "Why?"

"You don't seem very happy to be bringing us in," he admitted. "I would figure that such a good catch as this battleship would excite you."

Tabitha looked around the thirty or so control stations on the large bridge. It was quiet, and it should be. More than twenty of the *ArchAngel II*'s Guardian contingent were stationed throughout the ship.

Here on the bridge, it was her, Ryu, and Hirotoshi.

At the very start of the trip back to Yollin space, there had been a problem. Tabitha had handled it by slapping the Skaine into next week for giving her lip. Then Captain Bok had ejected that Skaine into space for trying to break the surrender agreement.

All issues quickly died down after that event.

"Captain Bok," Tabitha eyed the Skaine captain, "to be fair, I prefer to blow up Skaine ships. I like them best as little pieces of flotsam in the ever-increasing enormity of space. That you treated us as honorable combatants and yielded was a bit annoying."

"You expected me to try and fight the *ArchAngel II*?" he asked, surprised. "Or the other eleven ships with her?"

She shrugged. "Well, to be truthful, I didn't know about the other ships until they arrived," Tabitha told him. "I just knew *ArchAngel II* was coming."

"It was a message," Bok told her. "We were in an out-of-the-way place, yet your Empress sent a force that large for just *one* of her Rangers."

Tabitha smiled, then leaned over to the Skaine captain and whispered, "Bethany Anne would do that for any of her people. But if you *ever* fuck with her friends, just kill yourself right then and there, because the universe won't be big enough to hide you."

Tabitha leaned back and resumed filing her nails as the captain sat and thought about what she had just said.

CHAPTER NINE

"Nathan?" R'yhek asked, his mandibles clicking nervously as he looked to confirm that Ecaterina and Christina weren't concerned. "Why are you opening the door to space?"

"The question, R'yhek, should be," Nathan told him as he hit the last button and the door started to open, "what space are we opening into?"

As the doors separated, R'yhek's eyes widened as it became obvious they were in the hold of a much larger ship. Nathan waved R'yhek forward, and he walked out of the *Prometheus* onto the ramp that led down to the deck. Behind him, the three humans smiled as R'yhek kept looking around at the hold of the obviously new ship.

"Welcome to *Prometheus Major*," a voice came from the speakers. "I am the EI for this band of heroes and outlaws."

"Wait!" R'yhek turned back as the three humans caught up to him. The two ladies kept walking toward a door that swished open for them, and they both turned right.

"Where are they going?" he asked.

"Spa." Nathan clapped the larger Yollin on his back. "They love to soak after an operation."

"I am an operation?" he asked.

Nathan thought about that a moment. "In a way. Recruiting is our operation currently, and we need to get a move on. We are half a day behind already."

"Before I ask why we are behind," R'yhek continued, "why did the voice say that we have heroes and outlaws?"

Nathan scratched his cheek. "Well, that's because PM read the lyrics to the song, and for some reason has a rather romanticized view of what we are doing."

"PM?" R'yhek butted in, feeling the avalanche of info he had asked for starting to hit him.

"*Prometheus Major* is the name of this ship, and the EIs of the Empire tend to take the names of their ships. I don't think it is mandatory, but I can't recall one yet that hasn't."

R'yhek turned to look at what he previously thought was a large ship. It had to be at least fifty meters long, and he thought it could comfortably fit twelve of himself.

The voice came back through the speakers. "I consider myself Prometheus Minor when I'm active on the Q-ship."

"Q-ship?" R'yhek asked, his shoulders drooping a little.

"I'll catch you up on that later," Nathan told him. "Here is the fast rundown." He pointed to the smaller Q-ship. "We use that ship anytime someone will see us, and to do all of our planet-side runs." He pointed at the ceiling of the large deck. "The *Major* is for our transfers between systems."

"Wait, between systems?" R'yhek started to comprehend what kind of ship he was standing in. "This ship can create Gates?"

Nathan nodded. "Got it in one, buddy."

"This ship is more valuable than many worlds, Nathan." R'yhek spoke softly before turning to eye the human. "If anyone finds out we have it, we will be chased and have to fight our way out of systems."

"Well then," Nathan answered, "let's make sure no one finds

out, okay?" He pointed to the doors the ladies had gone through a few moments before. "Come on, we have more to talk about."

"What about getting the stuff off..." R'yhek left the question a moment as he tried to remember the names.

"We call the small ship the *Minor*, the large ship the *Major*, and the EI is Prometheus, or PM for short," Nathan told him over his shoulder as the doors opened. The hallway beyond was larger than the big human's stature required. R'yhek filed that observation away.

They were expecting larger aliens onboard.

Where the ladies had turned right, Nathan turned left. "Don't worry about the product. PM has a bunch of service droids for that work. Bad Company has a very lean operation."

"You call this lean?" R'yhek asked as they passed another hallway. He wasn't sure yet how large the ship was, but it was large enough to surprise him.

"We are bodies-lean, support-help-heavy," Nathan admitted. "On my world, I used to do all sorts of operations. Usually, we could and would include what was called hum-int or human intelligence. Since that terminology doesn't work in space, we just call it soft intelligence vs. digital."

"Why soft?" R'yhek asked as Nathan turned right down a corridor.

"Because organics tend to be squishy." He put up a hand and stopped a moment. "I realize that some aliens have very hard exoskeletons, so the term isn't perfect."

R'yhek shrugged. "I was wondering, not questioning."

"Oh." Nathan turned to a nondescript door. "Prometheus, this is Nathan Lowell, Co-Captain of the *Prometheus* and honor-bound to Bethany Anne, Empress of the Etheric Empire. I present to you the Yollin named R'yhek for medical review and enhancement on my personal approval."

R'yhek listened and watched Nathan. He heard a tiny noise

behind him, and when he looked back, he realized that this portion of the hallway had been sectioned off.

Prometheus spoke to him. "R'yhek of Planet Yoll, do you willingly join Bad Company? A company built to acquire intelligence for the Empire and work to promote the Empire's creed? Will you consider yourself honor-bound to Empress Bethany Anne and fight for these, your brothers and sisters in the company?"

R'yhek tapped his mandibles together. "If I say no?"

The EI answered. "Then you will be allowed to get off at the next location, but I will still fix your back. You will also lose the ability to remember what has happened over the last week, so consider it an exchange."

R'yhek looked at Nathan, who was patiently waiting for R'yhek to be comfortable enough to answer one way or another.

"If I choose to not have my back fixed?" R'yhek asked.

Nathan shrugged. "Your back is getting fixed. You just won't realize you said *no* originally."

R'yhek nodded his head. "Mercenary," he commented. "I approve, Nathan Lowell. It is a hard galaxy. Sometimes the right answer isn't the nice answer."

Nathan's eyes flashed yellow and his demeanor took on a new cast. R'yhek resisted the urge to take a step back. "If you join my family, R'yhek, you will be my brother in this company, and Christina will trust you as an uncle. Consider your answer, because I have lived with hard answers for two of your lifetimes."

R'yhek's eyes opened wider. "You are truly this old?"

"I am, R'yhek." Nathan sighed. "I've killed more souls than I care to remember. I have a mate, a wife if you will, and a daughter who have told me we either do this together or I sit in an asteroid somewhere else by myself. Every person accepted into this company would give up their lives for each other. So let me ask you." Nathan pointed to the other side of the ship. "If Christina is in a building alone, it is on fire, and you know you will die rescuing her, what are you going to do?"

R'yhek's eyes drew down, mandibles grinding together. "I won't need to go into the building, Nathan Lowell," he hissed, anger in this voice.

"Why not, R'yhek the Red?" Nathan surprised R'yhek by calling him by his mercenary name, which he had acquired because he had come back from actions so often with the blood of his enemies coating an axe.

"Because I would never have left her side. We would be in the building to complete our operation together, or die side by side."

The doors opened as R'yhek held Nathan's stare until Nathan broke it. He nodded toward the room on the other side of the doors. "Then enter into the greatest secret of *Prometheus*, R'yhek the Red."

R'yhek turned and stepped into the room ahead of Nathan. It was large, the ceiling easily twice his height. In the middle were two large machines.

Nathan pointed to the blue tank to the left. It could hold four of R'yhek without any touching "The large one with liquid is for when we need to regenerate." He pointed to another, which seemed to be opening as one end lifted. "This one allows you to lie down." Nathan pointed to a bin sliding out of the base. "Throw your clothes in there, since we will have a new uniform for you when you finish."

"Uniform?" R'yhek asked as he started pulling off his shirt. He sniffed. "It is a bit rank."

"That's because the air is purified, so you don't lose the smell among all the others," Nathan answered. "We don't do that all over the ship all of the time. The uniform isn't standard, but then, nothing about Bad Company is standard."

R'yhek padded over to the machine. "You want me to do what?"

Nathan pointed to the bottom. "Set your feet on that large step and relax. The Pod will slowly close. Not that you will know about it, because you will be asleep. We are going to give your body a little tune-up."

R'yhek put his feet where Nathan pointed and laid back on the reclining bed. He noticed it was set up for larger creatures than himself.

Substantially larger.

Well, he thought as the Pod started closing and the lights started dimming.

He had said he wanted adventure.

QBBS *Meredith Reynolds*, Yollin System

"Addix, the only way to deal with this threat is cutting it out and cutting it off," Bethany Anne told the Ixtali legate. "The pissed-off group can get itself together, denounce your efforts, and leave the Ixtali nation. You remove the kill switches and allow them to go."

Legate Addix made a face. "It has been suggested we just use the kill switches to rid ourselves of them now, but we realized with the first group that if we did that, we would face a massive revolt. We might as well just kill all of us if we choose that option."

Bethany Anne said nothing.

"I am stalling, aren't I?" Addix bowed her head once. "How do we do this?"

Bethany Anne put her hands on each side of Addix's head. "Meredith, privacy, please."

Those outside of the Queen's area were surprised to find out there was a barrier that could change from transparent to an opaque white in only a moment, blocking all view of those still inside.

"Well, that is another surprise." Delegate Tomthum admitted. He desperately wanted to send a probe to find out if it could make it through the swirling mass that prevented him from seeing what was happening to the Ixtali legate.

Self-preservation held him in check.

"It seems," his friend told him as he looked around, "this trip has been nothing but surprises."

"That is good for us," Tomthum admitted. "Those against us have provided nothing but surprises for generations."

The two fell silent, both imagining what might be happening behind the veil.

Now, this shouldn't hurt. Bethany Anne spoke to Addix. *But then, I've not done this recently to your kind.*

Done what?

This. Bethany Anne told her. *TOM?*

Almost there, Bethany Anne.

Who is that? Addix questioned. *Am I speaking?*

A friend and no, this is all mental.

A new voice spoke, a male voice if Addix could tell anything for sure. **Done.**

Done what? Addix asked.

You physically cannot talk, Bethany Anne answered. *We had to first be sure to protect you physically as well as... ADAM?*

>>**Done, Bethany Anne.**<<

Okay.

Who is that?

Addix, you have promised me access to all things Ixtali, so in return I will trust you with a couple of pieces of information. The first voice...

Me.

Yes, him, is Thales of Miletus, or TOM. He took that name on my world what seems like forever ago. However, he is truly older than me by too many years to count. TOM is a Kurtherian.

Of the Five, if your kind knows the difference.

Addix positively sniffed in affront inside her own brain. *Yes, we know of the separation.*

Good, just confirming what I already knew, TOM explained.

Wait, how? No, never mind. You are the one who can understand my language, and you are reading from my... Addix's insights came quickly. *You are enhanced!* She spoke to Bethany Anne

I am, Bethany Anne answered. *I have evolved beyond the norm, you might say, for my people. However, even with the enhancements TOM has provided, I am much stronger for my association with him and ADAM.*

Addix seemed to listen, but then she was off answering questions to herself. *That is why you fight Kurtherians so much. You have a pact with one of the Five to protect others.*

Not...exactly. TOM broke her chain of thought.

No? Addix questioned. *I thought it would be a requirement.*

No. TOM explained. **I upgraded Bethany Anne to help prepare her to protect her own world from attack. The whole go-out-and-find-the-sumbitches-and-protect-others is all her.**

You speak oddly for a Kurtherian, Addix observed. *I thought your kind was more...dry?*

You seek the word meaning the concept of *boring*, TOM agreed. **I was a bit stuffy, but I have loosened up around Bethany Anne.**

What will you do if you find deceit in me?

TOM answered. **You will be terminated.**

So the Empress will kill me?

No, I will.

But, I thought those of the Five did not do violence?

Bethany Anne isn't the only one who has received enhancements, Addix. I am now capable of taking the fight to

the Seven. I have had many conversations and debates and had many deliberations with Bethany Anne, some at speeds of thought which allowed us to explore in a night what might have taken years before. And now, it is obvious.

Bethany Anne finished TOM's thought. *To fail to kill those who institute racial genocide is the bigger sin.*

Addix pondered that a moment. *Which is why you are willing to help. Those who are causing us problems will, at some point, consider using the power they wish to develop.*

Power isn't sought for no reason. You don't create a tool without a purpose. There are some who pursue offense to provide the best defense against using it. We know and understand that. However, there must be a counter or a check for that kind of offense. Until the Ixtalis give up their ability to indiscriminately kill their own kind, you are holding a sword over everyone's head. That time has passed. It is time to recognize that the Ixtalis need to choose a direction. Neutral is not a direction.

Addix pondered while the other three did something in her mind; what, she wasn't sure. For the moment, she gave up worrying if she was going to die. She was either going to pass… or she wasn't.

There were large changes in store that her own people had already started. Perhaps they could not have the bloodless revolution many desired. However, it was certain that if the agitators could force the Ixtalis away from true neutrality, then they would end up fighting the Etheric Empire.

Unbidden, scenes from humanity's past wars entered Addix's mind. Massive violence as these humans killed each other. They killed using their hands, metal instruments, and weapons that fired. Chemicals and bombs fell from the skies, laying waste to thousands.

Millions.

Cities were destroyed, and people cried in their streets. Lands were awash in the dead. In some scenes the dead looked similar, and in others, it was obvious that while the corpses were human, they looked dramatically different.

Different skins, sizes, colors, ages.

These people had known killing for eons. It was what they did, whether they had superweapons or bones with which to hit one another.

Then the scenes changed. She was shown scenes of compassion. Humans providing food and drink to those who needed it. Heroes pulling the weak from crumbling and dangerous buildings on fire. Physical affection amongst different types for each other.

A few humans standing against many others, protecting the defenseless from a mob.

The Empress' voice reverberated in her mind.

Those who wish to hurt the defenseless will always be the enemies of the Etheric Empire.

CHAPTER TEN

The milky white opaqueness dissolved, and those outside of the Empress' area could see inside once more. What they saw was the Ixtali legate, head bowed, face and mandibles still. Some moments later, her head came up. She turned, head held high, and walked toward her side of the room.

Two Guardians walked with her as she and what was left of her party were led to a door exiting the throne area.

Then the Empress looked at the Yaree and spoke clearly, without shouting.

"Tell me," she asked. "What do the Yaree have for me today?" Bethany Anne turned and walked back up the steps to her throne as Delegate Tomthum took a deep breath. As she took her seat, he turned one of his three eyestalks to his friend and performed the silent dip of goodbye.

"Oh, no." The Empress caught their attention. "I want all of you over here."

Gabrielle waited until the tram had come to a complete stop. She stood as the doors opened and waived the Estarians toward the door.

Estarians were taller and more stately than humans They had thick, smooth skin with a blue tinge and an underlying effervescence. These attributes would often make other species a little envious due to the Estarians' almost magnetic charisma.

It was having no effect on this woman as she smiled. "Yes, you are still inside the *Meredith Reynolds,* and I am taking you to a private interview. Bethany Anne, I'm told, is running late with the Ixtalis, and then will meet with the Yaree. She will join us as soon as she can."

"Two groups most distant from each other," Senior Delegate Cannock agreed as he ducked his head and exited the tram.

Gabrielle waited for the entire group to leave the tram before she allowed the doors to slide shut. It continued toward the final station inside the *Meredith Reynolds.*

This stop was rarely used, and frankly, Gabrielle wasn't sure why Bethany Anne wanted to speak to the Estarians privately like this.

But Gabrielle had to take it easy during her pregnancy and absolutely wasn't allowed anywhere near sparring. To have something to do, she was trying to help in the diplomatic area.

Normally she would be happy to use non-threatening tactics, but her emotional control was occasionally weak, and instead of smiling, she would imagine ripping a table leg off and shoving it up the ass of the nearest annoying alien.

Often for no logical reason.

Sometimes Bethany Anne would view the video with an exasperated Gabrielle and chuckle. Then she would show the segment that had incited the incident and pat Gabrielle on the back. "Nice job not killing the messenger, Gabrielle."

Afterward, Bethany Anne would leave, not realizing how close to the edge Gabrielle really was.

Or so the mother-to-be thought.

Bethany Anne, TOM, and ADAM were constantly trying to figure out how to help Gabrielle with her pregnancy. Apparently, the nanocytes TOM had used and the ones Eric had transferred the good old-fashioned way were mixing in the twins inside Gabrielle, and there were...

Complications.

Gabrielle knew none of this as she explained to Senior Delegate Cannock the status of the Etheric Empire and the people in it.

QBBS *Meredith Reynolds*, Throne Room

Bethany Anne was tired. So damned tired.

Tired of being pulled in all these damned directions. Make peace here, solve a problem there, all in the name of trying to create a tidy little area of the Galaxy where people could feel safe.

When was she ever going to get a chance to leave this hocus-pocus talk behind? Couldn't people simply realize that her side was good, the other side was bad, and just fucking *dance*?

If her father told her one more time, that Empresses weren't supposed to be at the front of the attack group, she would remind him of the heroes of all the stories he had told her as a young and impressionable girl. *They* hadn't sat back in the middle of a damned asteroid as their people risked life and limb.

As the Yaree group came toward her, she crossed her legs and put an elbow on her knee, wondering what a nomadic group like the Yaree might have for her this day.

The Ixtalis, she was sure, were going to prove interesting in the long run, but that was for another time, after Legate Addix went back and spoke to her council.

TOM?

Yes?

Nomadic group, kind of like Earth's Gypsies with the same

concern from those they trade with. Namely, often accused of stealing when they move on?

Yes.

>>But their history as a nomadic group only goes back about five hundred years. Before then, there are rumors and counter-rumors about who they were and when they came into the systems to trade.<<

No one knows?

>>No, they are an insular group.<<

Yeah, just like our Gypsies.

There were five in the Delegate's group, now striding onto the carpet. The Yaree were an interesting bunch. Three eyestalks, tallish and thin. Their large feet had two toes, but they had five fingers on their hands. Their skin had a purplish hue. Two of the Yaree had little clothing on their torso, and two wore voluminous robes.

The three eyestalks of the two with little clothing were constantly looking around. Bethany Anne pegged them as guards for the two in the middle. That left one for her to be curious about.

"Greetings, Empress," one of the two in the center bowed with only his eyestalks.

Bethany Anne worked very diligently to stifle the snort of surprised laughter that wanted to erupt from her throat.

Seriously? TOM asked.

It was CUTE! Bethany Anne argued. *Those tall things all just bowed in the middle like...like...*

Like three eyestalks bowing on the top of a head. I get it.

Grumble Gus, she shot back before she replied to her visitor.

Bethany Anne smiled. "Greetings, Delegate Tomthum." She tipped her head to all of those with him. "I apologize for asking all of you here, but since there's no one else left in the room to speak with me today, I figured this way, you wouldn't have to retell the story to the rest of your team."

"The story?" Tomthum asked, one stalk turning to the other prominent individual in the group.

If she viewed their fashions as a statement of importance.

"Yes, the story," Bethany Anne answered. "And may I have the names of your group?"

Tomthum, his rather large mouth smiling, turned to his left. "Certainly!" He waved a hand. "Let me introduce you to Sub-Delegate Caspise."

Bethany Anne received another three-eye-stalk bow. She nodded in return, and fortunately, TOM didn't say a word. She wasn't sure if TOM understood that he had just missed an opportunity to make her laugh at an incredibly inopportune moment. "Greetings, Sub-Delegate Caspise."

"Greetings, Empress," he replied.

"These two," Tomthum continued, "are Keth and Bonn. Their role among our people is support."

"Don't you mean they are guards?" Bethany Anne wondered aloud as all six of their eyestalks swung in her direction before they returned to scanning the room.

>>Wow, talk about physical cues.<<

It could be a natural reaction. However, some of them probably use it against those that assume too much. Easy to believe they mean one thing by it, and the next thing you know, you come against a master who uses physical cues to deceive you.

>>Has anyone informed you that you have a very suspicious mind?<<

Of course.

>>Lately?<<

I'm sure.

>>How lately?<<

Uhhh... Bethany Anne blanked a moment.

TOM jumped into the conversation. **Three days ago. Stephen mentioned it at lunch.**

That's right!

>>Almost made it seventy-two hours. That might be a record.<<

Et tu, *ADAM?*

>>Not really. I just needed to know for the betting pool.<<

Bethany Anne kicked him out of the conversation for a second, annoyed that not only was she a part of yet one more betting pool, but her damned AI friend had just gigged her.

He could be entirely too smart by half sometimes.

"I suppose you could call them guards, but you have to forgive us. We aren't always seen in the best light." Tomthum smiled once more.

Damn, that's a lot of teeth.

>>Imagine the toothpaste commercials for their race.<<

Bethany Anne sighed mentally. *Wow, the shit that goes on in my head at these meetings. It's a shame no one will ever know.*

TOM sent her a gentle mind-bump. **It's how we keep you sane.**

Yeah, unfortunately, that's too damned true, she agreed.

"I've been informed about that," Bethany Anne agreed. "But let's save that discussion for a minute." She nodded to the last person in the group. "And the last in your party?"

"May I introduce you to Ship's Captain Teth?" Tomthum waved to the shortest Yaree in the group. His eyestalks bowed, but Bethany Anne could swear he was a bit vacant.

"Welcome, Ship's Captain." Bethany Anne nodded to the last of the group. She had five bodies and fifteen eyes, not all of them looking at her. She couldn't imagine what she would do with three eyes that could look in different directions.

Imagine if I could just use one of those eyes. TOM mused.

Let's not and never mention that idea again.

Why not?

I can only imagine the interesting comments if suddenly one of my eyes went straying off to look at God knows what. You could give something away.

Like what? I'm not interested in alien bodies, so no one is going to wonder about you checking out the latest piece of alien tail.

No, worse.

Okay, you are going to have to help me out here a little, Bethany Anne. I could understand if I looked at the wrong person or alien...

TOM, what is most interesting to you?

Math.

Exactly.

There was a slight pause.

Oh. TOM's mental voice was soft. **Everyone knows you hate math.**

Yup. Might as well put a damned "Kurtherian in residence" sign above my third eye.

"Thank you, Empress." The reticent Yaree took a step back.

"Okay, guys." Bethany Anne paused as she eyed each in turn. "I'm assuming you're all males of your species, right? I'm not trying to offend anyone here."

Well, hell, TOM interjected. **You just killed an Ixtali in front of them, kicked another's ass, and did all sorts of stuff that probably would make a grown bistok pause before attacking you. Even if you offended them, I doubt you would get any lip.**

And Dad says my version of a political discussion doesn't have an upside! Bethany Anne retorted.

Tomthum turned his two outside eyes in separate directions as if he were confirming they were all males before all three eyes turned back to Bethany Anne. "Yes, all males, Empress."

"So, let's get down to business." She pointed behind them. "I'm not terribly happy with gabbing for its own sake, and I've been informed that information has been shared with the universe's various races."

"It has," Tomthum admitted. "That is one of the reasons we requested an audience."

"Because I don't like to chat?"

"No, because the usual sycophants that would be around leaders are absent, to be truthful." Tomthum's large lips pressed together. "Empress, you have said that you do not know much about our people. How accurate is that?"

Bethany Anne sat back in her chair and crossed her right leg over her left. "It's as accurate as it needs to be, Delegate. I *don't* know much about you since I don't have a relationship with the Ixtalis for data downloads on everyone and everything. While I have the knowledge the Yollins have acquired, the data on your people seems to disappear between three hundred and fifty to five hundred years ago. And there is so much information in some places a person can't tell truth from dross. We can recognize a concerted effort to hide the truth."

Tomthum nodded his understanding.

"Now, I can guess a small part of your present needs, and I can admit something that will probably cause you to go catatonic on me. However, since the knowledge won't really affect these discussions too much—"

"What knowledge, Empress?" Tomthum interrupted as politely as he could. When the Empress started talking, all fifteen eyestalks turned toward her, including the guards'. The captain's eyestalks seemed to shrink just a bit.

"Well, the first is, your poison won't work on me," Bethany Anne answered. She pointed to Tomthum's partner. "And there is no way my team would allow any sort of explosives inside here, plus," she tapped her dress, "this protection from Jean Dukes can take any knife you can throw. Further..." She stood up and took one step down and disappeared.

The five Yaree turned around. Their two guards pulled out elaborate wires that started glowing blue as they whipped them in an elaborate pattern.

Only to fall to their feet a microsecond later when John casually shot them both. The captain dropped a second later.

Eric turned to John. "Wasn't me," John told him.

"Fainted," Bethany Anne announced as she reappeared a moment later, still standing at the top of the steps. "As I was about to say, Delegate," Bethany Anne stepped back to her throne and sat down, "my guards get really annoyed when someone comes here to have a discussion and then tries to kill me if they fail so their secrets don't get out."

"The only reason you haven't been spaced," Bethany Anne went on as the two left standing stared up at her, "is because I understand just enough of your concerns to want to know more about those that are attacking your world."

"Our world, Empress?" Tomthum swallowed but looked at his two guards. "Dead?"

"No, knocked out," the huge guard answered from Bethany Anne's right. "Killing, we have found, is always a damned mess to clean up. Much easier to stun and toss out the trash toward the sun when you need to."

Tomthum breathed in deeply. This whole day had not gone in any way, shape, or form as his team had planned.

The second group had been led away, the Ixtalis had something serious going on, the Empress' face had flared red before the meeting...

And now, she knew something about the Yaree that he was honor-bound to keep secret.

"Do you know the story, Empress?" he asked. "I presume you have some way of reading our thoughts to know this much."

Another voice came from the speakers in the room. "This is ADAM. Who says the Empress needs to read minds when you leave so much in your computer systems?"

Tomthum wanted to rub his eyestalks in annoyance. He was an idiot. Why assume she could mysteriously read minds if they had something that was powerful enough to get through the security of their systems and pull it straight from their ship?

"Ah, forgive me," he finally replied. "With all the powers you have demonstrated," this time, he nodded his head in her direction, "I just jumped to the conclusion you could read minds."

"So," Bethany Anne ignored his comment, "what is it about your home world that is so important that you need help? And if we don't give you that help, then you are willing to kill to keep it secret?"

The two guards were slowly waking up, with Tomthum's sub-delegate whispering to them as they opened their eyes.

Bethany Anne sure hoped he was telling them to settle the fuck down, or next time John might not be so lenient. He really did hate cleaning the floor. She had told him in no uncertain terms that if he killed someone who wasn't trying to kill her, it was his ass that was mopping up the blood.

That went for all of the Guards. So far, they had successfully stunned everyone when it had been a problem. However, one day she just knew that there was going to be blood and guts all over the place.

"First, let us do away with this charade," the Delegate declared. "We, the Yaree, as we are now known, were called by another name in the past." He pointed to his people. "Before Yaree, we were the Karillians."

>>**Oh, damn.**<< ADAM sent Bethany Anne.

CHAPTER ELEVEN

Five minutes later.

"Are you shitting me?" Bethany Anne asked, her voice reinforcing the shock her face was displaying. "You want to know if we can help with a set of aliens sent to destroy your world in *two* freaking months?"

Bethany Anne? TOM interrupted.

NOT NOW! she sent back.

"Well, we realize it is a fast turnaround," Tomthum admitted.

"FAST?" Bethany Anne wanted to pull out someone's hair. Not hers, because it was presently looking fantastic. Not stressing all the damn time had done wonderful things for her split ends.

She considered yanking Tomthum's eyestalk instead, since he didn't have much hair on his leathery purple body, at least not where she could see it. "*Fast*, for an effort to save a world, is not two months away in another *Gott Verdammt* galaxy! If I understand you correctly, you have had seventy years."

BETHANY ANNE! TOM repeated, more emphatically this time.

WHAT?

Do you remember the seven years with Kael-ven?

What? Oh... Are we talking six Earth months? Fuck, I get this shit screwed up all the time with the translations. Sometimes they seem to be using Earth, then Yollin, then standard date schemes. I fucking hate dates.

And math, TOM added.

Yeah, that shit too, she sent, then, thinking in a softer tone, *Sorry for yelling at you.*

No problem.

"Okay, I've had an update on the timing situation," Bethany Anne announced, her voice calm once more. "It seems the translation was telling me we had a third as much time as what you meant to tell me."

"That matters," Tomthum confirmed. "And it's better?"

"Well, I wouldn't say it was superb," she clarified. "But it beats the hell out of two months."

"Okay, new plan." Bethany Anne looked up. "Meredith?"

"Yes, Empress?"

"Provide the Delegate's team with quarters, set up proper security, and find out what we have to feed them. Let everyone rest and call the military leaders for a meeting in the morning."

Tomthum cleared his throat, his eyestalks watching the Empress.

"Yes?" she asked him.

"May I ask why you chose to help us so fast?" She thought Caprise's eyes did a fair imitation of rolling in disbelief that the delegate had asked that question.

"Because," John spoke up. "Our Empress will always and forever defend the defenseless."

Bethany Anne stood up. "Eric, please see to their needs and then meet with Gabrielle and me."

"Yes, ma'am," he told her and started down the stairs. "Okay, Karillians, grab your stuff and let me show you where you are going to be staying."

John moved next to Bethany Anne.

Tomthum turned to bid the Empress goodbye, but she and the large guard had already disappeared.

Damn, he sure wished he had kept an eyestalk on her.

John and Bethany Anne appeared in her personal quarters. "*Gott Verdammt!*" She practically vibrated with energy. "You know what TOM's telling me?"

"Nope," John answered, one eyebrow raised as Bethany Anne headed straight to an area that she had created a while back but rarely went into.

Bethany Anne spoke aloud, "Meredith, open the vault, please."

A solid door disengaged from the wall. In her bedroom Bethany Anne had a huge bed, more for Ashur and the others to jump on or for the occasional girls' movie night.

She also had a couple of dressers, and of course, her large clothes and shoe closet. Bethany Anne had continued to acquire pairs of shoes over the years and had finally decided that she needed to move out her weapons and armor to make room.

She'd had a separate room built for that purpose. Now the door was opening, and Bethany Anne strode into it with a spring to her step.

John reached down to touch the collar of his shirt. "ADAM, send code 222x3 to Dan, please."

In another part of the *Meredith Reynolds*, Dan Bosse was reviewing the latest information he could find regarding the surprise military meeting Bethany Anne had called in the morning.

"Dan?" the voice interrupted his thoughts.

"Yes, ADAM?" He looked up.

"John Grimes is sending you code 222x3 from Bethany Anne's room."

"Oh, shit..." Dan's voice sputtered.

"Dan," ADAM went on, "I don't have any records of this code. Can you illuminate me?"

"Yeah, but you have to promise to keep the meaning secret unless Bethany Anne expressly requires you to answer," Dan replied.

"I do."

"Okay. In short, he is telling me we are about to have an apocalypse."

"How? What does that code have to do with an apocalypse?"

Now how the hell were they going to deal with her? Dan wondered. If John sent the code, it meant that he believed she was preparing for one, and he didn't think he could change her mind by himself.

Dan tapped a finger on his desk as he thought about it. "Because if you use 'x' as a multiplier, it gives you the number 666. It means Bethany Anne has decided that the Empress is going into hibernation and the Queen Bitch is back."

Just what the fuck happened in her meetings today? Dan sighed as he started typing in the code to get Lance on the phone.

"Oh, shit!" ADAM replied.

Tabitha, Hirotoshi, and Ryu stood in front of Barnabas, who was eyeing his team lead and her top two assistants.

He had reached out to Hirotoshi and Ryu a while back to ask if they wanted to become Rangers, and the response on their normally calm faces had been telling, more telling than Hirotoshi's answer.

"No," Hirotoshi replied, a small smile playing along his lips. "There are Yin and Yang. And there is Kemosabe."

"And her Tontos." Ryu nodded his agreement.

Hirotoshi had winked to Barnabas, positively shocking him. "We are *her* Tontos, and we will *always* be with Kemosabe."

Barnabas had never brought it up again.

Now the three of them were standing in front of him in his temporary office on *ArchAngel II*. "Ranger Two, how am I supposed to commend you for bringing a Skaine battleship in?"

Tabitha shrugged. "Hey, they just wanted a piece of *Achronyx*'s tail."

"I've seen the video already," Barnabas answered drily. "But by accomplishing this feat, you caused poor Achronyx to require assistance to get into *ArchAngel*'s hold. You guys fried so many areas of his engines that the mech boys aren't sure what to do about it yet. You all could have been nothing but tiny little particles spread out over the universe right now. There is a reason, I'm told, that those limiters are in place on a ship."

Tabitha sniffed. "Not our fault they under-engineered Achronyx's body."

Barnabas just stared at his Ranger a moment. "They under-engineered the *Achronyx*? That ship design was state-of-the-art."

"It was when we received it, Big B." She smiled. "What say we get *Achronyx* some upgrades?"

Barnabas was exasperated. "To what?"

"I understand there is a Skaine battleship available?" Hiro-toshi asked.

"I can't believe he won't let us upgrade *Achronyx* to the battleship." Tabitha bitched after Ryu had shut the door to Barnabas' office. They all knew he could still hear them, but as long as they didn't complain directly in front of him, he could ignore it.

Anyway, it wasn't like he hadn't read their minds already.

"It would substantially up our costs," Ryu temporized.

"Yeah, but we could get fat and happy all the time eating popcorn and shit." Tabitha argued, "Who would fuck with us if we showed up in a battleship?"

"Which can't create temporal jumps," Ryu reminded her.

"Well, yeah, that kinda sucks," Tabitha agreed.

The three of them turned a corner, Tabitha's voice floating down the hallway. "Can you believe he told us to take a vacation?"

Yollin System

The alien moved easily between those walking on the sidewalk, his green skin marking him as alien, if nothing else. He had three earrings in one ear, and another two in the other.

He had been requested to meet a group at any bar of his choosing in the Yollin system.

So he chose All Guns Blazing as the meeting point. He enjoyed the beverage they had offered there the last time he went, and he never had a chance to start a fight with any of the feisty Torcellans. Okay, they were really called humans, he had learned.

He preferred his own name.

Shi-tan had checked the bona fides of the group he was

meeting with and found that it was one of the older companies on Yoll. They had apparently misplaced one of their founding members, who had disappeared with a large percentage of the company's assets.

Fortunately, a relatively simple data search, still expensive as hell, came back with information as to where that Yollin was located, and it wasn't very far from Shi-tan's location—only two jumps away. Shi-tan found the Yollin, Kiel, sitting and drinking some relatively expensive booze in a fairly middle-class bar in the nowhere space station.

It had been on the list of possible locations he had been provided, but it was the third one down in the secondary section. It had taken Shi-tan most of the day to locate the Yollin.

Shi-tan walked up to the small table. "Here, let me pay for your drink." He spoke as he tossed down enough credits to catch the Yollin's inebriated gaze.

"What?" the Yollin asked, then narrowed his eyes to take a better look at Shi-tan. "You're green." He looked higher. "And tall."

"The power of your eyes to discern the obvious serves you well, Yollin," Shi-tan replied. He was rather wishing this Yollin would pick a fight. Unfortunately, he would lose half his bounty if he unnecessarily beat up the mark.

Shi-tan looked around. There weren't enough drinkers in the bar to start a good brawl, and from what he could tell, they weren't drunk enough at the moment either. For a Shrillexian to go too long without violence was painful. Somewhere in their past, Shrillexians had been tweaked genetically to fight as often as they could. Their people would often sell themselves as mercenaries.

Why do that? Then they would get paid to fight. What could be better than that? Unfortunately, the plan had killed off a significant portion of their male population, and a sizeable number of their females, too.

Shrillex had started to die. Shi-tan watched as the males in his family went into the great mercenary companies, one after another. They reaped massive rewards and often helped those same companies decimate their opponents.

But in the end, the results were the same.

The family received either some money and a note about their loss or were given a body damaged beyond recognition. If the mercenary was lucky, only individual body parts were harmed. Two uncles came back one summer, each missing an arm or a leg or both. They were still learning to use the artificial limbs they had been provided.

When it was Shi-tan's turn to either stay on his world or leave, he had left. But he left with a determination that his body would not force him to become something to be used and then discarded.

So he became a bounty hunter. The thrill of the chase helped him keep his need to fight under control. With the occasional bar fight, or by walking around the wrong side of an area to incite some thugs to try and mug him, he had been making do.

So far.

Shi-tan cracked his knuckles as he looked down at the Yollin. "Kiel, I have been contracted to bring you back to Yollin space. There you will be—"

That's when the little puke sucker-punched Shi-tan in the gut, pushed back his chair and started running in the other direction for what looked like a side door.

Shi-tan yanked out a trim-pistol and shot the bastard in the neck, between his two shoulder blades. He flopped down, smashing a table and knocking a chair over, which hit a patron.

Shi-tan sighed. If it wasn't so much money, he thought as he walked toward the Yollin, he would have chased him and punched him a couple of times. But Shi-tan didn't care to go back to his home planet.

And to stay out among the stars, Shi-tan, scion of a great

warrior line and successful bounty hunter, had to take care of expenses.

He confirmed the Yollin was out cold and turned toward the barkeeper who was eyeing him suspiciously. Shi-tan lifted his hands. "He punched me and ran. I'm a licensed bounty hunter, and he," his right hand pointed at the comatose Yollin, "is my mark."

"You got the money for the damages?" the barkeeper demanded. The Shrillexian tossed him a credit voucher. The barkeeper knew enough about Shrillexians to know he really didn't want to push this alien. If he got out of it with enough money to make it all better?

Well, then that would be a bonus.

Three tedious hours later, Kiel felt the vibrations of the bounty hunter's ship disconnect from the space station. It had taken all of his admittedly shitty acting skills to pretend to be asleep the whole time.

Fortunately, this operation was going to be over soon, and Nathan would owe him big time.

He hadn't punched the Shrillexian as hard as he could have, but even so, hitting that bastard's stomach was like punching a damned wall.

Dan? Kiel sent out.

Yes?

It's Kiel. We are on our way back to Yollin space. Bounty hunter took the bait.

Good. There was a pause. *How did it go for you?*

I got to throw a punch before he darted me. I've got some bruises, but nothing that won't be healed by the time we get there.

What are you going to do now?

Kiel considered his options. *I'm going to go to sleep.*

Okay, I see we have our shadow ship following you. So be a good little mark until you are here.

Dan, I'm always good, Kiel sent before closing the Etheric connection. He slowed his mind, allowing the drug to take a little more control before he dropped into a light sleep.

CHAPTER TWELVE

QBBS _Meredith Reynolds_, Estarian Delegate Meeting Room

Senior Delegate Cannock heard the door open and turned to see the Empress come in. She was dressed in a casual blue shirt and a pair of white pants with shoes that increased her height.

She came up to his chest. The male human, however, was almost as tall as he was. Cannock wasn't weak, but he wouldn't care to fight her guard. As the Empress came closer, he found his body responding to her.

Physically.

He looked to see if she was doing something to excite him, but he failed to find anything overt. From the research his team had provided previously, this didn't seem like a tactic the Etheric Empire would try.

Or perhaps, they just hadn't had another species to try it on yet.

He bowed as she came close. "Greetings of the day to you, Empress Bethany Anne."

"And to you, Senior Delegate." She pointed to his chair. "Please sit."

Cannock took his seat again as she placed herself at the head of the table in the meeting room, her guard behind her. Gabrielle sat on the other side across from him.

Her first comment surprised him. "First, let me apologize for changing the location of our meeting. However, I have a lot of issues that need to be addressed, and your system might be able to help."

"Us?" he replied, a little surprised that their out-of-the-way-system could provide *anything* for the Etheric Empire. Then his eyes flattened.

When anyone large or powerful wanted something you had, the question was how badly your people were going to be screwed.

"Yes, and before you freak out—"

"Is it that obvious?" Cannock asked, his blue skin lightening.

"No, it is something I've come to expect and ask," Bethany Anne admitted. "The Etheric Empire has acquired a reputation in the last few years, and unfortunately, most assume we like to go around shooting up space ships and blowing up worlds."

"You have blown up worlds?" Cannock asked, his surprise genuine.

"No," Bethany Anne admitted. "We blew up a Yollin super-dreadnought that was attacking us, and the tales have spread from there." She tilted her head slightly. "Meredith, please display the systems between here and Estaria."

"Wall or table, Empress?" A female voice came out of the speakers.

"Here on top of the table should work," Bethany Anne replied.

Cannock watched as faint lines began to shimmer in the air in front of him. They solidified, and he was viewing a three-dimensional map of space.

"We are here, in orange," the Empress started. One system lit up in the lower left of the hologram. "We will highlight the three core systems we control in yellow." Three more systems, near to but not contiguous with Yoll, lit up. "Now, we will tag those systems who have been basically friendly to most of their neighbors for the last couple hundred years in green."

A larger percentage of space lit up.

"Finally, let's paint our three annoying neighbors in red and Sark in white."

Cannock nodded slowly. The Empress was very well aware that Sark, out in the border area, was cut off from most of the green areas as well as the orange. There was a lot of empty space between the red and them, but the red systems were closer than any of the support.

"You can see from the map that Sark is in a good location. Far enough away, and there aren't enough resources to make it a target. Unfortunately," Bethany Anne moved her fingers, and the hologram spun slightly, "you can also see that if your unruly neighbors wished to cut you off, they could."

"Yes, we are aware of the situation," Cannock admitted. "One of the reasons I have come is to see what, if any, relationship we might form with your Empire."

"Good. I was hoping that was the case, Senior Delegate," Bethany Anne exclaimed. "There is a saying on our planet related to problems and solutions. One person with a problem is a problem, two might be trouble, but three often provide a solution."

"There are only two of us here." Cannock looked around the room. "Unless the Ixtalis or Yaree are about to join us?"

Bethany Anne chuckled. "Not likely," she told him. "I'm representing two sides, and you a third." She put her hands on the table. "I'm going to lay out everything I'm thinking about the situation, and you tell me where I'm wrong or how it might work, okay?"

Cannock just nodded his head in agreement.

"The Sark system has four inhabited worlds, two closer to your sun, Estaria and Ogg, and two farther away, Secoria and Teshovia, with a large asteroid belt between the inner and outer planets. Generally speaking, your worlds are happy enough, even though you have an inner-world elitist attitude." She put up a hand. "I'm not criticizing, I'm merely expressing what I've been told."

Cannock wasn't about to tell her that he hadn't been going to argue; rather he felt elitist was too weak a term.

The Estarians simply *were* better than others in their system. How can one not feel superior when it is the truth?

Bethany Anne continued, "So, Estaria is a bit difficult to inhabit, with dust storms that cause all sorts of problems at times. Your people are not all that militarized, and you don't have a strong connection with the other planets should you all need to come together to fight." She paused a moment. "Frankly, chances are that nobody will want your system in the first place. No major resources, the planets are okay but not spectacular, and you aren't on any major trade routes."

Cannock was silent. He bowed his head just a little. "That is a fairly accurate representation, Empress."

"Okay, making sure I had that right. Here are my problems, and let's see if we can find a possible solution."

Cannock straightened in his chair. Anytime the other side had problems, and they felt you had a way to help them?

Well, he was all ears.

Inside the rooms the Empress had provided, Delegate Tomthum walked toward a wide seat. It looked a bit low for him, but he turned and sat down anyway. His eyes opened in pleasant surprise.

It was very comfortable.

"Is there anything you would like?" the voice he recognized as the station's EI asked. His team went in search of their own rooms, which were connected to the one Tomthum had stopped to rest in.

"Information," he admitted.

"Such as?" Meredith answered. "I'm fully capable of providing information that would be very interesting yet not tactically helpful to your situation whatsoever."

Tomthum thought that was a very nice way to say, "don't be a dumb Yaree."

"Are we safe to speak in this area?"

"Delegate, I can hear anything inside the station. I believe you are asking if your domicile has spying devices?"

"Well, I guess you already answered that, didn't you?"

"Yes, I am capable of hearing everything. However, I am also commanded to leave those things which are of a personal nature alone. If you were, for example, to say that you had plans to blow up the station or cause harm, then that would penetrate my filters and I would look for context. If I should calculate that you intend harm to someone within my sphere of responsibility, I would notify my chain of command."

Tomthum thought about that answer for a few moments. "So, you hear everything, but you don't pass it all along?"

"Correct."

"Do you have records of what we say and do?"

"I have the ability to record, of course. However, I'm not a spymaster, Delegate."

Sub-Delegate Caspise came out of his room and chose a spot on the other end of the couch Tomthum was sitting on. Tomthum was amused to see the same look of surprise in Caspise's eyestalks. "Comfortable, yes?"

"Very," Caspise agreed, feeling the material. "This is natural?"

"Yes," Meredith answered. "They are natural hides."

"Frommmm…" Caspise asked, hoping the answer wasn't an intelligent species.

"Bistok," Meredith answered.

"Bistok?" Keth questioned as he came out. "Aren't those the dangerous creatures down on the planet?"

"The very same, Guard Keth." Meredith confirmed.

Caspise rubbed the seat cover again. "That is interesting."

"That is devious," Tomthum murmured. "They killed the mighty bistok to get their skins."

"They might just bomb them from above." Keth spoke over his shoulder as he checked out the various doors and cabinets in the kitchen. He found the cooler and looked at the options for a moment.

"They did not bomb them from above," Meredith interrupted. "That would not be acceptable to the group."

"Don't worry about the spy stuff," Tomthum told Keth. "We already know we are surrounded by devices."

Keth turned around, each eyestalk looking in a different direction. "We do?"

"Yes," Meredith confirmed. "I'm fully capable of spying on you if I choose."

"What stops you from choosing?" Keth asked.

"I work for the Empress, and she isn't big on spying on invited guests."

"What about uninvited guests?" Caspise butted in.

"Well, of course I spy on those," Meredith answered. "If Reynolds doesn't take the lead, that is."

"Reynolds is…" Caspise drew out the question.

"Reynolds," a gruff voice answered the three, "is the military EI associated with this battle station. If an issue is elevated above the normal security level, it becomes my responsibility."

"So, to sum it up," Tomthum summarized, as Bonn, the other guard, wandered into the room, "effectively we are spied upon and nothing is off-limits, except that the Empress really doesn't care what we talk about, and therefore it won't be noted. If we happen to trip any warnings on your side, Meredith, you will review to see if anything needs to be passed up the chain. If it does, then somebody will review the data and if necessary, point it out to those in charge."

"That is true," Meredith returned, in answer to his question. "However, there is no difference when you are in your own ship, Senior Delegate Tomthum. When you came into the Etheric Empire, you were in the zone of those who protect Bethany Anne. We take our responsibilities very seriously."

"How would you—" Tomthum started to ask, then threw up a hand in frustration. "Are you saying you knew everything about us before we even arrived here on the station?"

"Yes."

"How?"

"I'm not at liberty to answer that question," Meredith replied.

"Who is?"

"ADAM." A third voice came through the speaker. This one was male again, but he had a different nuance to his speech, a different cadence.

"And you are?" Tomthum asked.

"I am ADAM, of course." the voice replied. "I am the one that broke through the security in your craft, read your databases, confirmed your secrets, and then made the decision to allow you to dock, send you back, or discuss with Bethany Anne whether to blow you out of our space."

"And you chose to let us dock?" Caspise asked.

"No, I chose to discuss whether we should blow you out of space. Bethany Anne chose to let you dock," ADAM clarified. "Your operations plan suggested that killing Bethany Anne was one of three options. Option A, you decide she is not the right person to discuss your needs, then negotiate a trade deal and leave. Option B, tell her your secrets and work out a solution, and Option C was tell her your secrets, find no solution, and kill her."

"Yet, you allowed us to dock?" Guard Bonn asked.

"You were no threat, Guard Bonn," ADAM told him. "I'm not saying this to belittle you, and I have compassion for the state of your world, but you were not a danger to Bethany Anne at any time. I had already defused the bombs inside of your ship before you arrived. The poison you wished to use on her doesn't work on her physiology. The martial skills of both you and Keth are inadequate to hurt an Empress' Guardian, much less a Bitch or the Empress."

"What you are saying," Tomthum sighed, "is we are woefully inadequate when it comes to fighting."

"Against the Empress, yes," ADAM confirmed. "However, you are merchants, not mercenaries. Why would you expect to be able to accomplish her death in the first place?"

Caspise leaned over and placed a hand on Tomthum's shoulder. "Don't worry about it, Tomthum. Our job was to see if she and her people could fight." He shook his head. "What, you wanted those who helped us to be someone whose ass we could kick?"

Tomthum's eyestalks twisted a second, "Well, it does show a glaring flaw in our plans."

Caspise looked up at the ceiling. "ADAM?"

A slight hesitation occurred before they heard his voice. "Yes?"

"Am I right in thinking you are another enhanced being, like the Empress today?"

"No, not in that way," ADAM answered. "I cannot fight like she does. My abilities are in the digital realm."

"There you go, old friend," Caspise commiserated as he patted Tomthum's shoulder twice before pulling his hand back. "We were played before we got here."

"If it matters to you," ADAM spoke once more, "Bethany Anne had already determined she would try to help if it was possible. She just needed more details."

"Like what?" Caspise asked as he settled back into the comfortable couch. "Did she get all she needed?"

"Oh, yes," ADAM confirmed. "She was just confirming with another advisor who might be behind the attacks."

"We know who. The damned Leath and their thrice-damned gods."

"Yes, but the Gods of the Leath have another name," ADAM responded.

"Really?" Caspise asked. "What is it?"

"Kurtherians," ADAM replied.

CHAPTER THIRTEEN

QBBS _Meredith Reynolds_, Estarian Delegate Meeting Room
Bethany Anne pursed her lips for a moment before she moved a few strands of hair out of her way and continued her discussion with the Estarian Senior Delegate.

"Sir Cannock, we are but a few years here, and there are families who have a desire to stretch their legs on another planet, away from the fighting if possible. Some have loved ones who didn't think through what living in a big rock in space truly meant. Some are migrating to Yoll, but frankly, the Yollins are still a problem."

Cannock nodded his understanding. "Too alien?"

"That might be one way to put it. Another might be 'too crustacean.' However, between the Estarians and the Oggs, your physiology seems to resonate with certain groups."

"Resonate?" Cannock asked.

"Yes," Bethany Anne thought a moment. "Your body types are easier for some to get accustomed to seeing. To us, Estarians look like a tall blue human with a flatter nose. Even many of your gestures are not dissimilar to our own."

"And Oggs?" Cannock asked, curious about her answer.

"You won't understand this easily, but I'll try." Bethany Anne made sure not to roll her eyes. "The Oggs remind many of those here of a life-sized cartoon character named Spongebob Squarepants."

Cannock just blinked at her, not comprehending.

"It's due to their mottled yellow skin. I don't see it myself," Bethany Anne admitted, "but there you go." She looked up. "Meredith, please take away the hologram model and replace it with a short video of the cartoon on the wall for the Senior Delegate and his team."

The Estarian delegate and team members turned to see what looked like an underwater scene. Something with a yellow character whose skin, if you squinted just right, did resemble the Oggs' skin. Obviously, Oggs were not square, but Cannock had to fight a smile anyway.

They seemed to him to be just as slow in the mind as this character was acting, too.

"I...see," he finally replied as he turned back. The video disappeared. "This character," he pointed to the wall where the scene had played, "is harmless, so it predisposes a fondness for Oggs?"

"I wouldn't say fondness," Bethany Anne temporized, "so much as they don't feel negative toward them."

Cannock thought about what they had discussed so far. He leaned forward to rest his elbows on the table. "On your side," he nodded to Bethany Anne, "you have people who wish to immigrate, and our system has features they would like since Yoll is not a primary choice."

"Correct," she replied.

The delegate thought a moment. "We need a way to connect with the Etheric Empire, but since we are not heavily militaristic, it needs to be a friendly, maybe a slightly distant relationship."

"We would call it an arm's-length friendship. Not super-close, but you could tap us on the shoulder should you want our attention," Bethany Anne supplied.

"And what happens if it takes you too long to get to our system?" he asked.

Bethany Anne smiled. "Well, that is the other thing I would like to discuss with you."

"Why do I feel you have saved the most interesting for last?"

"Well, it isn't the most interesting, actually." She shrugged. "It's just the most clandestine."

"This word means?" Cannock asked.

Bethany Anne checked, and sure enough, the translator didn't know the right word to substitute. "Sorry, I am trying to say that this is the piece of the agreement we keep hidden from practically everyone."

Cannock swallowed slowly and folded his hands together. Here was going to be the information that changed his society.

When the Etheric Empire had arrived, it had caused ripples that traveled all the way to the Sark system over time. Now, the three other races that were unruly were making noises about exploring alliances. It was only a matter of time before one of them decided that even a militarily useless system like Sark was still something that would make them seem bigger.

Frankly, the Sark system had enough troubles dealing with Estarians and Oggs. Adding some humans to the mix, provided it wasn't too many, shouldn't cause too much disruption. At least, that he could see at the moment.

"And what are you thinking?" Cannock asked.

"Meredith," Bethany Anne called. "Please bring up the Sark system as a hologram again."

Sark (their sun) was in the center of the image. Then planets Ogg and Estaria, a huge asteroid belt, and then farther out, planet Secoria, and finally Teshovia.

"What I am thinking…" Bethany Anne spoke slowly. Fingers on both of her hands touched, then slowly separated. Cannock watched as the hologram zoomed in. When it reached the desired size, she reached out to touch the area labeled Asteroid Belt. "Is that this area of your system does not have much activity outside of some limited mining. Is that correct?"

"Yes," Cannock answered, not sure where she was going.

"If you were attacked," she gestured with her right hand, and suddenly a large group of warships appeared inside his system, "assuming they have the ability to Gate in...." The ships emerged outside the asteroid belt, as most ships wouldn't want to get too close to the belt before appearing.

Given the small chance of a ship coming through inside one of the asteroids.

"They would arrive outside the asteroid belt and then navigate through it to attack the two inner worlds, yes?" She turned to look at him, but he was still watching the hologram: the lifelike ships, the three-dimensional aspects of the planets he felt he could reach out and touch. He wanted to play with the wisps of clouds.

His mind finally caught up with her question, and he saw she was waiting for an answer.

"Yes." He pointed to the warships making their way through the asteroid belt. "We believe this is the most likely scenario."

"Okay, then we would like to request seven asteroids as secret bases." Seven green dots materialized at designated locations in the asteroid belt. "Some of them would be for stashes of equipment, some for missile defense outposts. We would not tell you what we are putting there, and you don't ever ask us. Basically, you are gifting title to those asteroids to the Etheric Empire. In return, we promise to use our assets, should anyone ever try to attack Sark, to protect your system, because by attacking Sark, they would be attacking humans, too."

Cannock leaned back in his chair and watched as little missiles leapt out of the seven asteroids and attacked the ships crossing through Sarkian territory. There was a mighty struggle between the warships and the missiles before a third of the ships were destroyed. Many others showed damage, and all of them turned to leave the system.

He had to admit, it was a very effective demonstration.

"And if no one ever comes to attack you, no one needs to know we already have weapons there."

"How would you get them there?" Cannock asked, still staring at the hologram.

"We won't be ready to immigrate for a while, but we are willing to stage what we call a *show of force* on the edge of space and make a big deal out of you guys being our friends. If our demonstration gets no special response, then we will allow immigration to happen however it unfolds. If we get a lot of negative responses from your neighbors, we will make a lot of special trips."

"What happens between your trips?" Cannock questioned, then turned to Bethany Anne.

"Cannock, each trip will be us bringing more of our weapons and people to build the bases. Each time we leave, the system will be just a little bit safer. One of the reasons we won't start with humans immigrating is that I want a solid defense for the Sark system before the first families move to your worlds."

Cannock was thinking diligently about how this would affect his people, and so far, he wasn't finding the gotcha.

"Any special rights for those immigrating?" he asked.

"What, humans?" Bethany Anne shook her head. "They need to have basic rights, including the ability to own land, create businesses, and trade. They can't ever become slaves." She tapped her finger on the table to get his attention. "Cannock, understand what I am saying here." She took a deep breath. "If you, or those who come after you, ever try to create a state where humans are slaves, the Etheric Empire will come and beat the ever-loving shit out of your political leaders until they realize that is a no-no. So, whatever we agree to, make sure that piece is iron-clad, or I will be visiting your planet."

She waved a hand negligently toward the hologram, and Cannock turned to see the mighty *ArchAngel II* arrive in the Sark system. Except this time, the ship appeared very near Estaria, bypassing the asteroid belt.

There were a lot of military ships with her.

"I won't fool around," Bethany Anne continued. "I will come in, figure out who is trying to fuck over our people and get rid of them. Your people will have to fix the problem before our military presence leaves your skies." As she spoke, the *ArchAngel II* had disappeared, but a few large ships stayed behind.

A few moments later, the other ships left.

Cannock continued looking at his world for a while after they left, thinking about the consequences to his people. While they *could* be considered elitist, they weren't slavers. They weren't Skaines or any of their ilk.

The Empress was providing what he wanted: a way to create a friendship pact, along with a reason for protecting his people by integrating some humans onto the worlds. The information, as limited or factually inaccurate as it might be, still spoke of a leader who took care of her people.

At least, those who abided by the rules.

He pointed toward the asteroid belt. "Are any of those seven special in any way?"

"Only one," Bethany Anne replied. She moved her hands in the gesture that zoomed the map. She pointed to a larger asteroid. "That is Gaitune-67."

Cannock squinted. "I don't recognize it," he admitted.

"No reason to, yet," she told him. "It has been a temporary shelter for ships from time to time. We wish to build a special little town there and house a few dangerous toys. We are willing to install technology to help create atmosphere on that asteroid."

"How will you do this without drawing attention?" Cannock asked, intrigued.

Bethany Anne winked. "We create an Estarian company. Isn't that how everyone hides a government's activities?"

Personal Ship *Powerdrive*, Exiting Commercial Gate Five, Yollin System, Ring Three

Shi-tan was impressed. The company he was contracting with was able to speed him through the approvals process once he exited the Gate.

He looked at his controls and moved one to confirm that the ship couldn't approach closer to the human's *Meredith Reynolds* without his personal physical confirmation. He didn't need to be accidentally blown to atoms by a ship's automated mistake.

At least if *he* made the mistake, then he had earned the death.

He had checked on the Yollin twice, and both times he had been sleeping. He had alerts set up should he stop breathing or start to become violent.

"*Powerdrive*?" A Yollin voice came over the speaker. "This is Ring Two. You are scheduled to approach the QBBS *Meredith Reynolds* at location one-seven-seven, where there is a private commercial landing hanger rented for your use. Please contact QBBS *Meredith Reynolds* for details."

"This is *Powerdrive*. Understand approach QBBS *Meredith Reynolds* location one-seven-seven and contact ship for landing specifications."

"Correct, *Powerdrive*. Ring Two out."

And that, Shi-tan thought, *was that*. Efficiency in action. His ship started to turn as he felt the engines kick in.

The last time he was here had been another rundown. When he left, he thought he had started an interstellar war. He had actually laughed about that once or twice. The other group had shied away from attacking when the Etheric Empire melted a much larger warship than any they had in their fleet.

Now he was back, and he had asked to meet in All Guns

Blazing because, try as he might, he couldn't find Coke anywhere else in the systems.

The drink was damned good. This time he was going to store three of those barrels if he could, or find out how he could keep it for a while if it went bad too quickly. The last batch he purchased had lasted him a mere two weeks, and he had suffered a terrible head pain for half a day after he ran out.

Apparently one of the very minor ingredients in the drink was slightly addictive.

He didn't care. It was too good not to get more.

A little while later, his speaker came on. "Ship *Powerdrive*, this is Control for the *Meredith Reynolds*. I have you slotting into Commercial Hanger five-five at location one-seven-seven. Is this correct?"

Shi-tan leaned forward to push his talk button. "That is what I understand, Control. Ring Two suggested you would have additional information," he finished and released the button.

There was a slight pause. "Yes, the hanger has been rented for seventy-two local hours. Should *Powerdrive* stay beyond that time, you will be responsible for the additional charges."

"*Powerdrive* understands. Seventy-two local hours, and charges beyond are my problem."

"Correct. Welcome back to the *Meredith Reynolds*." The audio clicked off, leaving a slightly annoyed Shrillexian.

They knew he had been here before. Personally, Shi-tan was a big fan of governments that didn't know every time you showed up. Not that he had done anything bad last time.

But eventually, they would have enough information on him that he might find it annoying.

"Gabrielle, wait." Bethany Anne put a hand on her arm as they wished the last of the Estarians a blessed evening.

"God, Bethany Anne," Gabrielle murmured. "I've had less pain after a workout with you than having these twins in here." She pulled out two chairs. One she sat in, the other she would use to elevate her feet. "Are you about to tell me why, at a mere five months, I look like Mount Olympus, here?" she grumped as she lifted both feet into the chair.

There was a knock on the door. "John, open the door if that is Eric."

"It is," he replied as he opened the door. Eric was surprised to see John step out and close the door behind him after Eric stepped in.

"Family meeting?" Eric asked as he came up behind Gabrielle and massaged her shoulders.

"Mmmm," she moaned. "You may stop doing that sometime next decade."

"Sure, baby," Eric agreed.

"I know that you know that I know you are lying, Eric," Gabrielle whispered, her eyes closed. "But don't remind me that I know anytime soon, okay?"

"Who's lying?" Eric asked.

Gabrielle just reached up and patted the hand that hadn't stopped massaging.

I really, really don't want to do this. Bethany Anne sighed.

>>**We don't know it won't come out okay, and this is the only logical solution we have come up with.**<<

I would never hurt either of them, Bethany Anne. However, if we want the best shot at fixing this, we are going to have to go through the surgery. The Pod-doc is having issues with the different nanocytes' programming.

I know, TOM. We have already been through this too many times. I just... Fuck. I hate my life sometimes.

Bethany Anne tapped the table to get their attention. "Listen you two, we need to have a discussion between you, TOM, ADAM, and me."

Gabrielle turned, her mouth dropping. "The babies?"

Bethany Anne nodded. "Yes. Although we aren't at the crisis stage yet, there are some problems, and we need to make some decisions."

Eric lifted Gabrielle's feet, sat down in the chair, and put them into his lap. He pulled off her shoes and started massaging her feet. "We talked about it some," Eric told her. "You guys have had her in the Pod-doc once a week from the beginning, but twice in the last two weeks. What is going on?"

TOM's voice came out of the speaker system. "The Pod-doc is having trouble manipulating the programming for the twins' nanocytes while they are inside Gabrielle."

Bethany Anne noticed that Gabrielle was surreptitiously wiping away a tear, and wanted to scream. She could throw fireballs and destroy hundreds, but she couldn't wave a hand and make sure life was fair for two of her closest friends.

Gabrielle's voice was soft. "You *told* me that the birth would be tricky and possibly challenging, TOM." She looked at Bethany Anne. "BA, I can feel your emotions from here. We knew this might be a problem when we talked about changing the programming to allow me to get pregnant."

Eric nodded his agreement.

Bethany Anne looked at them both, and her voice cracked as she spoke. "The team of ADAM and TOM believe the best chance for them to be healthy would be to put them into the Pod-doc now. That way..." Bethany Anne wiped away a tear of her own. "That way, the analysis can continue twenty-four/seven." She noticed Gabrielle circling and rubbing her stomach repeatedly.

"What is the earliest a baby has been safe, being born prematurely?" she asked.

"Twenty-one weeks back on Earth," ADAM answered from the speakers. "Technically, the Pod-doc can handle it earlier, but the longer the gestation, the better. These babies are advanced for their age. They can be born safely now and placed in the Pod-doc."

Eric's eyes were vacant, Bethany Anne noticed. She thought he was staring at the future.

"Look, we didn't try to hide information from you, but this last week has been crazy, and we have been waiting for ADAM to finish the simulations before we told you anything."

Eric stirred. "What are the simulations saying?" he asked. He moved his chair closer to Gabrielle, who grabbed his outstretched hand and squeezed it.

"That is the good news," TOM answered. "Most of the simulations show an eighty-seven percent chance of success."

"Yeah," Gabrielle sniffed, "but thirteen percent is too damned high when you're the *mom*." She looked down, hair falling across her face, her shoulders silently shaking, as Eric gently laid her feet down and enveloped her in his arms.

Bethany Anne's heart was dying.

ADAM spoke up. "We will constantly be watching and adjusting as we go, Gabrielle. I promise you, my personal promise, that I will dedicate my resources to watching over your children until they are delivered into your arms in good health."

Gabrielle reached under her hair to wipe away the tears. "Thank you, ADAM." She sniffed. "That means a lot to me."

Bethany Anne put her hand on Gabrielle's shoulder. "We have your back, Gabrielle. These two will join us safely."

Gabrielle just nodded her understanding silently.

CHAPTER FOURTEEN

QBBS _Meredith_ Reynolds, Military Meeting Room

When Lance walked into the medium-sized meeting room, he nodded to Dan, then Admiral Thomas, John, Frank, Gabrielle, and Patricia in turn, then pulled out the chair at the head of the table and sat down.

"Good morning, everyone. I hope you brought your thinking caps this morning."

The quiet laughter did nothing to assuage his concern. He looked around the table. "Okay, someone say it."

"Well, we've talked," Dan spoke up, "in twos and threes, and we just don't see a way to keep her out."

"John? Gabrielle?" Lance directed his stare at the Empress' guard and guard captain, who were sitting next to him.

Gabrielle beat John to the answer. "No fucking way. Not an ice cube's chance in hell."

"Well," Lance sighed as he eyed her, "no need to sugarcoat it for me."

"If you want me to sugarcoat it," Gabrielle started, but Lance put up a hand.

He grimaced. "No, I've got the same feeling." He looked

around again. "Okay, now that we are all agreed Bethany Anne is going to be in the fight on the Karillians' home planet against a Kurtherian-modified race, what are we going to do about it?"

"Well, let's first determine why she will be there," Patricia spoke up.

"She needs to fight," John answered. "There is only so much Empress-ing that we can hope to get her to do. Her Bitches, including me, are there for her if she needs something done up close and personal. Or she has Dan's team go in, or the navy, or whatever. She has been slowly pressure-cooking, and she is going to blow her top sooner or later. When you have the Kurtherians in the fight, you are *not* going to be able to keep her out of it."

"She's the damned Empress," Lance groused.

"She's your daughter," Patricia shot back. "Maybe you shouldn't have told her so many 'leadership is from the front stories.'"

"Duly noted," Lance agreed. "Next daughter, I'll work on that."

"Oh?" Gabrielle perked up, looking between Patricia and Lance. "Do you have something to announce?"

The room started chuckling at Lance's expression when Patricia didn't answer right away. After a few seconds, she winked. "Not at the moment, but trying is still fun."

"*Gott Verdammt!* Give me a heart attack, woman," Lance mumbled.

"Wouldn't do you any harm. You would just heal from it," Dan told him.

"It would still hurt like a sonofabitch," Lance replied.

"Well, I want to be there when you tell Bethany Anne she has a sister on the way," Gabrielle informed Patricia.

"I'll let you know first, honey," Patricia confirmed.

"Okay," Admiral Thomas interrupted. "We know she is going to insist on being there, so why don't we sequester her in a low-risk area? We have the Bitches protect her. That way, she's there more or less safely, and if a few combatants come along, she gets a little action."

The table quieted down. Dan looked at Lance, who turned to Patricia.

She just shrugged her shoulders, so Lance glanced at Frank, who was taking notes but spared a second to flip his hand back and forth in a universal *maybe* gesture. Finally, he raised an eyebrow at John and Gabrielle.

The two of them looked at each other. "What do you think?" she asked him.

John scratched his jaw for a moment, then spoke to the whole table. "That's about the best we are going to get, I think. She will see through it in a moment, so keep hammering the message that she isn't supposed to be there in the first place. It might mollify her."

"Okay." Lance looked at his wristwatch, an anachronism from Earth. "We have ten minutes until our meeting with the Karillians. Let's not all hit the door at the same time."

The meeting adjourned, and Lance waited for Patricia to step around Frank before he pulled her over to the side for a personal conversation.

Frank closed his notebook and winked at Dan.

Dan shook his head and hoped Frank wasn't feeling the winds of the future again. Maybe the Yollin breakfast this morning just gave him gas.

At least, that is what Dan hoped was happening to Frank.

QBBS *Meredith Reynolds*, Large Meeting Room

Empress' Guardian Peter walked into the semicircular room, where rows of chairs ascended like an old university auditorium up to the top row. At the bottom was a table that could seat eight if they needed to face the people in the seats, or eighteen if they sat around the table.

There were already people from all over *Meredith Reynolds* in the seats. Bethany Anne was a big believer in allowing second- and third-tier support personnel to listen in on major discussions. They might not get a chance to contribute at the meeting, but history had shown they would speak with their bosses later.

The Karillian delegation was led in a minute later by Eric. Bethany Anne was already speaking with a small group of her military whom she didn't normally interact with.

The Karillians' eyestalks were darting all around, trying to take in everything at once.

Tomthum leaned over to Caspise. "This is more than I expected."

Caspise nodded. "Not quite a Festival of Assembly, but she is committing a lot of resources to this discussion."

"Notice how she is laughing with them." Tomthum pointed with his eyestalk. "Her people do not fear her."

"Not in the regular sense, that is true." Caspise glanced around as Eric provided seats for the two delegates. The Karillian guards Keth and Bonn stood behind the delegate and sub-delegate. Eric took their ship's captain over to the first row of seats facing the table at the bottom of the auditorium.

Bethany Anne looked around the auditorium, then raised her voice a little. "Park them, ladies and gentlemen." She nodded to the people she was speaking with. They turned and went toward their own seats.

Bethany Anne walked to the side of the table closest to the seats, opposite Lance, Dan, Admiral Thomas, and the two Karillians. There was a seat for her, one for Frank, and an empty one.

"Peter?" she called.

Peter looked up from his conversation with Todd and blushed.

"You're up here this time," Bethany Anne told the Were. "Todd, we're short one chair for you, sorry."

"No worries, ma'am." the captain of the Guardian Marines smiled. "I'm good with Peter shouldering the load."

She watched as Peter squeezed Todd's shoulder, causing his friend to wince. "No worries." Peter smiled at Bethany Anne as Todd surreptitiously rubbed his shoulder.

Bethany Anne turned to the assembly after Peter passed her. "Okay, folks, we have some good news and some bad news. The bad news is, we have less than six months to prepare."

Bethany Anne's smile turned harsh. "The good news is, we know where some Kurtherian lackeys are going to be."

She allowed the resulting hubbub to continue for a minute after that declaration, then put her hand up for quiet.

Conversation stopped. "Now, I realize that we won't be going against the Kurtherians right away. This is an enhanced and select group. From my understanding, the Karillians were first attacked some five hundred years ago. They were able to beat off that group, and since there was no follow-up attack, they allowed themselves to relax after thirty or forty years. Unfortunately, seventy years later, a second attack occurred, and killed a quarter of their population. Between the second and third attacks, the Karillians figured out enough to get into space. Since that time, they have kept their world's location a secret, fearing that all aliens were evil, but there have been three more attacks. That's six attacks so far."

"The seventh attack will be launched in about six months." She faced the front wall of the Auditorium. "Meredith, show us the map." Those at the table could look at the smaller screens hanging from the ceiling to see what was being displayed up front, or turn in their seats.

The screens at the front had merged to become one, showing the Etheric Empire and the three systems that had previously been part of the Yollin Empire. A blue dot appeared directly at the bottom of the Straiphus System. "That is Karillia. It's actually

MICHAEL ANDERLE

easier to get there from a secondary system rather than Strai-phus, for gravitational reasons that include a lot of math."

Bethany Anne turned toward the audience and gave them a thousand-watt smile. "I don't do math."

They chuckled along with her. Their Empress might not do math, but she kicked ass like Einstein did math, and that was enough for them.

She turned back to the map. "We know amateurs talk tactics and professionals talk logistics, so that is why many of you are here." This statement caused more than a few of the people responsible for logistics to sit up a little straighter.

Lance covered his smile with a hand. His daughter rarely missed a chance to compliment even those on the operations side of her organization. Perhaps she was a bit of a pain in the ass about fighting on the front, but he wouldn't change one damned thing about her.

There was only one thing that had kept her alive so many decades ago, and that was her deep-seated belief in fighting *hard* for what she believed in. It had caused Michael to choose her when she was dying, and it was the quality that brought the Guards to surround her and fight for her with their lives.

It was why everyone loved her to this day. Well, not everyone, but many. Those who didn't appreciate that violence was an appropriate answer to some questions would never love Bethany Anne.

And that was just fine with her.

"We will need to figure out the number of fighters required based on past experience, the enemy's probable enhancements based on the delta between each invasion, and what they need to get in and back out again. I've spoken with the Karillians, and we think this is their final push."

She looked at those in the seats. "They are here to exterminate the population of the Karillians' world. We don't know if they intend to occupy it or just leave it empty. Our consultant on the issue believes they might use the planet as a forward base."

Caspise leaned over to Tomthum, who met him in the middle. He whispered, "They have a consultant?"

Tomthum's eyestalks made the gesture that conveyed he had no idea what she was talking about.

"The Etheric Empire has sent Articles of Agreement to the Karillian leadership, informing them that they are now members of the Etheric Empire." This caused a murmur in the group. Bethany Anne put up a hand. "This wasn't necessary for our help, but rather recognition by those in the delegates' party that it was the least they could do to repay us for the blood and effort we would be expending."

Bethany Anne's face grew somber, her eyes looking across as her voice became firm.

"Let everyone know the Etheric Empire will *forever* defend our own, forever defend our friends, and forever defend the helpless!"

Her eyes flashed red, the energy causing her hair to lift and float as the men and women in the auditorium stood up and started cheering.

"*AD AETERNITATEM*!" Her voice rang clear both in ears...

And minds.

QBBS *Meredith Reynolds*, Personal Ship *Powerdrive*

Kiel's eyes opened at the slight nudge. He focused on the large green hand poking him. "I'm awake," he spat.

"You are a light sleeper," Shi-tan mused.

"You provided a shitty bunk for me to sleep on," Kiel told him. "I realize all you Shrillexians are supposed to have a personal code of loyalty."

"Not loyalty," Shi-tan corrected the Yollin. "Honor. We only give loyalty to those who are superior to us in battle; people for whom it would be an honor to fight."

Kiel sat up, his hands bound and small chains on his feet. He looked down and split his legs.

The damned metal was strong.

"So, is it honorable to get paid more than your contract by your mark and let that mark go free?"

Shi-tan just looked at him.

Kiel shrugged. "Okay, is it honorable to beat the crap out of you and put you under obligation to let me go free?"

"Little Yollin," Shi-tan bent over, the red in his yellow eyes more pronounced, "I've had many try to get me to let them go free. None have succeeded, and I must say, your effort is pitiful."

Kiel shrugged. "Hey, I gotta ask. It's required. Personally, my family will forgive me and, while my holiday is going to be cut short, give them five years and I'll be back in their good graces."

Shi-tan pursed his lips. "I was wondering why you were not more worried."

"Well, I'll admit this was a bit of a test of their forgiveness," Kiel ad-libbed. "And if it is all the same to you, I'd rather extend the vacation. But I'm the favorite child, so I'm expected to do crazy stuff."

Shi-tan looked at the screen on the wall, which was telling him the hangar had been filled with air and he could lower his doors safely. "Well, your family reunion will happen soon, so stop your bellyaching. We need to finish this."

Shi-tan reached down to pull the Yollin up by his arm. "You *are* dense, aren't you, Yollin?"

Kiel considered letting his muscles relax and forcing the bounty hunter to hold him up, but with his luck, Shi-tan would let him drop, and Kiel would bounce his head off the seat. So he stood up.

"Oh, you mean 'heavy,'" Kiel got out as he stood. "Not 'stupid.'"

Shi-tan laughed, his voice sounding like a wheezing human.

"You are about to be delivered to your group for stealing the company's money. That has already demonstrated that you are stupid."

Kiel kept quiet.

———

The trip through Security took Shi-tan a little longer than he would have hoped, but not as long as he'd expected. The humans apparently knew about bounty hunters, and had a procedure for handling them and their captives. Once they confirmed his mark was the Yollin on the bounty and that Shi-tan was a legitimate hunter, they switched out his personal restraining cuffs for their own and provided Shi-tan with the key.

He was sure they could open it too, but such was life.

Interestingly enough, they gave him directions to All Guns Blazing when he was finished processing, which was nice of them.

When the two came to a public hallway, Shi-tan watched the door they exited from melt itself back into the wall. He frowned.

No going back that way.

"Let's go meet your family." Shi-tan pulled on Kiel's arm.

William was working the door at the entrance to the bar. It wasn't busy, since it was the third shift for most on the *Meredith Reynolds*.

William put up a hand. Kiel hoped someone had thought to tell the owners of the bar they were pulling this operation. "Hold up." William glanced at Kiel's hands and feet.

William looked at Shi-tan. "License?"

The bounty hunter pulled out the paperwork the other human had provided. William took it, turned it so he could read it, and started mumbling.

"Blah blah blah," William's eyes kept going down the page.

"Bounty Hunter Shi-tan." William looked up. "That would be you?"

Shi-tan nodded.

"Okay." William looked down at the paper. "Don't speak much." His eyes kept roaming. "Blah blah blah, Kiel, a Yollin to be delivered to…" William looked at Kiel. "Bad Company?"

"It's a family thing," Kiel answered, looking embarrassed.

"I'll bet." William turned. "Bobcat!"

"Here!" The two aliens heard another voice respond from inside the bar. William continued, "We have the guests for Bad Company here!"

"Oh?" Another human came out of the bar. "All right, walk with me." He gestured to Shi-tan and Kiel and headed back into the bar.

Shi-tan grabbed Kiel's arm and pulled him along. Hopefully, this meeting and the money transfer would happen quickly.

He was dying for a Coke.

CHAPTER FIFTEEN

<u>**QBBS** *Meredith Reynolds*, **Medical Wing**</u>

Bethany Anne sat down by Eric, her hand rubbing his back. "I know that no percentage is small when your kids are the ones we are talking about, Eric. But really, we are going to make this happen for you both."

Eric nodded, not saying anything. Darryl and Scott were her guards for the afternoon, but they stayed outside the room.

Eric looked at her. "We always come out the other side, boss." He nodded to the Pod-doc that held Gabrielle. "Now we are messing with the same technology which gave us our abilities. And without our world's first true AI and an alien I've never physically met, my first babies would probably die."

Bethany Anne took the one hand off his back and clasped both in front of her. Right now, her heart was so damned heavy. They were protecting the defenseless, but all they could do was rely on her friends.

"They are as real as you or me, Eric," she started, but his tiny nudge stopped her.

He looked her in the eye. "Bethany Anne, I'm not saying anything against them. They are as real to me as they can be

153

without touching them. I know, as we all do, that they are helping you hold it together. For that, I'd go into battle for them any time."

Bethany Anne could feel ADAM's shock and TOM's determination.

"So, I know they have our back." He nodded to his mate. "Gabrielle is trusting them with everything right now." He sighed. "Our babies…"

"Your boys, I'm told," Bethany Anne added, almost in a whisper.

Eric turned. "Say what?"

She pointed to her head. "I'm informed by ADAM and TOM that you guys have twin boys. The Pod-doc is delicately transferring them to their location, as it helps Gabrielle's healing. There is some nanocyte reprogramming being done as well."

Her shoulders slumped. "There is always a new fuck-up with technology. I just wished it wasn't with…"

This time, Eric's hand on her knee stopped her.

"It might as well be us, BA," he told her. "We are here to protect our family and more. I wouldn't wish this situation on another couple just so my own family wasn't in danger."

Bethany Anne nodded her understanding. She felt like dirt for even suggesting that was where her thoughts were going. "I know, Eric." He put an arm around her shoulders, and she leaned in.

"Boss, don't think we haven't seen you struggle the last few years." He took a deep breath. "Want to talk about it?"

Bethany Anne chuckled just a tiny bit. "Lay the worry of the Empress on the father's shoulders as his two boys are being pulled from his wife, who is also my friend?"

"No," Eric told her. "Tell your friend that you fucking hate all of this jibber-jabber-walkie-the-talkie-bullshit and you are ready to give some fuckers the just desserts they really have earned."

"Was it really so easy back on Earth?" Bethany Anne asked. "It sure seems that way."

"Well, you allowed the governments to take care of the people then, and you still do."

"Yeah, and they went and fucked it up good, didn't they?" She sighed.

"That's what has you down the most?" he pressed.

Bethany Anne's tears rained down her face, and she turned into him. Eric strained to hear her as she sobbed into his shoulder. "Those fuckers didn't last ten goddamn years!" She stuck her hand out, and Eric grabbed a cloth on his right and gave it to her.

She reached under her hair to wipe her tears. "The very short message we got from Akio and Yuko... I can't believe those fuck-heads killed so many of our people."

"It's not on your shoulders," Eric told her. "You can't protect them from the Kurtherians and other assorted assholes on Earth. You know the Kurtherians are going to fuck us up any time they can." He breathed in. "The ones on Earth fucking us up was a possibility, but it had seemed like they had walked away from the brink each time."

"All our friends, Eric." She spoke quietly. "What could I have done?"

"After the Gate exploded with the data we needed?" he asked. "Not too damned much."

The two stayed like that for a while, just sharing in their pain. "It will take us some time to build another Gate and figure it out," Eric told her. "Even the new *ArchAngel* can't Gate that far, and that Kurtherian asshole you killed had some of the knowledge we need inside his head, so he fucked us once more from the grave. So be it." He smiled. "Pencil prick is still a dead motherfucker."

Bethany Anne chuckled, then hiccupped. "Watch your language!" she told him.

"What?" Eric asked. "You're going to deduct points for lack of creativity here?"

"No," Bethany Anne slowly sat back up, "but Gabrielle is going to be pissed if you curse around the kids."

There was a pause before Eric breathed out slowly and whispered to her.

"I'm fucked."

TOM's voice came out of the speakers a few moments later. "Mother and babies are doing well. Gabrielle is being infused with additional Etheric energy, and the reprogramming of her nanocytes for future integration is almost complete. She will be up within thirty minutes."

Bethany Anne stood up. "Let me get some water to wipe my face." She looked down at Eric. "Thank you, I needed that little bit of release."

He nodded his understanding. "Me too."

QBBS *Meredith Reynolds*, Barnabas' Office

Barnabas steepled his fingers as he sat behind the desk in his office, watching the emotions play across Tabitha's face.

She finally decided which one to lead with.

"ARE YOU FUCKING KIDDING ME?" she yelled, slapping her hand on his desk. Barnabas had long ago upgraded his desktop to stone.

Bethany Anne often had a similar reaction to his pronouncements, and he had lost two desktops to cracking so far. He was hoping this one would last longer.

"I am not, Ranger Tabitha." Barnabas spoke normally, ignoring her outburst. "You are an officer of the law, *NOT* the military!"

"But EVERYONE knows that BA is going to be fighting!" She threw a hand out behind her, pointing toward the core of the battle station. "It's a done deal. Hell, even Team BMW is starting to pull their thumbs out of their asses and get busy with new technology!"

"I agree," Barnabas answered, "that everyone is worried about her, Tabitha. I can understand your frustration. However, our *job* is to protect the innocent. Do you think you and the Tontos are going to add anything to the battle between the aliens and the Karillians to make her safer?"

"FUCK YES!" Tabitha spat back, her eyes starting to glow red. "I won't allow another fucking asswipe to kill one of my friends, Barnabas!"

"Tabitha." Barnabas stopped a moment. "I'll tell you what. If I can prove that you could potentially hurt Bethany Anne by trying to get in on this, will you consider settling down and thinking it through logically?"

Tabitha was breathing heavily. She wanted to shove the desk down her boss' throat. He wasn't arguing with her, and it wasn't a fair fight.

"What?" she asked, then caught up with what he had said. "How can I hurt Bethany Anne?"

Barnabas nodded. Now he had her mind instead of just her emotions engaged. "Who is the baddest fighter we have?"

"The Empress," she answered, then her eyes narrowed. "You aren't about to tell me someone is better, since she hasn't fought much lately?"

Barnabas chuckled. "No. She might not have been in any engagements, but she still routinely kicks everyone's ass." He put up a finger. "That's Bethany Anne's level. Now, who is next?"

"The Bitches, Gabrielle, maybe Stephen." She sat down in one of the two chairs facing his desk. "Then probably everyone in Nathan's league is three, and the Guardians and Guardian Marines, if you take them together, are four."

"Where is your team in that hierarchy?" Barnabas asked.

"Oh, we are level three, no problem," she told him. Her stare dared him to contradict her.

"I've been talking with Lance, Tabitha. I can truthfully tell you that no one except the fighters at level two have been assigned to accompany her."

Tabitha blinked a moment at him. "Nathan?"

He shook his head. "He has another task. He won't even be on the world, which is the front lines."

"So, if we are with them, we are the weak link." She sighed. "That fucking sucks."

"Plus, need I remind you for the thirtieth time," Barnabas leaned forward, his elbows resting on his desk, "you are law *enforcement*, not military. And frankly, I don't want to lose you."

Tabitha's face was emotionless for a moment before a small smile played at the edges. "Are you saying you like me, Big B?"

"I'm saying," Barnabas leaned back in his chair, "that you've grown on me, and your brand of trouble would be sorely missed."

She raised an eyebrow.

"In about a decade or so," he finished, a small glint of humor in his eye.

Tabitha finally started nodding her acceptance. "Are you really sending us on vacation?"

Barnabas raised both eyebrows. "It depends on your definition of vacation," he answered. "Do you remember the description of the town of Mos Eisley?"

"What, the wretched hive of scum and villainy?" she asked, perplexed at the change of direction.

Barnabas reached into his left-hand desk drawer and pulled out a packet. He tossed it to her.

"Exactly."

Personal Ship *Powerdrive*, QBBS *Meredith Reynolds*

Shi-tan got up from his bed, trying to remember why the hell his body felt like it had been beaten.

Senseless.

He groaned as he stood up and padded toward his medical closet. Before he could open the door, he stopped.

There was a dark red folder with a white emblem on the cover on a small table nearby. There shouldn't be *anything* on his ship he hadn't put there.

He reached up to his face, but yanked his hand back down, opened the door, and stepped into the medical closet. He looked in the mirror.

His face was...damaged. *This*, he thought as he examined it, *was really bad*. Had he been in a bar fight last night?

That's when the memories came flooding back.

He had delivered Kiel, the supposed mark, to the bar and had been led to another area that wasn't out in the open. In fact, he thought it might have been rather recently added to the bar, and the human had needed a key to get into the room.

Inside, he found a Yollin and six humans. Three looked maybe like one of their blood families. Three were not.

One of the latter three was the Empress, and the other two were definitely her guards. He whispered to his mark, "You are not getting out of this so easily this time."

The mark just shrugged.

"Kiel," The Empress had nodded. "Nice to see you back in one piece."

"I do my best, Bethany Anne," he admitted.

She turned to Shi-tan, who was now on guard. "First, please check your account and confirm we have paid the bounty."

That wasn't what he had expected to hear.

Shi-tan ignored the feeling in his stomach and pulled out his tablet. It took him a moment, but he confirmed that the money was there. While he verified the transfer, one of the humans came up and unlocked Kiel's cuffs.

Shi-tan looked a second time. "Why is there more?" he asked.

"A small bonus for arriving quickly and keeping the mark in good condition," She replied.

He looked around. "Why do I get the impression this isn't a company issue?"

"Well, it kinda is," one of the male humans answered him. "I'm Nathan, by the way."

"My apologies," the Empress replied. "Shi-tan, please be introduced to Nathan," she pointed to the female next to him, "his mate Ecaterina, and their daughter Christina Bethany Anne Lowell. And this is their company employee, R'yhek."

He didn't fail to catch the Empress' name in the younger human's moniker. Warning received: hands off that child.

She turned to her right. "This is John Grimes."

Shi-tan was proud of himself. He didn't grimace. Shrillexians loved a good fight, but they didn't love a good ass-kicking if they couldn't get a few licks in. He had seen enough of the John Grimes videos.

Even *he* doubted he would get more than one good punch in, and that was only if he was enraged.

She turned to her left. "And this is Darryl." Both humans nodded in his direction.

He nodded back.

"You have met Kiel, of course," she continued. "However, you might want to know that he is the captain of the Empress' Yollin Mercenary force, not a family member who stole a bunch of money."

Kiel looked at Bethany Anne. "Just remember you lost the bet."

"Yeah, yeah, no one knows the mercenary faces," Bethany Anne agreed. "You were right."

She focused on Shi-tan. "This has actually been a recruiting operation, Shi-tan."

"For a company," Nathan told him.

Shi-tan glanced at him. "Mercenary?"

"No," Nathan told him. "Profit."

"And for me, loyalty." Bethany Anne added. "Let's see if we can provide enough assurance that your Shrillexian desire to fight will be amply served, shall we?"

For the next four hours, Shi-tan had his ass handed to him so many times it was brutal. He had done well against the Yollin, Kiel, once he tried.

However, that Yollin must have trained with the humans, because no Yollin Shi-tan had ever fought before had done so well against him.

Kiel deserved honor.

Then he fought the little human. He was able to win that bout too. He was told he could use anything but killing moves, and twice he had hit her hard enough to toss her across the room.

"You lost, Christina," the one named Ecaterina called when she stood up and started heading back into the fight. "He beat you two-zero."

"But," she turned to her mom, "we were having FUN!"

What race's youth enjoyed an all-out battle? he wondered. *Other than Shrillexians, of course.*

She received honor.

Then it was his turn against the mom. That was going well until she changed, then it went to shit for a little while. It was everything he could do to hold her off until he finally, barely, took the third point. Honestly, it could have gone either way.

Ecaterina received honor too.

Next he got his ass handed to him by Nathan. Ecaterina was a bit miffed when Nathan used tactics she didn't know about. "You should practice with the Bitches more often, honey," he growled.

Nathan might possibly receive loyalty, but he wasn't sure yet.

He was allowed to rest for a while to recoup his energy and come down off his fighting high.

And they kept bringing him as much Coke as he wanted to drink.

When Nathan held out a hand to help him stand back up from

a particularly hard landing, he whispered, "We will make a Pepsi drinker out of you yet!"

Shi-tan grimaced. He had tried Pepsi, and it wasn't the same. But if there was nothing else to drink but Pepsi, maybe he could stomach it.

When the break was over, Shi-tan was surprised that the Empress stepped up. "Tell me, Shi-tan," she asked him. "Who has received honor and who loyalty?"

Shi-tan reached up to scratch his throat. "All have honor." He pointed at Nathan. "I'm not sure about loyalty yet. I need to see if I can learn his tricks."

"Yes," Ecaterina looked at her mate, "me too."

Nathan just shrugged. "All it takes is to be willing to take an ass-kicking from John, Scott, Darryl, or Eric."

Ecaterina waved that off. "Maybe I'll talk to Gabrielle."

Bethany Anne took control of the conversation again. "Now it is my turn. This is a full-contact fight, Shi-tan. You came into my base and took information related to Aerolyn, the son of the king, and sold it to his enemies. They then decided that perhaps it was time to attack us, that we were weak."

She looked at him. "They chose to turn around."

Shi-tan had actually been proud of the fact that he might have started an interstellar war, but now that he was in front of the Empress, maybe it had just been his blood talking.

Bethany Anne continued, "There are no rules. You may try to kill me. You will submit your loyalty to me, or I will break so many bones in your body you will take a year to heal."

She raised an eyebrow. "Yes, I know you Shrillexians heal fast, so I'll break the bones into enough small pieces that it takes a while."

Shi-tan watched as everyone stepped back.

Shi-tan had shrugged. *How well could an Empress fight, anyway?*

Looking at his face in the mirror now, he had to figure the answer was "too damned well."

He stepped back out of his little medical closet and turned toward the table that held the folder. He opened it, pulled out a document, and smiled. It was the agreement he had signed.

He was a member of the Bad Company now, and he had given his loyalty to Empress Bethany Anne. Fighting, he had been told, was expected.

No more bounty hunting for him.

It was time this Shrillexian kicked ass for someone who was hands-down the baddest leader out there. He looked at the clock and frowned.

He had three hours to patch himself up and leave. The *Powerdrive* had a ship to catch.

CHAPTER SIXTEEN

QBBS _Meredith_ Reynolds, Military Meeting Room

Bethany Anne dropped into the head chair as she looked at her father, Admiral Thomas, Dan, Frank, Pete, and Todd.

"We have four months to go, gentleman." She put up a hand. "I've heard you guys tell me eight different times," she looked at Todd, "actually nine if you include the sneaky way you badgered me during the Guardian Marine challenges last weekend."

Todd just smiled and shrugged.

"The answer," she looked around the table, her gaze going hard, "is still HELL NO! I _will_ be on that world, and I _will_ be fighting, not stuck in some sort of box where nothing can hurt me. Am I painfully clear?"

"Yes, Empress." Lance made a face before looking up. "Meredith, please bring up a map of Karillia."

A large world came into the hologram over their table. "We expect all the initial fighting to happen on the main landmass." The world showed a planet with about eighty percent water, one landmass that represented another sixteen percent, and then more than a thousand islands that made up the last four percent.

"ADAM and his team have reviewed the previous data they

were provided. We will be speaking with their representatives when they get back in two weeks. By then, we will have the communication protocols set up. The attackers have always arrived on the same date, but we will be setting up the first defensive arrays in two months. That leaves us less than eight weeks to dig in."

"Chance they come early?" Bethany Anne asked.

"Negligible," Frank supplied. "I've gone through all the data, and it seems this group is very prompt. I've spoken with TOM about this. He believes the Phraim-'Eh clan is behind it."

"That means what?" Bethany Anne's eyes went distant for a fraction of a second. "Okay, TOM says they would be like our conception of the Germans at one point in our history: *very* organized, *very* punctual, *very* much a pains in the ass as opponents."

"The Germans were conversant with trickery," Frank pointed out.

"Maybe I should say it is a close metaphor for those of us who need an anchor to ground the conversation." Bethany Anne paused a moment. "Okay, that gives us eight weeks to dig in. Jump Gate issues?"

Admiral Thomas spoke up. "ArchAngel is going to be damned busy. We have one new superdreadnought just about ready to load, but her crew won't be battle-ready soon enough to be part of the fight."

Bethany Anne turned to her admiral. "Plans for her?"

"I've spoken with Defense Minister E'kolorn. He would be happy to have her stay here while you are out of the system."

"Uh-huh," Bethany Anne nodded. "Who is supposed to know I'm out of town?"

"Only the closest," Lance answered. "But you have to believe damned near everyone with two brain cells is going to know you aren't here."

"Why?" Bethany Anne looked at her father. "If we aren't announcing it, who's breaking operational security?"

This time it was John Grimes, speaking from behind her. "Really, boss?"

Bethany Anne turned around to see John raising one eyebrow at her. She shook her head as she returned to the conversation. "Okay, I wasn't seeing the obvious. They know me, they know the Bitches, they know if those guys are gone, so am I."

"Well," Frank shrugged, "sure. However, the other part is these people know you aren't going to take this shit lying down."

Bethany Anne eyed one of her Intelligence guys. "I blame your books for that, Frank."

"Maybe, but I think the books keep you real. Otherwise, the tall tales about you would just get bigger and bigger, and nothing would be true anymore."

"Is that such a problem?" she asked him.

"It would be for those who are trying to kill you, Bethany Anne," Dan admitted. "If the stories get too big, eventually someone is going to find a way to kill the fake Bethany Anne in those stories, and that kind of power and/or technology would be able to take the real you out."

John spoke up from behind her. "Well, that would make for a bad day at work."

Bethany Anne grinned. "They can try!"

"And they will, Bethany Anne," Dan continued. "If someone stops someone else from being a complete megalomaniacal douche bag, that person or race will retaliate against the ones stopping them."

"Not to put too fine a point on it," Lance pointed to the world. "Like we are about to do for the Karillians."

Bethany Anne was in her working office near her quarters.

"Empress," Meredith began.

Bethany Anne closed the paper book she was writing in. Not

only was it impossible to steal data out of it without physically stealing the book itself, but she was writing in a forgotten language from a culture TOM had visited from over two thousand years ago.

On a world most considered a mudball.

It was the best she could do to keep her notes secret even from her closest friends and guards. She knew they would do their best to keep her safe.

Just as *they* knew she would do her damnedest to be in the middle of the fight.

Their latest meeting, just that morning, had them just four weeks from first deployment. That meant there was a month to go before they started shipping assets to a brand-new system in preparation for defending a group of aliens most considered thieves and malcontents. Sometimes, if you knew someone's true history, it changed your opinion of them in seconds.

Something only the truth can do.

"Yes, Meredith?" she answered.

"Ixtali Legate Addix is requesting permission to arrive in four weeks."

Bethany Anne's mouth thinned in annoyance. Was this happenstance, or a plan on the part of her people to keep Bethany Anne out of Karillian space?

"Tell her to get her ass here in three and a half weeks, no later." Bethany Anne replied.

"Exactly like that?" Meredith asked, her voice going up an octave.

Bethany Anne smiled. Apparently, ADAM had been working with Meredith so that her inflections carried more reality.

"No, work out something generous, but be emphatic that it must be no longer than three and a half weeks, and that they shouldn't expect more than two days with me. If they want more, they will need to arrive sooner, or push the meeting back another quarter."

"Yes, ma'am." Meredith closed the connection.

>>**You do realize the twins are scheduled to be released from the Pod-doc during that timeframe, right?**<<

Bethany Anne made a face. *Yes. No. Shit!*

What happens if you miss the first deployment? TOM asked.

I have to wait two weeks until they're back. Her shoulders slumped. *ADAM, tell Meredith we have four weeks, no problem.* **Gott Verdammt** *Mother Nature!*

She wasn't about to ask if the boys could be pulled out earlier, and no fucking way she was going to request that they stay another two weeks in the Pod-doc.

She blew out a frustrated breath.

Eric needed to be here.

Prometheus Major

Nathan dodged the kick and rolled out of the way. Knowing the follow-up attack was coming, he pushed up with his legs and jumped horizontally over Shi-tan's head.

He kicked the green head on his way down. This time it was Shi-tan's turn to roll out of the attack and come back up, dodging just in case Nathan had been able to chase him.

He hadn't.

The two combatants, who were smiling at each other, heard R'yhek tell them to break. Each bowed to the other before they bumped fists.

"That was a good bout," Shi-tan exclaimed. "I thought I might lose my skull there at the end."

"Pulled my kick," Nathan admitted. "Can't have you in the Pod-doc if we have to go on an operation."

"Something coming up?" R'yhek asked, tossing both men a towel. Today was Shi-tan's weekly-scheduled full-contact bout.

Christina had affectionately named it, 'Shi-tan's weekly ass-kicking.' Shi-tan was kind enough to refer to her matches with him as her ass-*kicked* sessions in return. It gave her additional encouragement to beat the green-skinned alien, but so far, he was keeping ahead of her easily as he learned how to fight more effectively from Nathan.

R'yhek was no pushover either, especially since he had gone through multiple Pod-doc updates and was now at the same physical level as someone half his age with many fewer years of the damage the mercenary work had caused.

Torcellan Passenger Ship (translated) *Luxurious*

"This is the captain speaking."

Tabitha held up a hand to stop the workout and cocked her head toward the speaker. They had turned it down as low as it could go, which, by damn, was pretty low.

Ryu nodded his understanding and dropped his arms. He was quite happy and relaxed at the moment. He turned and winked at Dio, who had been watching the bout.

Dio got to his feet and jogged over to Tabitha, who started petting him as she waited for more information.

Ryu glanced at Hirotoshi, who was practicing with Kouki and Katsu. Hirotoshi glided in between two kicks and delivered a backhand to Katsu's face while grabbing Kouki's ankle and twisting it.

The pop could easily be heard back where Ryu was standing. The team had paid extra to take over a shipping area on the passenger liner, and they had set it up as a practice gym to keep in shape.

Most people on the ship didn't even think about the strange group of humans, because almost none of them ever saw the five of them. The team had decided they would practice their stealth skills during the voyage. They wouldn't rely on Achronyx, who was tagging along with Tabitha on a special tablet while the ship that was his mobile body was being upgraded.

Presently, though, the team would rely on Katsu's computer skills.

"We are going to suffer through some general antigravity issues as we slow down for a few hours. There is a distress call coming from this sector of the System, and we are required to check it out and report the message. Captain out."

Tabitha looked at Ryu and Hirotoshi. "We could not really get this fucking lucky, could we?"

Hirotoshi started toward her. Ryu joined him as they met up with Tabitha, who had gone over to the nearest wall. She bent down, unzipped a pocket on her bag, and pulled out a tablet. "Achronyx?"

It took a second before she got an answer. "I'm here."

Tabitha considered asking Katsu to do this, but time might be a factor. She looked at the blood all over Katsu's face before returning to the tablet. "Hey, I want you to jump into this ship's systems and see if there is a legit distress call, or if it's pirate or slaver action."

"The Skaines aren't known to be in this system," Ryu commented.

Tabitha looked at him. "Doesn't have to be Skaines," She shrugged. "If someone came looking for trouble," her eyes flashed red, "it looks like they found it."

It took a couple of minutes, the team mulling over potential solutions as Kouki and Katsu took time to heal and clean up before Achronyx came back from eavesdropping.

"Ranger Tabitha, there are two very faint sensor readings I suspect are located near the distress signal."

"Does the captain see them?" she asked.

"Doubtful. I'm using advanced algorithms on the raw sensor data."

Tabitha thought about it a moment. "Can you enhance their data and feed them the readings for the two suspected ships?"

"Yes, but if we are wrong, then we have potentially interfered with a legitimate distress call."

"*Dammit!*" Tabitha hissed. "Okay, take over their sensors and provide the real data as best you can." She ripped open her second bag. "Suit up, Tontos!" She started pulling out weapons and clothes. She laid out her black leather-like suit, then reached into the bottom of the compartment and unzipped a special pouch. She pulled out a necklace and put it around her neck.

She looked at Dio. "I know you weren't happy being left out of the last takedown, and you can't come with us on this one either." Dio gave her a *look*. "I'm sorry! I promise I'll get with Jean to have her make you armor. You could die on these operations, and…" Tabitha stopped talking a moment.

Dio came up and nudged his partner. *It's okay. I understand. I got your back, Tabitha.*

Tabitha reached over, pulled Dio's head closer, and kissed him between his furry ears. *Thank you. I've been able to cope better because of you, but I've been completely selfish. My fear for your safety has kept you from being able to grow into the partner you could be.* She grabbed Dio's head to look him in the eyes. *I'll change that now. I'll send a message to Jean so she has something for us when we get back.*

Dio barked once, and all of the Tontos congratulated him.

Twenty-five seconds later, five humans left the workout area, heading for the bridge of the ship.

CHAPTER SEVENTEEN

"Where the fuck is the black cat?" Bobcat asked, looking around the team's development and manufacturing area. The cat, which was the second generation of a cat that had snuck aboard with their beer supplies run, had been hanging around for a while, getting into stuff it wasn't supposed to.

The team couldn't figure out what to name it. Bobcat wanted "Beer" so he could run around yelling, "Where the hell is my Beer?"

William's answer to that had been an emphatic *NO*. They would never know if it was the cat or his beer that Bobcat was asking about. William had suggested "Master," since the damn thing seemed to treat the three of them as slaves.

Marcus wanted to call it "Dog Food" because it had ripped his papers up one time when he was ignoring the cat to get some work done. He'd left for dinner, and when he got back...

It had been worse than if someone had used a paper shredder.

"Haven't seen it since," Marcus thought about it, "about two days ago."

"Uh," Bobcat scratched his chin, "wasn't that when we crated up the new weapons the Bitches were taking to the Karillians?"

William was the first to acknowledge what they were all thinking.

"Oops?"

Marcus shrugged. "I sure hope the Karillians don't like cat." He thought about his comment for a moment. "On second thought, I hope they *love* cat."

"You know Christina would kick you in the shin if she heard you say that, right?" William asked his friend.

"What Christina doesn't know won't hurt me," Marcus replied. "And if either one of you tells Christina, I'll be sure to make up something suitably horrible to tell her about you."

"You would lie about us like that?" Bobcat asked, his face showing shock.

"When you are talking about a young woman who has the ability to create a hand that can rip you apart," Marcus shaped a clawed hand and ripped through the air, "and doesn't quite have the ability to control her emotions?" He looked at the two men. "Absolutely."

William turned to Bobcat. "You know," he reasoned as he pointed to Marcus, "I can't really fault his logic."

Bobcat made a face. "That's because he is a scientist and they are full of logic. Anything they spout is sure to be logical." He pointed at Marcus. "He could recite a grocery list and it would sound logical."

"Doesn't mean it would be right," Marcus argued. "Just ask my first wife."

"All wives," William replied.

"And how would you know?" Bobcat asked.

"Sounds like you and Yelena are having problems, perhaps?" William replied. "Is there a problem or two in beermaking heaven?"

"Not something I care to discuss," Bobcat admitted. "But for what it is worth, everything is fine."

"You screw up the last batch?" Marcus walked over to his friend. "It was the yeast, wasn't it?"

Bobcat blew out a big breath and looked at Marcus like *'which part of not something I care to discuss didn't you understand?'* Finally, he answered, "It was supposed to be a surprise birthday present, and I got a little excited. I didn't realize we hadn't done a full sterilization of the equipment that last time we'd used it, and damned if some bad yeast or some other bacteria didn't get into the batch."

There was a moment of silence among the men. William broke it. "She tried it first because she trusted you, didn't she?"

Bobcat nodded. "Yeah, she tried it first."

"God," Marcus whispered, "you are so fucked, and not in a good way. You will never live this down."

Planet Karillia

"What the hell?" John Grimes looked around the small landing zones, then grabbed the box and started over to Dan Bosse's location. A minute later, the door was opened for him by a private, and he walked inside. Dan's large operations tent was open in the middle, with the monitors on tables around the sides. While everyone's helmets had HUDs capable of displaying most anything, the team preferred to share a set of monitors for larger operations and use their HUDs for personal views.

John set the box down on a table. No one had really noticed his arrival, but when he set the box down, it meowed.

That got everyone's attention.

Dan left the conversation he was having with the Guardian and the Guardian Marine commanders Peter and Todd and walked over to the table. "How," Dan asked John, "did we manage to bring a cat down to the surface of this planet?"

"There were only two groups that have animals on the *Meredith Reynolds*. Team BMW and the food and animals group," John replied. "I'm going with Team BMW. I imagine they didn't even realize they had shipped one of their cats down here."

Dan reached into the box and lifted out the black feline. "Since those guys never noticed when the cats infested a pallet of their beer supplies," he scratched the cat on the head, "I believe you to be correct."

"What do you want to do with him?" John asked.

"Her," Dan corrected.

John made a face. "Shit."

"Don't stress it," Dan told him. "So long as we don't have any tomcats, I think we are fine."

"Yeah." John turned around and started back to his post. "I've got to go get ready for Bethany Anne's arrival." He waved at Dan. "You just watch that little hussy stick her ass up in the air. If her tail is to the side and there is a male cat within a continent of here, grab her!"

Dan looked down at the purring creature and wondered if there was a way to spay a cat easily down here on the planet. He pursed his lips.

He'd have to talk with ADAM.

Torcellan Passenger Ship (translated) *Luxurious*

"Achronyx, open all doors necessary for us to reach the bridge." Tabitha's tablet was safely back with Dio, but she had her operations comm turned on.

The first group of Torcellans were shocked to see the humans, who looked very much like them, running through their hallways.

Their purple eyes followed them as they got out of the way.

"Tell us what's happening on the bridge," Tabitha requested as they took a left down another hallway.

Two Torcellans, their white hair flowing down their backs, lifted their hands as their eyes opened wide.

"Halt!"

They had barely spoken when Tabitha yelled "Rangers!" and the five of them dodged around, through, and over the two Torcellans, who had armbands labeled Security.

"Shut them down!" Tabitha commanded.

The two security guys behind them tried to use their communicators but found they weren't working.

"The bridge," Achronyx answered Tabitha's original question, "is concerned. The captain is well aware that pirate activity, or worse, slaver activity, is possible in this vicinity. The two extra sensor readings are causing him a lot of heartburn."

The five of them dodged a startled couple and took a right.

Tabitha asked, "Any news on the two faint readings?"

"They seem to be using a form of cloaking. The two contacts are starting to break from their positions and change direction, which is supporting the assertion they are not false readings."

The five turned the last corner to the bridge. There were two alien guards in front of the doors.

"Fancy that...Tulets!" Tabitha commented. The opening of the bridge doors startled one of the two alien guards, who turned slightly to see if someone was coming out. They had large black eyes with sandstone-colored leathery skin. Tabitha noticed they had donned their ceremonial white clothing under their armor.

Both Tulets were surprised when Tabitha damn near appeared between them. They reached for their weapons, but her hands had pinned their arms by the time the other four humans reached them.

"Permission to enter the bridge, Captain," Tabitha barked, then walked in.

The Torcellan captain turned to see who was yelling on his bridge and narrowed his eyes. "I did not give permission, and who are you?" he asked. He glanced up, only to see his guards covered.

"Ranger Two, Etheric Empire," Tabitha answered. "And the request was simply me being respectful, to let you know I was coming in."

The bridge crew was concerned as the captain eyed the dark-haired and darker-skinned alien.

She definitely wasn't a Torcellan.

One of the support officers on the bridge cleared her throat. "Sir, we have incoming communications."

The captain eyed Tabitha, who told him, "Go ahead. If we are right, it will be a pirate or slaver. If we are *wrong*, then we will help rescue the ship in distress. Either way, you have the best possible support to help you in this situation standing right here with you on your bridge."

The captain made a gesture Tabitha assumed was at least accepting. He moved towards a large chair in the middle of the bridge and sat down. "Put it on screen."

Yollin Space, Fifth Gate, Third Ring

This time, the Ixtalis' small ship was met at the fifth Gate by an honor guard that flew her directly to the QBBS *Meredith Reynolds*.

"It's better to be on her good side than her bad," the pilot mentioned as he matched speed and confirmed the coordinates.

Senior Legate Addix had to agree, but she told him, "We are expected, and the Empress wants this conversation done quickly. Don't expect this treatment every time."

"One could hope," the pilot replied.

QBBS *Meredith Reynolds*, Meeting Room

"Welcome back, Senior Legate Addix." Gabrielle nodded as

the Senior Legate was escorted in by a Guardian and her two Guardian Marines.

Addix nodded, remembering that the humans were not accustomed to her mandible responses. "Thank you, Empress' Captain Gabrielle."

Addix saw that this room they were meeting in was smaller. The table could possibly fit six humans if they weren't large.

The Empress herself arrived with two Guards.

Like those two, Addix thought to herself.

Bethany Anne greeted Addix. "Welcome, Senior Legate." She pointed to the large dark human on her right. "This is Darryl." She turned her finger in the other direction. "And this is Eric."

Both nodded at her. "I've got outside," Eric told her as he turned around and stepped back out of the room, closing the door behind him.

"Take a seat, Addix. Let's get down to business." Bethany Anne waved to a chair as she pulled one out for herself.

Addix clicked her mandibles together. "Before we start, may I ask why you shut down my kill switch?"

Bethany Anne raised an eyebrow towards her. "Did someone check?"

Addix's four major mandibles came together. "I was in a meeting when one of the usurpers stood up, yelled at me, and clicked a device. He seemed quite upset when I didn't slump down on the carpet and die. Then he reached for a weapon, but Security already had him in their sights and they shot his arm."

"Bad aim," Bethany Anne commented.

"They shot his arm off," she amended.

"Well, better aim, then." Bethany Anne smiled. "It seems like maybe we forgot to turn it back on when we conversed with you last time."

"Or perhaps you expected the attempt, and protected me against such attacks so I could take my offer back to the council?"

"Well, wouldn't that be self-serving?" Bethany Anne countered.

Addix tapped two of her minor mandibles together. "Yes, but I have enough information to think you might have done it for more altruistic reasons."

Bethany Anne shrugged. "The answer is more complex and yet simple. All those reasons are good and partially right. I disabled it for you, as I have for other Ixtalis who have boarded the *Meredith Reynolds*." Bethany Anne was amused when she noticed the Ixtali's mandibles stop mid-movement.

"Plus," she continued, "we left it off to protect you against your enemies, who obviously didn't want you to live. That was just prudent on our part." Bethany Anne's good humor faded. "Finally, it was a message that we won't put up with any modifications like that, so the Ixtalis should expect it to happen everywhere we go."

Addix was nodding her understanding until the last comment. "I'm sorry, do you mean every time an Ixtali comes here?"

"No." Bethany Anne tapped the table. "Every time an Etheric Empire ship is close enough to disable the kill switches, we will do so."

Addix slipped farther back in her chair, her spider-looking face blank. Bethany Anne was waiting when Senior Legate Addix put both hands on the table in front of her. "You really aren't happy with my people, are you?"

"Addix, I'm neither happy nor unhappy with how your people chose to make their future better. However," Bethany Anne leaned forward, "I won't put up with something like a kill switch."

"May I ask why?" Addix asked.

"Your council had to figure this out," Bethany Anne replied. "If we could turn off your kill switch, we could just as easily activate it if the Etheric Empire wants to win a war against the Ixtali."

Bethany Anne waved a hand towards the legate.

"I could just send the commands necessary to kill your race," she finished.

"Yes," Addix's minor mandibles started touching each other. "We thought you would have that ability. There is a plan in place to change the coding."

"ADAM?" Bethany Anne called.

A male human voice replied from the speakers, "Yes, Empress?"

"How many different commands are possible, related to the hardware we have investigated?"

"Over two million permutations on three channels. So, call it about 6.425 million permutations. I'm assuming your next question is, how long would it take me to break it? Perhaps as much as one and one-half days."

Bethany Anne turned back to Addix. "Now you know why the Ixtalis must turn off those kill switches. Our planet has a saying." Bethany Anne shrugged. "Once the genie is out of the bottle, you can't put it back. Now that *we* know about the kill switches, your whole race can be killed from a distance. We don't even need to be anywhere near you."

Addix sighed. The council was not going to be happy with her message. "Okay, assuming the council takes your advice, what does the Etheric Empire want from the Ixtali nation?"

"You need protection, and we can supply that," Bethany Anne answered. "And in return, we need general intelligence so we aren't attacked while we are absent."

"Why are you going to be absent?" Addix asked.

Bethany Anne's smile wasn't gentle. "We have some Kurtherians to find and kill."

CHAPTER EIGHTEEN

QBBS _Meredith Reynolds_, Medical

Gabrielle was flanked by Eric on her left, and on her right was Stephen, with Jennifer next to him. Bethany Anne had decided to stand to the side so she could see their faces.

"You are going to be a grandfather, Dad," Gabrielle whispered as they all waited for the Pod-doc to finish checking the twins one last time.

"Oh, my God!" Jennifer whispered. "I'm going to be a grandmother!"

The hushed chuckling around the room caused Jennifer to blush. As a Were, she still looked to be in her twenties, even if she was older and had seen a lot of tough action in her life.

Bethany Anne thought back to the fateful time she was banging on Stephen's door to either get him to deal with Petre, kick his ass, or kill him.

Maybe all three. Instead, she had won her first sworn follower.

She reached up to wipe away a small tear as she watched her team bring two new souls to meet the universe.

Souls she was determined to keep as safe as she possibly could.

Stephen spoke up. "Unlike Jennifer, I know I'm old enough to be a grandfather and am ready."

There was a soft *whoomp* when Jennifer punched Stephen in the ribs. "Never tell a woman she is old enough to be a grandmother," she hissed. "She will let you know when it's okay."

"Duly noted, and possibly ignored," Stephen stage-whispered back.

Everyone listened as the two kept the antics going. "You are impossible," Jennifer told him.

"I've been impossible every day since you fell in love with me."

"That was hormones."

"Hormones are definitely out of the picture after a couple of years," he told her smugly. "What is your excuse now?"

"You've had a thousand-plus years to find every weakness a woman has."

"Are you saying you would rather I bore you?"

"Maybe," Jennifer admitted. "But give me another century or so to figure that out."

Stephen chuckled. "As you wish."

Their byplay halted when a light appeared above the Pod-doc. Everyone took a step forward.

ADAM's voice came over the speakers in the medium-sized room. "Eric Escobar and Gabrielle Nacht, it is my—"

"And mine as well," TOM jumped in. They finished together, "Pleasure to announce your two healthy boys."

"We just need their names before you pick them up," ADAM finished. "It's part of the paperwork."

Gabrielle and Eric moved to the Pod-doc and held each other a moment as the lid finished opening. "Stephen Michael Escobar." Gabrielle reached in, gently lifted her first son, and kissed him before turning and handing him to Eric. "And John Michael Escobar."

She tenderly lifted her second son and kissed him before the new parents turned to those in the room. Gabrielle held one son and laid a hand on Eric's shoulder. "We would like to announce that I'm changing my name. I will be Gabrielle Nacht Escobar since I'm taking this man as my husband." She looked at Eric, the shock plain on his face. "You better understand any divorce will be more than painful."

"Never," Eric whispered as he leaned over to kiss his soon-to-be wife. "But I never asked."

"And you never would," Gabrielle answered. Stephen Michael chose that time to start crying, and everyone took a moment to wipe their eyes.

Jennifer was caught kissing one of Stephen's tears away.

Bethany Anne leaned on Scott's shoulder as Cheryl Lynn walked up to play with the babies.

John was coming back in two days, and she wished the young couple a happy forty-eight hours.

She had a moment of sadness, thinking of Michael. She knew in her heart he was alive. She could feel something when she was in the Etheric, but it was too nebulous to track, as it had been since he had disappeared in the explosion.

She believed he had slipped into the Etheric, but she had no idea *where* in the Etheric. She'd tried to find him back in Colorado, but it had been hopeless.

He felt more alive now, but he certainly wasn't there for her to find—yet.

Faith, she was learning, was a challenge she had to meet fresh every morning.

So she did.

Space Station Ekuled, Eubos System

"That is a beast," R'yhek commented as the team watched the huge space station come into view on *Prometheus Minor*'s screens.

"Have you ever been here?" Nathan asked him.

R'yhek ignored the fact that everyone turned to look at him. "About thirty years ago. It was maybe half as big back then. We had a small uprising on one of the slavers' asteroids to put down."

"Did you kill the slavers?" Christina inquired.

R'yhek shook his head. "Mercenary, Christina, remember? We fought for the paycheck, not which side was right."

Shi-tan kept his mouth shut. He had been part of a couple of conversations with R'yhek in the past month and now understood the mercenary attitude a little better. It boiled down to, *"The universe is a Bitch, so take what is yours and protect your brothers- and sisters-in-arms because the universe doesn't give a shit about you."*

Shi-tan understood. His bitterness over his family coming back dead or maimed had kept him out of any mercenary group. If he was going to get hurt for something, it was going to be for himself.

In a way, a bounty hunter was just another form of mercenary. He just got to choose the ethics of the job.

Now that had changed, and frankly, he was still feeling his way around this new paradigm in his life. He wasn't sure it would all shake out completely positively, but he knew one thing.

Whether he wanted it or not, this team had his back.

He cracked his knuckles. "I wonder if they like a good bar fight?"

Nathan chuckled. "Well, since our contact is a bouncer at one of the more violent bars, perhaps we should consider that a good way to interview her?"

"Her?" Christina asked.

Torcellan Passenger Ship (translated) *Luxurious*

The captain looked at the black screen. "This is the Torcellan

Ship *Hythethaneuk* answering Distress Signal Four-one-one-five. Why have you not answered before now?"

The video slowly faded in, and multiple gasps occurred around the bridge.

Skaines.

"We haven't answered before now." The Skaine captain sneered, "because we didn't want you rabbiting. It seems you were keeping your speed high and might have been able to dodge our little welcoming party."

"The Torcellan people will not take this lying down. We will have—"

The Skaine captain laughed. "Have what? Another mercenary company come after us? We are Skaines, and we don't run from any Torcellan just because you threaten us. We run from noth—"

Tabitha stepped into the camera. "Hello, Skaine."

The captain's eyes narrowed, then opened wide in recognition. "*You!*"

Tabitha nodded, her eyes flaming red. "That's right, me, and the Tontos too, you fuckwit asswipe. You and your two other ships need to prepare to be blown out of space into enough small particles to—"

The video died.

Tabitha yanked her head around to stare at the comms officer. "Bring back that damned video!" she shouted angrily.

"I'm sorry, ma'am, I can't," The comms officer replied, looking between Tabitha and the captain.

"Tabitha," Achronyx spoke through the bridge's speaker, "I'm picking up the three Skaine ships breaking from their locations and leaving in separate directions."

Tabitha slapped a nearby desk. "SON OF A BITCH!"

The captain turned to his right. "Bring us back up to speed!" He calmly asked Tabitha, "Who is that?" as he pointed to a speaker in the bulkhead.

"That's Achronyx," Tabitha answered, her eyes slowly

returning to their normal color as she started to come down from her fight response, which had been triggered by seeing the Skaine.

"Where is Achronyx on my ship?" He was doing his best not to shrink from the hostile woman in front of him.

"He's..." Tabitha was about to point outside when she remembered that their ship was back in the Etheric Empire. Her eyes completed their transition as she realized she had just bluffed the Skaines with bravado, arrogance, and anger. "...in the shell," she finally answered, waving her hands around. "He is an AI."

"I'm an EI." Achronyx spoke to the team on their operations channel.

Tabitha subvocalized, "How about we make it mean Anonymous Intelligence?"

There was a slight pause before Achronyx answered, "I think I like that."

The captain made a general broadcast to the ship to tell everyone that the distress incident was over, they were resuming their flight and they would not lose any time. When he finished, he turned to Tabitha again. "Care to join me in the captain's meeting room?"

She shrugged. "Why not?"

The captain nodded to his second, then stood up from his chair to walk towards his meeting room.

Captain Gaheel opened the door to his meeting room and waved the five Etheric Empire agents inside. Three went in, and two nodded to him but took guard positions outside the room.

He sighed as the door closed behind him and turned to the three humans. "You are from the Etheric Empire, correct?"

"Yes," Tabitha admitted.

"Is my ship under your control?" he asked.

She looked confused, if he was reading her facial expression correctly. "No. Why would you think that?"

"You did a fair job of breaking through my security and affecting my ship's computers, and getting involved in a discussion with the Skaines."

She shrugged. "Your point?"

Gaheel looked at the woman a moment. "Young female," he managed before she put up a hand.

"If you talk down to me, I'll take offense. You won't have to worry about me seizing your ship," she lifted a black boot above the table a second, "when I put my size-eights up your ass."

The captain swallowed. "Your kind is a bit aggressive, aren't they?"

"You mean we don't accept others pushing us around?" Tabitha twisted his words slightly. "No, we do not."

"Why did the Skaines run?" Gaheel asked.

"Because they know us," she answered, crossing her arms over her chest.

"But *why*?" Gaheel asked. "I assume you have fought them lately and won?"

"You could say that," Tabitha temporized.

Ryu spoke up. "Capturing the Battleship *Shllet* probably caused some commotion."

Captain Gaheel turned to Ryu. "And you are?" he asked, swallowing as he replayed the answer the man had given him.

They had taken out a Skaine battleship?

"He is Lead Tonto Ryu, and the other even quieter individual is Head Prime Tonto Hirotoshi."

"Is that a form of rank?" Gaheel asked.

Ryu smiled. "Only for the day. She tends to change the titles to fit whatever is going on."

Captain Gaheel noticed the female pulling something out of her shirt. It was a circle medallion on a necklace. "This," she told him, "is an official Ranger Medallion. You may use your ship's communications system to contact this medallion and acquire whatever information you need."

The captain leaned forward and held out his hand, but the woman didn't take it off her neck. "You can examine it, but if you try to remove it from my neck, I'll break your arm, understand?"

He nodded.

He held the medallion. It was solid, but only slightly heavy. "What is this designation?" His finger was playing over a portion of the medallion.

"That is the number two in our script. It means I'm the second in the Ranger group," she answered him.

His eyes looked. "So, up at the top?"

"Probably close enough," she admitted. "I only take orders from either Number One, who is my boss, or the Empress." That was true for any other Ranger as well, but it wasn't necessary to explain that to him. *She* considered it a flat organization, and that was enough. If this captain wanted to make any positive judgments about her status in the organization, that was fine with her.

"You are authorized to negotiate with me?" he asked Tabitha.

She shrugged. "Sure. Although if there is something you want from the Empire, I will have to get additional permission. Anything involving my group is good to go."

She hoped.

"Are you aware of Torcellan agreements regarding efforts against our shipping?"

"Sorry, no," she admitted. "I've been busy in the Etheric Empire's areas, and most recently, in an unaligned area of space."

The captain looked at her strangely. "May I ask why your team is booked on our ship then?"

"Sure," Tabitha answered. "We were forced to go on vacation."

CHAPTER NINETEEN

<u>Space Station Ekuled, Eubos System</u>

"She's pretty," Christina commented when she saw the small feline-looking female who sat in a chair at the entrance to the bar.

"I agree," Ecaterina murmured, allowing the cacophony from the bar to wash her voice away.

"The cat-people are notoriously picky about their friends." Shi-tan sipped from the glass holding his non-alcoholic beverage. The bartender had asked Shi-tan twice whether he really wanted a *non-alcoholic* drink, and when Shi-tan's eyes narrowed, he poured him a local juice that wasn't fermented.

"Says a Shrillexian." R'yhek chuckled.

"We aren't picky, we are very open about how it works." Shi-tan turned to the Yollin. "I understand your main focus in the company is business, so I cut you some slack with your fighting. However, I will observe your abilities are good and getting better." He waved his glass. "It would do you good to test your abilities every once in a while."

Nathan grabbed a couple of nuts from the table the five of them surrounded. "Pain is a great teacher."

Christina turned to her father. "You stole that phrase from Auntie BA."

"Who stole it from someone else, but that doesn't make it any less true," Nathan told his daughter.

"I can't believe the Empress is your aunt." R'yhek tipped back a small bottle of local alcohol. It was actually more like another fruit drink than liquor, but it allowed him to keep his wits while drinking something alcoholic.

R'yhek explained to Christina that he was just trying to fit in with everyone else. Shi-tan found it humorous when the small human looked around the bar to see if R'yhek was telling her the truth.

"I can't believe I beat you yesterday," Christina shot back. "And I'll bet I will take out more people than you today."

"No, you won't, young lady," Ecaterina interrupted her. "Your job is to stay on the outside and watch."

"But *you* get to fight!" she argued.

"That will be fifty pushups for being obstinate during an operation," Nathan told his daughter.

She turned to her father with a fresh argument on her lips, which died when she caught the look on his face.

"Well, bistok shit," she muttered. "We somehow went into ops mode and I missed it."

Nathan looked at Shi-tan. "Okay, this is your gig more than mine. Who is going to start the bar fight? This is our third night here," he asked as he allowed his eyes to wander around the bar. It was two stories, with the upper balconies opening to the main floor below. There were easily over a hundred and twenty people on the lower level. He figured the top was half full, so maybe another thirty upstairs.

The area around the bar was crammed with Yollins in mining clothes or variants thereof, with a strange-looking alien or two around the outside.

Shi-tan sighed. "I'll give you my professional opinion, but I'm thinking you won't like it."

Nathan shrugged. "I want the truth. I'll deal with the rest."

"Okay." Shi-tan nodded over his right shoulder. "See the miner there, with the red hat?"

Nathan kept his eyes on Shi-tan. "Has about seven lackeys around him supporting his ego?"

"Yes, the very same." Shi-tan smiled. "Have Christina bump into him and apologize, and then have R'yhek say something that upsets him. He'll throw a punch, but R'yhek ducks, and he hits me instead."

"I like that plan!" Christina's eyes lit up.

"I like the ducking part of the plan," R'yhek agreed. "Not so much the you-being-in-the-middle part."

Nathan's eyes had a distant look. "No, we can't start the fight ourselves. That pushes us too much, I think, for this operation. However, I'm okay if we go over there and see if we can hear anything. If a fight starts, so be it." He nodded to the women. "Make sure you ladies duck if something comes your way."

"Am I still expecting a punch?" Shi-tan asked.

"Of course." Nathan smiled. "That's the best part of your plan."

So far, Bastek's night had been rather slow, which was what she preferred. Too often, fights occurred at the Dirtside Bar, where she bounced.

Just last week, she had been required to stitch herself up after a melee that had sent seventeen to the infirmary. Fortunately, her medical skills allowed her to not only keep her costs down but her reputation up. She was rarely in the infirmary, no matter how much blood covered her.

And she really hated to get blood on her white fur. Her chest down through her hips on the front was almost black, but the rest of her was as white as ice drifting from the sky.

If she had just been all white, she could have done more hunting in the snow on a planet. It was the perfect camouflage.

In this job she had to wear clothes, which rubbed her hair the wrong way. She didn't mind shorts and a mini-top, that was fine in civilized society, but long pants and long sleeves were annoying as hell.

She was working her way through Gronnick's *Third Edition of Alien Physiology* when her ears picked up the beginning of the altercation.

Her head whipped around in time to see the first punch being thrown by Zikie'kol, who was a pompous ass. She was already wincing when he reared back to slam a fist into a human, when he ducked and he hit a—

"Oh, fuck no!" she whispered as she tossed her book under the desk, pounced up on her chair, and jumped to grab the second-level railing.

That ass had just hit a Shrillexian!

"Fornicating boots!" she bitched, as the fists started flying. She noticed a small human being pulled out of the middle by the larger human lady. Probably a kid and her mother.

Bastek jumped from the rail into the middle of the fray and started howling.

―――――

Shi-tan was having a blast!

He took that first punch, moving only enough to allow it to hit his chin, which split open. He popped his horns out of his face and sent a punch back at that buffoon. A mug flew past the front of his face and cracked into the head of a Yollin at a table nearby, causing the three of them to mess up their drinks.

High likelihood those three had just drawn a ticket to the

fight. Shi-tan turned to his left and saw R'yhek dodging a punch, his left hand grabbing another mug.

He approved. The old mercenary was a sneaky bastard.

Shi-tan noticed the cat-woman jump onto and bound off her chair, reaching the balcony and running along the rail. She occasionally grabbed a handhold to keep her up there before she howled and jumped into the fight.

She hadn't even landed when an errant kick caught her in the hip.

"Zikie'kol!" She yelled as she went under. A second later, someone screamed as he got pulled down, and Bastek jumped on top of him. "You started this shit, and I'm tossing your ass out!"

"No one speaks to me like that little runt did, so get the fuck out!" the large Yollin yelled back, as he punched out a smaller Yollin who had grabbed a chair.

Zikie'kol grabbed the chair from the downed Yollin and threw it towards Bastek. She ducked but winced when she heard the crunch as it hit someone behind her. At this point, the people on the second floor were leaning over the banister, cheering the fight on.

That's why she charged them three times the normal entry fee to go up there. Too many came just to egg on a fight.

The altercation went on for a few moments, chairs and fists flying, and then it went all to hell.

Someone had pulled a laser.

Bastek saw the beam pass to her left, then heard a shriek of pain.

This fight was going downhill fast.

"We have guns!" Nathan announced when he saw the laser blast go through the smoky area. "New plan, put everyone down fast!"

"HUMANS!" came from his left somewhere, but at that moment, Shi-tan was occupied dodging a knife slice.

"Oh, perverted canines!" Bastek heard someone yell "Humans" and turned to see four younger miners head toward the two females. Her eyes narrowed as she tried to place the four, and then she remembered they had been sent out to mine when they had caused political problems on the main Yollin world.

Apparently their political beliefs included hating on humans, usually a no-no in an Empire ruled by those same aliens.

Torcellan Passenger Ship (translated) _Luxurious_

Tabitha was confused. This captain kept asking her questions that didn't seem to lead anywhere directly. She sure hoped that answer about negotiating didn't come back and bite her in the ass.

That would be embarrassing. However, the Skaines had attacked, and frankly, she had been too pissed off to remember that her team didn't have any backup here. She had just started to really lay into that Skaine captain when he broke the connection and left.

She wished she could be a fly on the wall at their after-action meeting. Someone was bound to ask whether she had been bluffing. She had been, as it turned out, but she had sold it because she had absolutely believed she was going to kick their asses. That would have been a problem if they had called her on her arrogance.

This time her version of dropping off the three-story building had been taking over the situation, which fortunately had turned out okay. But she was sure Hirotoshi would have some words for her when they were alone, and _fuck-all_, he would be right.

Better to be lucky than good, sometimes. However, considering they had almost gotten blown to atoms by a damned battleship on the last operation, they were due a little luck.

Still, the conversation with Hirotoshi was going to suck.

"You are on vacation?" The captain had finally come back from wherever her answer had taken him.

"Yes. After the last operation," she nodded to Ryu, "where we grabbed a Skaine battleship, Ranger One decided my team needed a break."

"And he chose this liner?" Captain Gaheel asked her.

She nodded. "Yes, he tossed us the tickets and told us to move our asses and make sure we weren't late..." Tabitha's eyes narrowed, and she turned to Hirotoshi and Ryu. "That rat bastard didn't set us up, did he?"

This time, it was Hirotoshi who answered. "I don't think he did. Or, it was a small chance, but not large enough to provide us with backup, because what could Dio and the five of us do?"

"Apparently your reputation alone was enough to scare off three Skaine ships," the captain interjected. "However, may I confirm for the record that you had no plans to be here to help my ship?"

"That is correct," Tabitha admitted.

The captain nodded, turned towards the wall next to his chair, and touched two buttons. A red light flashed twice, then went solid. He turned back to the three of them. "I am recording this for our files. This is Captain Gaheel of the Torcellan ship *Hythethaneuk,* and I am sending the primary record of an attack on my ship by Skaine enemies. We have video backup, which will be attached. Presently I am speaking with Ranger Two, Tabitha, from the Etheric Empire, and confirming information about the attack. Detailed follow-up documents will be attached or sent shortly."

"Hope you don't think I'm gonna fill out paperwork," Tabitha told him. "Because I'm on vacation and there is strict 'no paper-work on vacation' rule enforcement."

Ryu looked at Hirotoshi, who rolled his eyes at their Ranger's comment. She didn't do paperwork at the best of times, even when on assignment. Why would a vacation be any different?

"I just need you to answer some preliminary questions on the record," Gaheel told her, "so that I may move forward with another form of paperwork."

"Better you than me," she told him and winked.

"Very good." He looked at the three of them. "I have three representatives from the Etheric Empire in front of me, and two more outside the door. First, may I have the names of those outside the door?"

"Katsu and Kouki," Tabitha answered.

"They are part of your team?" Gaheel continued.

"Yes."

"And in here we have Tabitha, Ranger Two of the Etheric Empire, Lead Tonto Ryu, and Head Prime Tonto Hirotoshi."

Tabitha smirked as she glanced towards the two men with her. "That is correct."

"Can you tell me where you were and what you were doing at the time you first thought something might be wrong regarding the safety of this ship?"

Tabitha shrugged. "We were in our workout area training when the Ship's Captain said over the speakers there was a distress signal. I've read about, seen in entertainment, and been in too many operations where those with nefarious intent used a fake distress signal as bait to slow down or stop their targets."

"And then?" he prompted.

"Then, I had our EI Achronyx check to see if it was legitimate, or a possible ruse."

"How did Achronyx accomplish this? And I understand that Achronyx is a program, correct?"

"I wouldn't call him a program if you don't want something

bad to happen to your ship. Rather, he is an Entity Intelligence or EI. Far superior to a program."

"On what basis are you making this claim?" the captain asked.

Tabitha snorted. "Because I am a programmer. If you would like to see how I can program your ship to ignore you, just keep barking up this tree."

"My apologies," he told her. "We do not have many of these types of programs. They were outlawed over two generations back."

"Perhaps that was wise of the Torcellans," Tabitha temporized, "but we *do* have them, and it was Achronyx who cleaned up your signals enough to show you had cause for concern."

The captain's eyes opened wide. "Oh," was all he said.

"At that point, we traveled from our workout room to the bridge, and made entry."

"By 'made entry,' you mean you took out the bridge guards, asked permission to join me, and then walked in before I answered?"

"Operations require decisions to be made quickly," Tabitha answered. "I determined through the information I was provided by Achronyx, coming from your sensors, that time was of the essence, and that as a Torcellan, you might need our type of help."

"Which type of help is that?"

"The kind that can scare a Skaine asshat with just my angry-as-hell face." Tabitha's eyes started to burn in the middle.

"So," the captain swallowed, "you felt that you could protect the *Hythethaneuk* better than the security already in place?"

Tabitha just stared at him.

"Yes, I see...of course you do. May I ask for the record why you believe it?"

Tabitha chuckled; it was deeper and more dangerous than any of her speech to date. "Our team has captured many Skaine slavers and pirates, destroyed more than twelve, and attacked and helped capture one Skaine battleship. To my team and me, the only good pirates or slavers are those pirates or slavers that are either in jail, or dead. No matter the race."

Tabitha looked at the captain, her beauty edged with fire. "How many kills or captures do your teams have?"

"None," the captain answered before he realized he was supposed to be doing something good for them here, and it had gone off track. He cleared his throat. "My apologies, Ranger Tabitha. I am not trying to irritate you. On the contrary, I'm trying to set up the prerequisites for the reward you and your men will receive for the altruistic support of a Torcellan ship without regard for your own lives."

"In short," the captain smiled, "I want to help you secure a lot of money and acclaim from my people along with free rides for your team anytime you need to ship somewhere."

Tabitha stared across the table at the captain before turning to Hirotoshi with a raised eyebrow. "Do you know of any reason we can't accept this?"

Hirotoshi pursed his lips, then shook his head.

She turned to the other Tonto in the room. "Ryu?"

He also shook his head.

Tabitha took a deep breath. "Well, I'd rather we didn't have an official meeting about this, but if your company wants to provide us free rides on your liners and money? Well, we will accept."

He smiled. "It will make you and your team very rich, Ranger Tabitha. Some have retired from the proceeds of mercenary compensation. This gift will be almost three times that amount."

Tabitha shook her head. "The team will figure out something to use it on, I promise you. Plus, I like how the free rides get 'known security' to use you guys again. Nice touch." She pursed her lips. "How much is that in Yollin credits?"

"Do you already have a plan for the money, Kemosabe?" Ryu asked.

"Yes, if the team approves," she told him. "I'm thinking we

need to have a Ranger Team Two plot of land we can call our own."

"Where?" Ryu asked.

Tabitha smiled. "How about some world that needs cleaning up? Grab some worthless land due to the crime, clean up the area, then sell it at an appreciated value because it is safe?"

The two elder vampires turned to each other, a small smile on each of their faces.

Oh yes, this was a Ranger who would keep them interested in life for a long, long time.

CHAPTER TWENTY

<u>Dirtside Bar, Space Station Ekuled, Eubos System</u>

Bastek turned toward the two humans and jumped, clearing ten heads before she landed on the back of a random Yollin and pushed off him to jump again. She hoped he wasn't hurt much when her jump shoved his head down to slam into the table.

Where the miners had located an old slugthrower Bastek didn't know, nor did she much care when a slug caught her in the chest as she landed. She was thrown into the adult human, who caught her.

"Go, Christina!" The mother, whose eyes flashed yellow once, held onto Bastek as the bouncer moaned in pain.

"Ohhh, Torcellan titties, that hurts," she cursed. The human threw herself in front of Bastek as the weapon was fired again.

Bastek saw the woman jerk, then turn and throw a hand up, catching the slug thrower and easily sliding it behind her belt.

Then she heard the woman's guttural voice.

"Here she comes, Mom!" Christina yelled, and pointed toward the cat-woman as her mother swore. Christina turned in time to see an old weapon trained on the two of them, and the young Yollin yelling something as he aimed. A moment later, Bastek landed in front of the two as the pistol went off.

"Go, Christina!" her mom shouted as she caught the wounded woman. Christina's eyes flared yellow and she took two steps before jumping into the mix of fighters. She grew claws on her fingers, but her damned shoes were armored, and she couldn't do anything about that. The idiot was able to get one more shot off before Christina's clawed hand ruined his eyes. Focused on his pain, he didn't feel much more when Christina broke some of his fingers yanking the pistol out of his hand.

She tossed it to her mom.

That's when another fist came in from the side and punched her hard. She rolled with the punch and had just been knocked off her feet into another free-wheeling slug-fest when she heard the growl.

"Well, shit," she grumped as she dropped to the ground and dodged around the guys hammering each other. "Mom's going to take away my options!"

Dedek hadn't meant to shoot the bar's bouncer, but she had landed just as he fired. This time he aimed at the human female who had jumped in front of the cat female, and he fired a second time.

Then his face was on fire, sight gone, his mind registering something wrong with the hand that had held the pistol, as well.

Bastek saw the small child get pummeled, but then she lost her behind the back of the woman protecting her.

"Attack my family?" the guttural sound came out in Yollin. "Eat it!"

The woman took a step, and although she seemed to mass less than the Yollin she hit, he went down with one punch. With the same hand she had used to punch the Yollin, she backhanded the shooter, who was now holding his eyes.

Reaching forward, she grabbed the mandibles of the one who had punched her child and yanked him into the knee she brought up to meet him.

Instead of the human's knee shattering on the hard carapace as she had expected, Bastek heard a crunch and a sob of pain from the Yollin.

Ecaterina then tossed his whole body into a nearby wall. The Yollin's motionless body slid down the side to lay in a heap on the floor.

Bastek was starting to stand when the young female showed back up. "Lay down, we got this!"

Bastek pointed behind the human. "Chair!"

The young woman turned as she reached up with her left hand to catch the chair that had been thrown across the room. She turned it right side up and slid it next to Bastek. "Can you move?" Bastek nodded her agreement. "Let's get you sitting up. Hope this doesn't hurt too much!"

Bastek was going to push with her legs, but it wasn't necessary. The human was certainly stronger than she looked. Bastek's eyes narrowed when she saw the claws.

"I'm Christina, you are Bastek, and are you okay?"

Bastek nodded again. Christina turned and dodged a body coming from Bastek's right.

Her mom showed up right after the thrown body. "I swear," she commented to no one in particular, "she gets that from her father!" She turned to Bastek. "I'm Ecaterina. Nice to meet you, Bastek."

A large Yollin came running up to the two of them. Ecaterina slugged him in the face, stopping him cold, then lashed out with a kick, sending his body back into the fight as so much dead weight.

"Who *are* you people?" Bastek asked, watching the body flop around when it hit the mass of those in the middle of the floor, all pummeling each other.

"Bad Company!" Ecaterina laughed, looking around for her daughter. "I thought Nathan was stupid for naming us that, but I have to admit he was right."

Ecaterina's focus was captured by something on her right as the large Shrillexian came up quickly on her left.

Bastek tried to get up, but couldn't. The pain in her chest was too much, although it didn't feel like she had been hit in more than bone and muscle. "Fuck Shrillexian Kateriana!" Bastek shouted, trying to get the human's attention to warn her about the alien fighter behind her.

"I don't do humans," Shi-tan snarked as he caught the arm of a Yollin trying to use a club to hit Ecaterina in the back. He twisted the arm right, then left. The Yollin flipped in the air to land on his back, cracking his head hard on the ground.

That Yollin was out of the fight.

"Down!" Ecaterina yelled, so Shi-tan ducked low as a chair whistled over his head from Ecaterina's direction. He was about to stand up. "Not yet."

This time both Shi-tan and Bastek were surprised when a whole table went flying over the top of him.

That's when the roaring started.

"Oh, fugnuts!" Ecaterina cursed as Christina came running back, eyes afire.

"Dad's pissed!" she warned.

Ecaterina pointed to the second floor. "You, up there!"

Christina stepped into her mom's clasped hands, and Bastek watched as she tossed the girl up to the second floor.

"Shi-tan, you got R'yhek?" Ecaterina asked the Shrillexian. He looked around before he pointed toward the stairs.

"He saw Christina go up to the second floor, and is going to join her."

"Good!" Ecaterina told him and came over to Bastek. "I've got you, so hold still." She reached down to pick up the bouncer. "Sorry you took that bullet for us!" She turned around, holding Bastek. "Make us a path, Shi-tan, before the shit hits the fan!"

Bastek wondered how it could get worse. It wasn't until they had navigated the outside of the floor and gotten halfway up the steps that she saw the tall monster in the middle of the fight tossing bodies and slicing them up.

His eyes glowed yellow.

When the two women had made it to the top, Shi-tan yelled, "You three got her?" Bastek wasn't sure if he meant Christina or herself. When Ecaterina nodded, Shi-tan growled, "Make way!"

Those on the balcony turned to see a large green humanoid running toward them. It was all any of them could do to duck out of the way. Shi-tan jumped over the banister and right back into the middle of the fight, landing on and taking out three Yollins as he reached the floor.

"Bornnn with a shotgunn innn my hands." Nathan tried to sing as he tossed punches and dodged various assaults, but his activities were doing shit for his voice. Not that it mattered to any of those around him.

They had never heard the song before, anyway.

He saw someone lash out at Christina, then someone else caught her and tossed her ten feet into another group of guys pounding each other.

"Get back to your mother!" he ordered, his eyes flashing. "NOOOWWWW!"

Where there had been a human a moment before, a seven-foot-tall Pricolici now stood. His roar caught most of those around him by surprise, and that's when the ones who weren't fighting each other started trying to get away from the beast in the middle of the battle.

Unfortunately, it didn't matter if they were still fighting or trying to get away. The creature's long reach allowed him to grab them by an arm or a piece of armor or clothes, and the next thing that Yollin or alien knew, they had been punched and were flying through the air.

Then the Shrillexian landed on the three Yollins, and it became a free-for-all to get the hell out of the bar.

It was all over but the moaning.

"I don't do the infirmary!" Bastek tried to argue as the male human, still in his monster form, easily carried her from the bar.

"Not going to the infirmary," Ecaterina told her. "We will get you healed up and drop you back off here soon."

"Yes!" Christina could be heard on the other side of the small party, speaking to someone on comms, Bastek assumed. "Bring *Prime* in closer. We need quick access to Medical."

"They are going to want to talk to you as witnesses to the fight," Bastek told them.

"Wasn't us that started that," Shi-tan told her.

Ecaterina cupped a hand to her mouth, but Bastek easily heard her conversation. "ADAM, need a quick review and erase from Dirtside Bar, Station 551, Eubos system."

Who is ADAM, and how is he going to erase the recordings? Bastek wondered.

Bastek didn't hear any response, but Ecaterina nodded her head.

It took the group another five minutes to get back to their ship. "Anything here you want before we take off?" Ecaterina asked.

"Why? Am I being kidnapped?" Bastek replied.

"No." She turned to the woman. "You are being offered a job, and we might not want to come back any time soon."

"My book, back at the bar," Bastek admitted. "Gronnick's Third Edition of Alien Physiology."

As the team boarded the ship, Ecaterina called, "We got that book, *Prometheus*?" A voice responded from the ship as they all trooped through the locks, and she was laid gently down on a chair Christina had changed from upright to horizontal.

"We have all of Gronnick's collection, including access to two originals, but those are untranslated works."

"Really?" Bastek asked, her eyes lighting. "You have Subverted Clinical Studies of Kahleck?"

"Yes," the voice replied, "but I don't believe Gronnick was accurate in his assertion that he could ascertain what was wrong with the race through the writings of two physiology doctors from the Pehterians who had studied them."

"Pull us out, *Prometheus*," Ecaterina ordered.

"We are being told to get into a queue... No, never mind. We've jumped the queue."

"How did you jump the queue?" Bastek asked.

"When you are with Bad Company," R'yhek told her, "amazing things happen, and will just continue to surprise you." He sat down across the aisle from her, handing a bottle to Christina, who had come to sit next to him.

He raised a bottle of some liquid that smelled like Pepsi and smiled. "I guarantee it."

Bastek heard a new voice and cut her eyes to see a human male come from the front of the ship. "ETA twenty minutes, and then we get her healed up. *Prometheus* has a location off the ecliptic he feels is safe enough. We land, then leave, so we aren't nearby too long."

"Wait!" Bastek raised her hand a couple of inches. "Are you the tall monster?"

Nathan nodded. "Nathan Lowell, President, the Bad Company."

Bastek's eyes started to close. "I have to be dreaming."

Prometheus Major

Bastek woke up and gasped.

She was in an enclosed space, a large part of which was transparent.

"Hello," a voice greeted her. "You are on *Prometheus Major*, and I have extracted the bullet that was lodged in your muscles. Your bone was chipped, not broken. We have corrected that issue and removed all extraneous bone chips as well."

Bastek remembered what had gotten her here. She reached for the bullet's entry point but felt no scars.

She had no clothes on but found them once the device opened. They were on a table that was obvious when she looked around. Once she got dressed, more for others than for her, there was a knock on the door.

"Hello?" Bastek called.

The door opened, and Ecaterina walked in. "Hello Bastek, I hope you are feeling better?" When she nodded, Ecaterina continued. "We felt it would be best if another female spoke with you."

"Because you are less scary than Nathan?" she guessed.

"Well, he's basically a big teddy bear, but someone hit Christina and he is still a very overprotective dad."

Bastek nodded. "You are married."

"Mated, but it is the same thing," Ecaterina agreed.

"What is this place?" Bastek asked, looking around.

"We call it a bunch of things, but essentially this is the heart of Medical on *Prometheus Major*. The little ship we used when on 551, or Ekuled, if I use the common name, is *Prometheus Minor*."

"That ship is little?" Bastek asked, but she was only half-listening. "How was I healed so well?" She focused on Ecaterina. "And how long did it take?"

"The first is a secret for now, but if you end up being a part of the group, you will find out. I understand it took a little over three hours to heal you. I'm informed by our EI that it will be cut by another thirty percent next time since he has your physiology mapped now. He went slower to understand what your body could handle."

"Why am I not tired?" Bastek asked.

"More secrets," Ecaterina answered.

"Did your people start that fight?"

"No," Ecaterina sighed, "but, to be fair, we had been waiting for a fight to start while you were working."

"What! Why?" Bastek was confused. "I'm nothing but a bouncer there."

"We needed to know more than if you could fight." Ecaterina explained. "We needed to know your *heart*. Frankly, we don't want you for your fighting skills. We want you," Ecaterina looked her in the eyes, "for your *medical* abilities."

Bastek stared back, then pointed to the Pod-doc. "You need *me*, when you have *this*?"

Ecaterina nodded. "We can't take that with us on business or operations, so we need a medical person. What we do can be dangerous, so we need someone who can be dangerous back, who isn't concerned with breaking a few heads even though they would rather heal someone than fight."

"Who are you?"

"A better question would be, who are you, Bastek?" Ecaterina countered. "You were sent to Eubos to be a slave, but—"

"But I was rescued by a Ranger and her team." She looked around. "I said I was fine with going to Ekuled when asked where I wanted to go." Bastek walked over and sat down on a chair, "But that was a poor decision."

"Because?" Ecaterina asked.

She shrugged. "Life is held in pretty low regard out here. I do fix some people up for money, but my real income is from bouncing." She made a face. "The jerk who owns Dirtside thought it would be both funny and a great attraction to hire a female bouncer. It has caused the number of bar fights to increase one hundred and seventy-eight percent over the last five months. Now we charge people higher entry fees if they want to sit on the second floor to watch."

Bastek looked over to the Pod-doc. "How did you find me?"

"The Etheric Empire looks after those they save. We monitor when we can to see if there is something further we can provide. It doesn't necessarily happen often, but you were flagged as possibly being a good match for Bad Company."

"Which is what, exactly?" Bastek asked.

"Family," Ecaterina started, when Bastek tensed.

"Family?" she spat. "My family sold me into slavery because of my desire to read, to learn, and to do, not listen to those so-called wise elders in my group who wished to marry me off."

Ecaterina's voice softened. "That only means *your* family is questionable, Bastek, not families in general."

Bastek thought about how this group had protected her when she took the bullet. She touched the location where the scar should have been. "Who do you work for, really?"

"The Empress," Ecaterina told her. "Mind you, if you choose not to work for us, you won't remember any of this."

Bastek stopped a moment to turn her attention back to Ecaterina. "Why not?"

Ecaterina pointed at the Pod-doc. "I'll have you lie back down in that Pod, and your memory of us will be removed. We will put you back on the station in your bed, and you will wake up healed, but not able to remember how. You will find your book, and your job, waiting for you back on the station."

"I'd say you and what monster could make me go back in there, but I've already seen him." Bastek's voice trailed off. She was on their ship, so what could she honestly do?

"Oh, inside we are all monsters, Bastek." Ecaterina's eyes flashed. "But some of us don't come out to play all the time."

Bastek's eyes opened wide. "Okay, that's not frightening or anything." She thought about it a moment. "Unless one is on your team."

There was a knock on the door. Ecaterina asked, "*Prometheus*, who is it?"

"R'yhek is on the other side of the door, Ecaterina."

"What the hell does he want?" she wondered aloud as she walked to the door, hitting the manual control to open it. "Yes?"

"If you are done speaking with her and she has not decided to join us yet, I would like a chance to talk to her."

Ecaterina's eyes narrowed. "Seriously?"

The Yollin just nodded. Ecaterina turned. "Are you okay with R'yhek here?"

Bastek nodded. "Yes, that is fine."

"Do you want to talk down in the galley, or somewhere else?" Ecaterina gestured to the room.

"No." Bastek looked around before she answered, "No, I'd rather it was here."

Three hours and three more conversations later, Bastek joined Bad Company as their medical officer.

Bad Company's *Prometheus Major* turned toward a point in space, and moments later, a small Gate opened. The ship slid into it and disappeared.

They needed to speak with Bethany Anne and get their team fully up to speed on their next project.

They had a large corporation to build.

CHAPTER TWENTY-ONE

<u>**QBBS *Meredith Reynolds*, Empress' Quarters**</u>

"If we are going to do this," Bethany Anne spoke from inside her armor and weapons vault, "we are going to do it right!"

"If you say so, boss," Cheryl Lynn answered from where she was sitting on Bethany Anne's bed.

Bethany Anne walked out of her room and was playing with the armor around her wrist. She looked up when she heard Cheryl Lynn gasp. "What?" she asked.

"Do you have to make everything look so good?" Cheryl Lynn complained. "Holy crap, it's like Barbie-goes-to-war in here."

Bethany Anne looked over to see her reflection and smiled. The added three-inch lift in the boots of her armor did make her look very good. The armor fit snugly over the cushioned leather suit underneath.

Which required her to sweat way more than she wanted to while wearing it, but way less than she should. "If you are going to fuck someone up, you should only wear the very best." Bethany Anne winked to her PR person. "Why do you care? I thought you public relations types always wanted us to look our best."

"Well, yeah," Cheryl Lynn admitted waving a hand at Bethany Anne. "But damn, woman."

"You can always join us at practice if you want to get this kind of body, Cheryl Lynn. You have the genes for it."

Cheryl Lynn rapidly shook her head. "But not the desire to suffer that much pain. I find it far more satisfying to occasionally bitch about it to you in private." She smiled. "Say once a month or so. It makes me feel good, versus a month full of…" Cheryl Lynn stood up, struck a karate pose, and punched a couple of times, then kicked once, "martial arts where everyone hits back."

Bethany Anne raised an eyebrow. "Those punches look remarkably practiced, and so did that kick. Scott been working with you?"

"Uh-huh," Cheryl Lynn blushed. "Seems appropriate, considering I am a weak link if something happens."

Bethany Anne nodded. "That's a good idea. I think you are right to do it."

Cheryl Lynn smiled when Bethany Anne added, "I think all the partners should have once-a-week training. We will start that as soon as this operation is finished."

Cheryl Lynn's smile faded to a grimace. "Patricia is going to kick my ass."

Bethany Anne chuckled. "Cheryl Lynn, I'm not above being bought to keep my mouth shut about where the idea came from."

"What's the price?" she asked. "I know it isn't money, so you must need something done." Her eyes narrowed. "And you want it done before you lift off."

Bethany Anne smiled. "Exactly!"

"Who's going to be hurt by this?" Cheryl Lynn asked. "I mean, who's going to be mad?"

"Well, I'm sure my dad will be, and probably Dan," Bethany Anne answered.

Cheryl Lynn pursed her lips. "And you promise to never tell where you got the idea to make us work out each week?"

Bethany Anne nodded.

"Okay, what do you need?" Cheryl Lynn sighed.

"I need you to go down to Team BMW's area. A bot will have a package for you. I need that package brought to me on the other side of the mall."

"A package?" Cheryl Lynn narrowed her eyes. "That's it?"

"Yup."

"I can do that."

"Good. ADAM will tell you more on your way. Now skedaddle. I've got to go act as if I'm an ass-kicking Empress now."

Cheryl Lynn looked Bethany Anne up and down in her red armor, swords, and what weapons she could see. Cheryl Lynn knew there were others that she couldn't. "So, you are just being yourself, then."

Bethany Anne smirked.

"How does it feel?" Cheryl Lynn asked, nodding at the armor and weapons.

Bethany Anne turned and took a moment to look at herself in the mirror again.

A calm rested across her shoulders. "Like I've put my own skin back on," she answered.

QBBS *Meredith Reynolds*, the Open Court

There had to be at least thirty thousand souls packed into the Open Court. The levels now numbered eight, with all but the last level occupied a hundred percent. There was presently a second court under construction to help separate the shopping and restaurants from the other businesses.

Many groups that wanted to conclude a deal in safety made the trip to the Etheric Empire's Open Court. What started as a way to get different groups of people to come together for food and shopping had turned into a major destination.

For some, it was a chance to see humans up close. For others, it was a safe location to meet. There had been three murders in the *Meredith Reynolds* in the first five years of her existence. Each time one was successful, the humans got better at identifying those who meant to hurt someone else.

No one who had killed another ever made it off the base. It was widely known to be a one-way trip, and it was believed that no one *could* successfully commit a large-scale killing in the Open Court, not that there weren't people trying to figure out how to pull that off.

Assassins and others who were willing to kill could make an enormous amount of money from a successful hit on the *Meredith Reynolds*.

If they could get away with it.

In the last twelve months, seventeen had attempted the feat. Nine had been tried and sent to Eubos to work as forced labor. Five had been remanded to their own governments for punishment. One of those five had been slapped on the wrist and let go, proving to the Etheric Empire that it had been the government itself trying to commit murder in their domain.

Three days later, the assassin, and the legate who had argued for his release and promised capital punishment "on pain of death" should it not happen, died at the exact same time in two different cities.

The Etheric Empire had never claimed the kills, but many believed it was by their hand that both had died.

The last three were ushered out an airlock without suits.

At the present time, there were no less than six businesses that rented their facilities out for impromptu meetings in the Open Court.

Bethany Anne refused to have any sort of music announce her entrance. She entered the Open Court from a hallway near All Guns Blazing with twenty-one Guardians and their Marines ahead of her, Darryl was in the lead, Eric and Scott beside her, and John Grimes behind her. Stephen and Gabrielle were behind John.

As soon as the first of her team came out of the hallway, the conversation in the Open Court hushed.

ADAM, give me access to the speakers.

>>**Done.**<<

"My people, and visitors to the Etheric Empire..." she started saying.

Johnny was eight years old, visiting his mom at her office on the seventh level of the Open Court, when people started setting up chairs at viewing spots on the levels below. "MOM!" he called over his shoulder as he looked down, his hands grasping the top of the protective rail.

She didn't answer.

Johnny turned to see his mom with her head still down, working on some sort of drawing. It seemed that every time he looked, she was drawing, drawing, drawing.

He'd rather stick one of her pens in his eye than draw.

"*MOM!*" He shouted again to get her attention, but he was too far away. He shrugged and went into her office. He grabbed one of the chairs, the four legs making a screeching noise as he half-carried, half-pulled it across the twenty feet from the front of her office to the balcony, where he pushed the chair up to the rail and sat down.

A moment later, he wished he had thought to get something to eat. He wasn't sure how long this was going to take, but he could see the fourth level getting full, and the fifth level was starting to stack up too.

He turned and slid off his chair, ran back into the office, and grabbed a bag and a drink out of the small kitchen. He looked at what he had picked up, then grabbed a second set. He ran back out and placed his loot on his chair, then went back in. He dragged another chair out and placed it by the first one.

Thirty minutes later, a very well-dressed man walked by. Johnny watched him, wondering if he would want to rent his little chair, complete with snacks?

The man continued his walk, and then, to Johnny's surprise, he turned around. "Young man?"

"Yes, sir?" Johnny replied.

"Would you happen to know if that chair is for rent?"

Johnny smiled. "Yes, sir!" He stood up. "I can let you use it for two credits, sir," Johnny looked down over the balcony, "but honestly, I'm not sure what everyone is so anxious to see down there."

"Is that so?" the man asked. He reached into his pocket and took out a tablet. "Who do I pay the two credits to?"

Johnny was stumped for a moment. He didn't have his own account yet. He looked around and back at his mom, but she was still working. "Um, my mom." He looked up at the man, "But I don't know how to make that happen."

The man pursed his lips. "I understand. That's her business name, right?" Johnny nodded, so the man tapped his tablet, then winked at the young boy. "ADAM? Yes, Barnabas. I need you to find the account of the lady who owns this business, so I can deposit two credits. Charge it to my account. Yes, that's correct. Make it so, and label it 'For Johnny's Chair Rental.' That's right, thank you."

Barnabas looked at the eight-year-old. "You have gumption, young man."

"Johnny?" a female's voice called. Both he and Barnabas turned in their chairs to see a woman looking at a screen, then at her son when she realized that he was sitting next to a man. She quickly grasped there were a few people standing around the perimeter.

She pushed away from her desk and moved quickly toward

the two of them. "Sir, did you just deposit two credits for Johnny here?"

Barnabas turned toward her. "I did, yes. Your enterprising young son had set up a rentable chair, complete with snacks, where one can watch the Empress come by below."

"The Empress?" Johnny asked, excited.

Barnabas nodded. "Oh, yes. She will be here in about five more minutes."

"How do you know this?" Johnny's mom asked.

Barnabas smiled. "I'm aware of her itinerary." He nodded to the people around them. "This time, I chose to be up high and let others be a little closer. It isn't often you get to see her as she was meant to be."

"How's that?" Johnny asked.

Barnabas looked down at the young man. "The Empress is going to come through here on her way to defend the helpless, to defend those who can't defend *themselves*."

"What's so wrong with that?" Johnny's mother asked. Then, having decided this man wasn't a threat to her son, she reached across her son. "Sorry, I'm Sarah."

"Barnabas," he replied, raising himself just a bit and then sitting back down.

"Absolutely nothing," the man answered her earlier question. "But I can tell you that the Empress most have seen these last few years isn't the Empress the Kurtherians will meet."

Sarah's eyes widened. "Oh…"

The hush caught their attention, and they all leaned forward so they could see down to the bottom level as a number of black-clad warriors entered the Open Court.

"Who are they?" Johnny whispered.

"Those are the Empress' Guardians and the Guardian Marines. They are always deployed in groups of three. One Guardian, two Marines. The Guardian handles close-range attack and defense, and the Marines are for distance attacks and Guardian defense. You can see the guns they wear."

Johnny turned to Barnabas. "Why don't the Guardians have guns?"

Sarah swallowed. She knew the answer but had never thought to teach her son this stuff. "They *are* the weapons, Johnny," she told him. He turned and looked at her. "They can change shape, son. They are there to attack for the Empress. The Marines are there to protect the Guardians."

Johnny looked back down. "THAT'S THEM!" he half-shouted, half-whispered. The people around them chuckled at his exuberance.

"Yes, those are the Empress' Guards. The one in front is Darryl, to the Empress' left is Eric, and across from him is Scott. Behind her is—"

"John Grimes," Johnny told him. "Everyone knows him."

Barnabas laughed. "I suppose they do."

"That's Gabrielle, their captain, right?" Sarah asked, getting into the spirit of things.

"Yes, and the man next to her is Stephen," Barnabas finished.

"No one knows much about him, do they?" Sarah asked. "I mean, we know he is with Jennifer."

"You have to love the grapevine. But gossip or not, it is true," Barnabas answered. "Stephen prefers to keep to himself when he isn't on an op. He doesn't mind being in the spotlight, but you won't find him there on purpose."

Johnny looked up at Barnabas. "Why's he doing it now?"

"Because those soldiers down there are going with the *Arch-Angel* to fight a Kurtherian-backed group."

"Coooool," Johnny whispered. "I want to see the *ArchAngel* someday," he murmured to no one in particular, then turned to Barnabas. "I have a model of it, you know."

"No, I didn't," Barnabas admitted, "but that is interesting,"

"I had heard rumors," Sarah whispered. "I guess I didn't want to know it was true."

Barnabas glanced at her. "Those who fight are trying to make it so those that don't fight have the choice to participate, or not. However, you should always support them with your voice and your support."

Sarah nodded, watching the procession. The Empress started her speech while continuing to move across the court.

Bethany Anne could feel the emotions awash in the group watching them. "My people, and visitors to the Etheric Empire, I leave you in capable hands as we do that which we left our homeworld to accomplish."

There was cheering as she started talking, and more as she added, "Getting rid of the Kurtherian threat!"

"The Guardians and Guardian Marines, the special teams, and those in our army, navy, Engineering, Operations, Intelligence, and Diplomacy, have worked to support our new friend and ally, the Karillians. It is time now to show our support by defeating the ones that would damage their world, and stopping them before they hurt another world such as ours, or yours."

STOP, she called to her people, and they all stopped instantly.

Bethany Anne looked around. "Some question whether Empress Bethany Anne should go out and fight. However, it is not the Empress who fights."

She looked around as her eyes starting to glow. Her hair rose and floated as her face was marked by visible red lines of Etheric energy.

"Well," Barnabas leaned over and whispered to Johnny as he pointed to Bethany Anne, "there is your answer."

She looked at those around her, and those staring down at her from above. "Before Empress Bethany Anne was ever crowned, there was another, someone who fought for others too. I am relinquishing my crown for this mission and will do so as needed in the future. Empress Bethany Anne is stepping aside, and the Queen Bitch is stepping up."

Bethany Anne's group started walking again.

"I do this because the Etheric Empire will defend those who need and deserve it!" she finished.

The people down on the floor had been pushing backward, feeling in their hearts that getting too close to the Empress was a bad idea.

Just then, a little boy on the seventh level started a chant that was quickly taken up by those on the eighth and sixth levels.

"QUEEN BITCH!" Johnny shouted. "QUEEN BITCH!"

Beside him, his mom joined in.

Soon, all thirty-plus-thousand souls added to their voices.

Bethany Anne swept out of the Open Court, heading toward the Etheric Empire's destiny.

A month later, Sarah was surprised to find an invitation for her and her son to visit the *ArchAngel* as guests of Ranger One, head of Empress Bethany Anne's Rangers.

He signed the invitation *Barnabas.*

CHAPTER TWENTY-TWO

<u>Planet Karillia, the Dying Plains, Twelve Days until Expected Return</u>

Bethany Anne's ship floated above the graveyard. The skeletons of Karillians and machines littered this area and had done so for close to five hundred years.

"Take me down, ADAM." She spoke softly, and her ship dropped. There were five additional G'laxix Sphaea-class warships with the *ArchAngel II* high up in the sky above them, keeping watch as the Empress surveyed the world.

Their ship hovered over an area that looked level, but it couldn't land because the ground was too soft.

It took a careful scan to find a place her ship could land safely. The team exited, and she walked the half-mile to a ship that had been destroyed and was now just a carcass that vines and other greenery grew on. Bethany Anne was able to see that it was clear inside the broken shell, and she entered.

She looked around, thinking about what it must have been like to be on the ship, under intense attack before crashing into your own planet.

Defending your people from aliens in the sky who were hell-bent on killing you. You beat them off, and then in time, your people got so lax that in another generation or two or three, no one believed the stories anymore.

Then, when the fire came down from the sky again, people cried as loved ones burned in the streets, all because they had failed to remember the past, deciding that believing it was over was better than staying prepared.

Since they had gotten into space, they had told no one their story until they sought out the Etheric Empire.

They were trusting the Queen Bitch and her people to protect them this time, and after they won, they would have seventy years to take the battle back to the attackers.

Bethany Anne looked around the ship and walked back out, taking in the vast plains and the many burned and broken husks that littered it.

This would be the last time that these aliens would ever attack this planet, she promised those who had died here.

Or she would be here with them, another skeleton who had died protecting it.

Ten Days until Expected Return

Lance walked over to Frank, who was sitting in a corner. "Got a minute?"

Frank nodded. "Take a walk?"

"Sounds good. Need to get these legs a little exercise," Lance agreed. Not true, but who gave a shit?

The two men left the control bunker and started walking the streets. "She knows the main landing zone is on the plains," Lance started the conversation. "They have attacked there six times."

"Yes," Frank agreed.

"So why did she agree to defend a different location?" Lance asked.

"She's *your* daughter," Frank answered.

"Whom you have studied like crazy to understand what makes her tick," Lance replied. "Trust me, if I had the answer, I wouldn't be asking for your opinion."

"Tried Dan already?"

"Yup."

"John?"

"Wouldn't answer if he knew anything. Bethany Anne put the kibosh on that."

"I don't even have a suggestion to offer," Frank replied. "She went looking for positions, and I'm told she found some damned weird pyramid-looking structure from a time the Karillians don't even remember. Looks like it's way out in the middle of futt-buck nowhere, and we're all scratching our heads."

The two men walked a little longer, deep in their own thoughts, before Lance pivoted, and they started back. He turned to Frank. "Think she will be okay out there in the middle of futt-buck nowhere?"

Frank's laughing turned into coughing for a moment. "Hell, no!"

"Okay, just making sure I'm not being stupid here."

"Well," Frank grinned, "I can't say you aren't being stupid, but I don't believe for a moment she will be okay out there."

Eight Days until Expected Return

Lance looked at Stephen and raised an eyebrow. "You know why I asked you here to the bunker to chat?"

"Easy enough to guess. You want to know Bethany Anne's plans."

Lance nodded his agreement.

Stephen shrugged. "Lance, if I knew, and she told me to keep it to myself? I would keep it to myself."

Lance bit down on his unlit cigar. "But you don't know

because she has kept you in the dark too?" He swore when Stephen just smiled at him. "She's making this *such* a pain in the ass."

"Did you stop to consider that she plans on staying fairly safe, and being available to respond quickly with support when we find a hot spot?"

Lance chewed a moment. "That's our most logical guess at the moment. That is the plan we think she is following, but no one is comfortable with that assumption."

"So, more intelligence efforts, like speaking with me?" Stephen nodded. "Smart."

"Yeah," Lance agreed, "but it isn't getting me anywhere."

Six Days until Expected Return
ADAM
>>**Yes?**<<
Connect me with Defense Minister E'kolorn.
>>**Yes, ma'am.**<<
And both of you are hereby commanded to keep everything you learn on a need-to-know basis. And as far as I'm concerned, no one has a need to know, understand me?
>>**Yes.**<<

I understand, TOM agreed. **I was wondering when the plan would be revealed.**

It took a moment for the Etheric connection to route through the ships on their private channels, bypassing the traps Command had put into place to covertly listen in.

Why they even tried to capture anything ADAM sent out, he could not calculate.

A Yollin's voice came on the line. "Defense Minister E'kolorn, awaiting your orders, Empress."

Bethany Anne smiled. "It's time to see if our little ship is ready to bring me my goodies, E'kolorn."

"Yes, Empress," he answered as the connection cut off.

ADAM or no ADAM, Bethany Anne figured there wasn't any reason to keep the call open longer than she had to.

Third Outer Ring, Yollin System Space Control

First Shift, First Class, Double-Starred Ship's Controller Yri-Keva tapped the command that would warn all traffic that a new super-dreadnought was departing for trial runs.

What no one knew was that the ship was being handled solely by Reynolds. Bethany Anne figured no one would even try to ask him anything about the spaceship since they all assumed his responsibility was strictly for what happened on the QBBS *Meredith Reynolds*.

What they didn't think about couldn't get Bethany Anne in trouble.

At least, she hoped not.

In another system, a queued message to Admiral Thomas was lowered in priority, per the Empress' orders. He could be upset with her later. The new ship would only be in the system long enough to allow thirteen ancient, to them, containers to float off. Then it would leave for another system before returning to Yollin and delivering the results of the testing for the yard to review.

Two Days until Expected Return

Gabrielle took a deep breath, then knocked on the door to Bethany Anne's suite on the *ArchAngel*. "Come in, Gabrielle."

She opened the door and stepped inside, closing it behind her. She was treated to a view of Bethany Anne painting her toenails.

Gabrielle blinked a couple of times. "Uhh," she pointed to Bethany Anne's feet, "is this a new way to get pumped for an alien invasion?"

"Not exactly, but you never know when your time has come.

Why not go out looking fabulous?" Bethany Anne asked as she finished her pinky toe.

"That's rather depressing, especially coming from you." Gabrielle stopped a couple of feet away from Bethany Anne, who had little foam dividers between her toes to keep them apart. "You wanted to talk to me?"

"Yes. Sit down. I'll hurt my neck looking up," she told her.

"As if." Gabrielle sat down, but wasn't fooled. "Let me ask, is this about me fighting on Karillia?"

"Yes, of course it is." Bethany Anne turned to her. "What color?"

"What color?" Gabrielle wanted to be annoyed, but when Bethany Anne picked up a box, she peered into it and found over fifty different colors of nail polish. "Oh, I'm digging this purple," she enthused, and pulled it out.

Gabrielle started taking off her shoes and socks. "Did Eric put you up to this?"

Bethany Anne snorted. "That man is a big Gabrielle pooh-bear." Turning, she picked up the bag of the foam dividers and handed them over to Gabrielle.

"Thanks." She started placing them between her toes.

"He won't ask you the hard questions because he was traumatized by your first experience." Bethany Anne told her.

"And because he loves me," Gabrielle added as she shook the purple bottle.

"Yeah, that too," Bethany Anne admitted. "Although, you taking his name was damned impressive. It meant the world to him."

"Yeah, I know." Gabrielle looked wistful. "You know that's the reason, right?"

"What is?" Bethany Anne asked, continuing to work on her toes.

"Why I have to do this," Gabrielle answered. Bethany Anne looked up and raised an eyebrow.

Gabrielle shook her head. "Why do you make me say these things? You can be a real bit— Queen sometimes."

"Yes, I can." Bethany Anne's face became stern. "I need to know why you are not back with your kids because it had better not be for me. You know I will be all right."

Gabrielle nodded. "I know that, Bethany Anne. In the end, I know you can walk out of any mess, and you will take everyone you can with you. However, what happens if Eric *isn't* near you?" She wiped a tear away. "I can't tell stories to Steve and John Michael about their dad who died when I could have been there to maybe kill the one who shot him or dragged him away from the danger in time."

She looked into Bethany Anne's eyes. "Don't make me go home, *please!*"

Bethany Anne smiled and breathed out. "I'll give you this one, but don't ever ask me again. When those boys grow up, I'll not be telling them I got both of their parents killed, understand?"

Gabrielle nodded. "I understand, and for what it is worth," she conceded as she started on the toes of her other foot, "Eric told me something similar."

Twelve hours until Expected Return

Bethany Anne listened to updates from all groups as her team boarded her ship to be deployed to the planet below. She had some toys she needed to position.

"Any idea who we are fighting?" John asked when he saw the massive quantities of ammo they were carrying for their guns and other weapons. They had even grabbed backup armor, previous generation stuff, although Bethany Anne had looked at it and made a face.

"Tell me that is the previous model, and you aren't secretly planning on stuffing me into Model One or Two? Because if you are," she glared at him, "let me just slit my wrists right now."

John chuckled. "No worries, last generation. Unfortunately, you won't be able to fight in high-heels like you can now, but otherwise, it's pretty powerful."

Two Guardians were carrying a case marked "Jean Dukes Q-Carbon Flechettes."

Bethany Anne eyed the designation on the box and put a hand up. "Stop, you guys." They stopped, wondering what they were doing wrong. Bethany Anne smiled to reassure them before looking at the case again. "Put it down for a moment."

They put it down as Bethany Anne waved the rest of those bringing supplies to continue loading the ship. She looked the box over until she located a way to pry open the top and examine the carefully packed boxes inside.

"Interesting," she murmured as she pulled one of her pistols out of its holster and ejected its magazine. "Come to me, my pretties." She grabbed one of the new boxes and opened it, revealing a magazine. She pulled it out and slid it into her pistol butt, locking it in place.

"You need to be careful with that," John told her.

Bethany Anne looked up at him. "Why, Mr. Grimes?"

John shrugged. "If those are the rounds Jean was talking about, they could probably punch a hole in the ship we're standing in right now. Those flechettes are that hard."

"Seriously?" Bethany Anne looked to make sure her pistol's safety was in place. "I like that." She turned to the two guys. "Wait one second," she told them and jogged to a pile of stuff fifteen feet away.

Returning, she pulled nine more boxes out of the crate and exchanged her mags. "You can never have enough ammo." Finishing, she waved to the guys to complete their task.

"The one thing I hate about the new weapons," Darryl commented as he loaded a box, "is you can't say that you love the smell of cordite in the morning."

"I don't know," Stephen contested as he walked by. "Who's to say the aliens won't use a form of gunpowder you can smell instead?"

Darryl stared at the man as he passed. "Way to ruin a good thought there, Stephen."

"Doing my best to expand your horizons," he called back, before entering the ship himself.

Bethany Anne looked around and smiled. She was feeling like herself again.

She walked over and grabbed her helmet and gear. It was going to be a good day, one way or another.

Planet Karillia, Northwest Quadrant of the Main Land Mass

The ship floated down to hover about two-thirds of the way up a pyramidal structure approximately five hundred feet high. There was a large gap at that level, where the top pyramid was held up by massive pillars on all four sides.

They started exiting the ship and pulling supplies off.

Bethany Anne surveyed the structure that was another two hundred feet above the canopy of the trees, which were themselves between eighty and a hundred feet tall, and nodded to herself. "This will do."

"Do for what, exactly?" Gabrielle asked as she brought in a large crate, straining a bit with the weight. "Where do you want these reloads?"

Bethany Anne waved toward the middle of the room. "Let's create three defensive positions."

"Three?" Eric asked as he brought in his own large crate, also straining under the weight regardless of the advances in the armor he was wearing.

"Yes," she agreed, turning around as Stephen came up behind her. "You bring the charges?"

"Yes, my liege." He smiled.

"Great," Bethany Anne muttered, giving him an annoyed glance. "Back to that again."

"Of course," he told her. "It wasn't that long ago that I took your blood and swore my allegiance." He opened a trunk and started pulling out small gray boxes. "In fact, I like to think of myself as the first person who saw the royalty in you." He turned and walked toward the large columns surrounding the open floor.

A total of twenty-eight massive columns held up the impressive pyramid above them. Stephen stopped and scratched his head, then retrieved the whole crate before walking back toward the columns.

"Going to need more explosives," he admitted.

Each of them looked at their HUD when the bulletin from Command relayed that ships were entering the system.

"Don't you hate it when they come early to the party?" Gabrielle muttered.

"Okay, first defense is at the columns," Darryl put his crate down in the middle. "Second defense is right here." He looked around. "Where is number three?"

"I was looking at the holographic representation of this area with Reynolds before we left," Bethany Anne told him as she came over. "I knew the guys were trying to placate me and keep me out of the fight."

She reached up and grabbed Darryl's arm. "Because fighting isn't what Empresses do." She winked at him, and the two of them disappeared.

John came in holding two crates under his arms as they vanished.

"Where the hell did she go now?" he asked no one in particular as he angled his approach toward the rest of the crates. "Shit goes in the middle, I take it?"

"Yup," Gabrielle answered. She looked at her helmet's HUD. "Okay, special incoming on one-three-niner."

The rest of the group looked at their HUDs to see what she was talking about. Scott placed the two crates he was carrying on top of John's. "What the hell are those?" He modified the video to take a closer look. "Shit, those look old-school."

"Oh, they are *very* old-school," Stephen enlightened them, smiling. "I see twelve offensive shipping containers I recognize from when we were on Earth," his eyes narrowed, "and one I don't."

CHAPTER TWENTY-THREE

Bethany Anne peeked out of the Etheric. "Okay, I've got this, Darryl."

"You've got what?" Darryl asked warily, his eyes widening a bit. Bethany Anne rarely said, "I've got this."

The two of them stepped out and immediately started falling.

They dropped about five feet before Bethany Anne pulled Darryl back into the Etheric. "Sorry, miscalculated. Here we go." She pulled him out of the Etheric once again.

"I really don't like it when she surprises me," Stephen murmured. Gabrielle patted him consolingly on the back.

"Welcome to our lives," John told him as they set up the crates they had brought in. They were creating an octagonal defensive position, placing some of Team BMW's new antigrav shields on three sides.

"Why aren't we placing them four-up?" Gabrielle asked.

John shrugged as he locked the third shield into place. "Bethany Anne will be on this side. It won't ever get turned on."

Gabrielle blinked. "What if she gets hurt or knocked out?"

She looked up to see John's eyes flash red. "Then all those motherfuckers better have prayed to their gods before they dropped down on us."

"Hoooollly crap." Darryl whistled as he looked around the cave. There was a square aperture about twenty feet wide some thirty paces away that was open to the outside. "Where are we?"

Bethany Anne started walking toward it, and Darryl followed. As she stood at the edge, he joined her and looked down. There were about a thousand steps leading into the jungle overgrowth far below.

"We are at the top of the pyramid?" He looked at the glass-like sides. "So those asshats are going to have to climb the stairs."

"Yup," Bethany Anne agreed. "Watch yourself, we have incoming."

Darryl turned to see what she was looking at, and raised his eyebrows.

There were twelve black shipping containers with the female vampire insignia of her Empire painted on the side floating towards them.

Along with one rusty old shipping container.

The twelve split off and started to settle into the jungle around them. Darryl could see five of them land but lost sight of the other seven. "They being placed in a circle?" he asked.

"Yup," Bethany Anne told him. The two of them moved to the side of the entrance. "Make sure you don't jiggle that one, ADAM."

Darryl watched the rusty crate slow just a bit as it slid down the large stone walkway into the pyramid itself.

After it was in place, Bethany Anne grabbed Darryl's arm. "Time to go back. I'm being told we have ships inbound."

"Seems like the party is about to get started," Darryl commented as they disappeared.

Leath Dropship *22-Cheezth*

Quarter Military Leader Grindlock nodded to his team as he stepped into the drop capsule. The Leath didn't believe it was every grunt for himself. Rather, everyone lived and died by the Quarter.

Four to a team, four teams to a section. All sections would drop together toward their target.

When you saw a full drop, it was impressive—as long as you weren't the aliens the Leath were dropping on. They looked like incandescent strings coming out of the sky and raining death on the unfortunates below.

With a half-gravity reduction on deceleration, a Pod holding a Quarter stood an excellent chance of landing safely.

Especially on Tournette, which the locals called Karillia.

This was the sixth time Karillia had been used as a training ground, and now it was time to finish this world and get rid of its defenders.

Permanently.

Previous generations of Leath had failed and had been left here to be torn apart by the inhabitants of the world. With each new generation, the attackers were a little better, a little stronger, and a little stouter of heart than the previous generation.

Not this time.

This time, the Leath had bred out any weakness held over from past generations. They had accomplished much with tools and training, and now they were truly a fighting machine fit to take out any Karillian defenses. Even if the defenders burrowed into the ground, they would pull them out and dispose of them.

The gods had commanded them, and the gods were not very forgiving. They had grown tired, or so Grindlock had been informed, and training was over. It was time to finish Karillia and move the Leath forces on to other challenges. Bigger challenges.

Richer challenges.

"Lock and load everything we need," Grindlock ground out between his two upthrust tusks. Muscular, bipedal, and brown, the Leath were masters of moving over long stretches of ground and through alternative terrain. Whatever it took, this new generation of Leath was sufficient to bring calamity to the Karillians as their gods had commanded.

As it was ordered, so it would be done.

Grindlock's team nodded, but only one, Tholt, turned in place and grabbed an extra ammo block. He locked it into his weapon and smiled at his Quarter Leader. "I didn't want you to have spoken for nothing."

Grindlock and the rest of the team chuckled. They had all heard the rumors and had set up their weapons appropriately. What they needed they had. What they might need in the field, or if they forgot something, their Pod would either deliver, or they would take from the vanquished.

The Leath had been fighting the Karillians for six generations, and the defenders' weapons were well-known. Frankly, Grindlock had been surprised, when he was taught Leath history, that the gods had been so forgiving of the amount of time it had taken his people to mature into adequate followers, with all the advances the gods had brought. Had they forgiven the previous generations their failures?

Hard for Grindlock to understand. But that was why they were the gods and he was the follower.

Now, it was time for his Quarter, their section, and ultimately their full complement of ground-pounders to prove to the gods they were worthy. Worthy of the patience that had been exhibited, of the enhancements their people had been blessed with.

Which removed the emotions which had been so limiting to their forbearers.

"Kill them all." Quarter Leader spoke right before the team both heard and felt the sudden jolt as the Pod was kicked out of the massive dropship.

Over one thousand pods were dropped into the darkness of space from each of the twenty ships spread out over the main continent, which was the only continent of consequence.

The final subjugation of Karillia had started.

The yellow eyes of his Quarter gleamed in the dark of the Pod, and Grindlock felt pride along with desire welling up in his heart.

He wanted to taste blood and taste it soon.

Dan Bosse looked at the screen showing all the incoming trajectories. "Well, I think that counts as a fuck-ton." He shook his head. "I believe our plans came up a little short, folks."

"Agreed," General Reynolds spoke up from behind him. "We are tracking," he turned to his right, "well, shit. Eighty thousand of the sumbitches."

Dan smiled. "Somebody better tell the Queen's Guardians to lock and load more ammo." He looked at the map as the tracks coming down from space started calculating landing zones. "*Gott Verdammt!*"

Lance turned to look at the screen Dan was watching. "How the hell did she call that so well?"

"Beats the fuck out of me," Dan muttered, then sent the command to talk over the private channel.

"Bethany Anne?"

"Here." Her voice answered immediately.

"Do you see what I see?"

"That the Queen Bitch is granted her wish and most of the tracks are heading this way?"

"The very same," Dan admitted, raising an eyebrow in Lance's direction.

"I do."

There was a pause before Dan asked the question he knew he wouldn't like the answer to. "How did you guess that would be the location?"

"Who guessed?" she answered, her humor coloring their connection before she closed it.

Dan turned slightly toward Lance. "Did you just hear her answer?" Lance shook his head. "I asked her," he told him, keeping his voice down, "how she guessed the right location, and she says she didn't guess."

Dan looked at Frank Kurns, who was busy re-routing a small contingent of special ops groups. "Frank!"

Frank looked up. "What?"

"Did you help Bethany Anne figure out where the Leath would be landing?"

"How was I supposed to do that?" Frank asked, perplexed. "When I myself am having to re-route support to her area?"

Dan nodded to Frank to let him know he understood his answer and turned back to Lance. "Okay, I'm officially out of ideas on how she accomplished it."

Lance chewed on an unlit cigar and gazed into the distance as he murmured. "Follow the money."

"What money?" Dan asked. "There is no money—"

Lance put up a hand and focused on Dan. "We tried to stick her in a back-ass area of the world where she could be defended, where we didn't believe the Leath would try to attack."

"Yes." Dan nodded. "That was the plan."

Lance took the cigar out of his mouth. "Sometimes my daughter is so damned devious." He pointed the cigar at the monitor. "I'm a pissed-off general but a very proud father."

Dan's eyes narrowed. "She isn't following the money. She is having the Leath follow the money."

Dan swore softly, then raised his voice. "All right, everyone! New fucking orders. Minimize teams around the continent. Everything we got, congregate on Bethany Anne's location."

There was a pause before Dan added, "And someone find out how Bethany Anne is telling the Leath they are a bunch of baby-loving, shit-slinging fucktards who couldn't catch and kill a cockroach."

Lance nodded. "You figured it out."

Over in the corner, Frank laughed and reached to his left, grabbing a new notebook.

The Bitch was *back*, and pulling stunts he needed to write down.

Once more.

Eric looked at the input from Command on the monitors and whistled. "Wow, you really pissed them off." He turned to view Bethany Anne, and his next question was instantly forgotten.

"Hey!" Eric exclaimed, causing Scott and Darryl to turn in their direction. "Where did you get gum?"

Bethany Anne turned and grinned. "You didn't read the notes on this little adventure, did you?"

Eric looked up for a second. "Ah, yes. Yes, I did!"

"Oh, well, then." Bethany Anne smirked. "The information must have only been in my copy."

Eric's eyes narrowed. "We have the same copy."

"Do we?" she asked. "ADAM?"

ADAM replied, using the speakers on her suit. "Yes, Bethany Anne?"

"Did Eric have the same copy of the notes I did?"

"Yes, of course. You were very explicit about making sure everyone had the same information as you."

While Bethany Anne was having that conversation, Scott,

Darryl and John were all quickly perusing their own copies of the notes. Over to one side, Gabrielle was smirking at Stephen, who was shaking his head.

Both of them surreptitiously pulled small packages out of one of the bags at their waists and popped a small chunk of purple substance into their mouths. It took Scott and Darryl only half a second to see them chewing and smiling at the rest of them.

"The hell?" Eric finally realized what Gabrielle was doing.

John issued a succinct curse. "Naturally concentrated lattices of vegetable origin?" He turned to Bethany Anne. "Seriously?"

"How are you going to learn to ask what everything means in a document if you just breeze through it?" she questioned him. "I mean, come on, I had to ask what every one of the substances we were provided were. Most aren't that helpful in this battle, but a few were. Also, I found out what terpene resins are."

"Well, that's going to be a pain in the ass," John replied, glancing at the screen. "Are we going to do anything about those incoming?" he asked as he mumbled a note to connect with ADAM after they (hopefully) made it back to the *Meredith Reynolds*.

He wasn't going to be caught flat-footed again. He had trusted he would be informed of anything interesting. Right now, his mouth salivated when he thought about chewing gum again.

"Sure, when we are absolutely sure we can hit the sumbitches," she told him.

Stephen reviewed a few screens on his heads-up display. "They really don't think too much of this world's people, do they?"

"Well, they thought enough to bring ten times more friends to the party," Darryl commented from his location.

"With about two-thirds of them coming here," Scott remarked, "seems like we are going to be having the party."

Stephen chuckled. "Jennifer is going to be pissed."

"She thought she was in the sweet spot for the fighting and you would be on the back lines?"

"Yes, that does sum up her logic," he agreed. "In fact, I would say she has been itching to be at the front since we began dating in Europe."

"That would be the date," Scott pulled out his favorite Jean Dukes EE102 Long-distance Semi-auto, "where you ran into trouble with the Weres and she jumped ship on you?"

"The very same," Stephen agreed.

"So, she has been training ever since?" Eric asked.

"Yup," Stephen agreed. "With me, Nathan when he has a chance, and Peter."

"All the boys," Bethany Anne broke in, "who were having hissy fits in the halls about her."

"She was becoming quite angry in practice," Stephen admitted.

"All practice and no action made Jennifer a bit of a bitch," Bethany Anne commented as she reviewed the screens in her HUD. She looked around and saw everyone staring at her. "What? She's a Were, so she *is* a bitch."

"You know..." Stephen paused, trying to pick his words carefully.

"Stephen?" Bethany Anne got his attention and pointed to herself. "You are talking to the Queen Bitch here. I wear my moniker proudly, so she needs to own hers, too."

They could hear hundreds of pods screaming through the atmosphere, then slowing and creating chaos in the vegetation as they crashed through the overgrowth surrounding the pyramid.

"Okay, time for our first welcome to the uninvited guests," Bethany Anne commented, and soon thereafter, all hell broke loose down below.

Planet Karillia, Command Base

"Should we make a few overflights?" Dan asked Lance,

watching the thousands of pods moving toward Bethany Anne's position.

"Nope, not unless she calls it in." Lance sighed. "Damn that woman. She can really sell an invitation to aliens hell-bent on killing and destruction." He reached up and wiped his face. "Someone better start feeding this information to ArchAngel."

Dan looked at Lance, who winked at him. "Two can play nasty."

Bridge, *ArchAngel II*

Admiral Thomas was sitting on the bridge of *ArchAngel II*, thinking about the shape of the Leath ships and how they had arrived in-system. He watched them appear, ship after ship, in a pattern of two ships, one ship, then two ships again.

There was a break. "Do we have them all?" he asked aloud.

"Negative, Admiral Thomas," ArchAngel answered. Bethany Anne's face appeared on the main screen. "We are still able to sense a disturbance in the space where they are arriving."

"Well, there are a whole lot of the fuckers," Admiral Thomas admitted. "I'm counting, what, twenty dropships, at least four or five ships that look like logistics, and three capital ships."

As the Admiral finished, there was a huge flash of energy and a final ship appeared.

It was round with an empty center and was fully three times the width of any of the capital ships.

"Well, I think we have found their method of arriving." Admiral Thomas rubbed his face. "Now, what do I do about you?"

CHAPTER TWENTY-FOUR

Planet Karillia / Tournette

Quarter Military Leader Grindlock kicked open the door that blocked his exit from the Pod. He knew they weren't following the original plan that had been designed for this useless world, because they were in a jungle.

"Who the hell decided we needed to play in the grass and trees?" he grunted, his two upthrust tusks rubbing his lip as he sneered.

"Turn to Comm channel 112.251, QML," Quarter Second instructed. He jumped out of the Pod while looking to the right, his section to cover.

Grindlock switched to the general frequency and listened a moment to the bullshit that was being spewed. He counted seven languages, but he only understood two.

"Seems someone is itching for a fight!" Grindlock smiled as he cocked his weapon. "About time we met an opponent with some backbone."

"True," Tholt added as he came around from the back of the Pod. "Easier to rip a backbone out of their ass if they have one in the first place."

"Even better than stomping on their little nasty larval heads as they mewl for their parents," Glot remarked.

"I've been looking forward to a real fight, anyway," Quarter Fourth D'thok commented.

Grindlock looked at his wrist comm for orders and smiled. "Looks like we have permission to seek and destroy, but be ready for traps."

"Like the idiot Karillians have a real clue about—" D'thock's comment was cut off as an object about two inches in diameter slammed into his armored body with enough speed to lift the five hundred pound Leath off his feet, armor and all, to slam into the Pod behind him.

Denting it.

Both the puck and the alien died together on an alien planet, far from the homeworlds that had created them.

Grindlock and his Quarter dropped to the ground as the Quarter Military Leader swore viciously.

Bethany Anne watched the data streaming in from below.

ADAM, filter this shit for me.

>>**Working.**<<

Bethany Anne's eyes narrowed. "Well, shit, the pucks aren't as effective as I'd hoped. The damn vegetation down there is a bitch, and they're being blocked by the trees."

Stephen joined Bethany Anne as he looked toward the jungle below. The screams of the Leath killed by the puck defense Bethany Anne had dropped with the twelve containers easily reached his ears.

So did the destruction of the undergrowth as he watched trees below start to fall. Most, so far, had been held up by their upper branches, which were intertwined with the trees around them.

"I'd say the vegetation is getting its ass kicked, Bethany Anne," he mused as openings in the canopy started to show across the landscape. The trees closest to the twelve containers were taking the brunt of the damage.

She looked away from her HUD to see what Stephen was talking about. "Well, this is one little tactical flaw." She chewed the inside of her cheek. "I imagine the General is going to point it out in the AAR."

"That's okay." Stephen pulled the rifle Jean had fashioned for him more than five years before. "Do you have some of those new cartridges on you, or shall I fetch them?"

Bethany Anne reached down to her belt. "I thought I was going to be an overachiever with all this ammo, but now I'm slightly concerned." She tossed him a magazine. "Here you go. One thousand rounds of Jean's finest Q-Carbon Flechettes."

Stephen caught the magazine Bethany Anne tossed him. He ejected his magazine, slid in the new one, and caught the other in the air, sliding the spare into his belt in one fluid motion while lifting his rifle to his shoulder.

Both of them ducked, their bodies almost disappearing as the stone around them started shattering.

"Can't believe this shit," Bethany Anne muttered. She and Stephen were both prone on the platform's floor. "ADAM?" she called over the team's comm.

"Yes?" he replied.

"Shut down the pucks on my side of the pyramid. I'm going down to have a look-see."

Before she could finish her statement, a boot appeared next to her head. She turned her head to see the sole of a boot, then followed the boot up its leg to the chest, above which she saw John's face staring down at her.

"What?" She smiled. "I wasn't going without you!"

"Damned right, you weren't," he growled.

Grindlock and his team remained flat on the ground as the cacophony continued around them. One moment, the noise was everywhere.

The next, it was distant.

Grindlock's eyes narrowed as he looked back over his shoulder. He checked his wrist comm and could see that the other three-quarters of the assault force were still under attack.

His eyes narrowed before he growled, "Prepare for attack."

"More?" Tholt asked.

"Different kind, dumbass," Grindlock told him. "They stopped bombing this area, so their people are coming in."

"Or just initiating a new kind of attack," Glot commented as he took a knee, preparing for the attack his Quarter Military Leader told him was coming.

"Nope, just two of us right now, Stephen," she told him. "You were voted off the team when you chose the wrong weapon."

Stephen looked down at the larger rifle and grimaced. She was right. For close work while running in a leafy jungle area, pistols were the better choice.

"Ready, Mr. Grimes?" Bethany Anne reached up and unlocked her sword.

"Born in fire and blood, Bethany Anne," he told her, his eyes starting to glow.

Bethany Anne glanced up and saw a fresh set of tracks starting to drop into the atmosphere. "Let's make this quick."

The two of them took off running toward the edge and then jumped, their angle impossibly acute for a human. However, as enhanced humans using the latest Jean Dukes powered armor, they easily cleared the base of the pyramid.

They had just about made it to the top of the canopy when a shell exploded near them, tumbling them both sideways flipping end over end into the trees.

High above them, Stephen shook his head and sighed. "Better keep your head down, Bethany Anne."

Her voice came back over the comm immediately. "Might want to make sure your microphone is off when you rag on me next time, Stephen."

There was a creak, then four more snaps and a thud. "Well, fucking ouch. That's one way to get down." Her voice spoke over the comm to no one in particular. "Not that I'd recommend it as an efficient method to reach the ground."

"Glad you found it eventually," Stephen told her. He eyed the arriving pods. "You have thirty seconds to get your asses back up here."

"Plenty of time," John answered.

This time Stephen made sure to turn off his microphone.

Grindlock's head pivoted right when all the shots seemed to be coming from one area. "Enemy right!" He turned and took a knee, using the Pod for cover as Tholt watched the other side and Glot aimed behind them.

Didn't want any annoying Karillians ruining the party by shooting his people in the back.

Assuming those three-eyed bastards could hit the side of a mountain. He had been told how ineffective their fire was even when they knew that the Leath would be back again, and they had had plenty of time to practice.

Once each generation his people came and kicked some Karillian ass, and they would continue to do so until this finally became a Leath world. Or a burned husk. Whichever occurred first.

Grindlock hated the dense vegetation in this location because he couldn't see his enemies. But he did appreciate the cover it provided when those enemies were attacking his team. A beep caught his attention, and he looked to see what was happening.

Good, the next thread was about to arrive.

He turned to look to his left at Pod *He'9114*, just in time to see the head of the Quarter Second explode inside his helmet. His body convulsed, repeatedly pulling the trigger as his rifle plowed holes into the ground before his body slid to the right, his finger finally off the trigger.

Grindlock dropped. "Open fire, three by three-five!"

"I've got nothing, QML!" Tholt told him.

"H114 Q2 just took something in his helmet," Grindlock explained as he ripped a short burst in the direction of the attack. "Pretty sure it came from enemy action!"

Grindlock could hear Tholt's own burst into the leaves. Both had pings on their HUDs and risked a glance to see where they were coming from.

Bethany Anne hit the ground with a thud. Perhaps the jump from the pyramid hadn't been the smartest move, but other than her ego, she and John weren't hurt.

It did underscore the fact that these Leath could hit them. "John?"

"Got your six," he told her as she stood up. She took off, running through the trees. Her HUD showed over two hundred tangos in the area around them. Springing upward, she landed on a limb about fifteen feet off the ground. She held on with her left hand as she took five shots, and five tangos disappeared from her screen.

She jumped down from the tree and saw that three more had been erased by John.

MICHAEL ANDERLE

"Five to three, Mr. Grimes!" She laughed as she took off again, jumping over a tree that had fallen due to puck destruction. She hit a branch, but it just broke when she slammed through it with her armor.

She stopped a moment, cricking her neck left, then right. She could feel John. "Let's do this!" she told him as he slotted in behind her. Both pulled out their pistols.

"Give them eleven!" she called and started pulling her triggers.

Behind her, John smiled and switched the level on his Jean Dukes to maximum. They bucked like a sonofabitch, but the sheer destruction was amazing to watch.

"TREE LEFT!" Bethany Anne yelled a few seconds later.

John turned completely around and ran after Bethany Anne, who shot twice as they dodged a tree that their fire must have destroyed. The crash behind them took two more tangos out.

Bethany Anne jumped on top of another trunk, then bounded up into the foliage.

"Son of a bitch," John muttered. "Fucking light people!" He dialed the antigrav up a touch to reduce his own weight and took off after her. As he jumped from the second to the third tree, bark exploded from the tree he was about to land on. The shot came from his right.

Although they had probably aimed for Bethany Anne, he didn't give a shit. He lifted his left leg and kicked off the tree instead of landing on it, and headed toward the location the shot had come from. John ended up in a small clearing with two pods and seven aliens.

That's when it got interesting.

———

Quarter Military Leader Beechton was irritated as hell. He had just lost his Quarter Third to what he figured was friendly fire when he saw something red moving in the trees.

248

He immediately snapped a shot toward the last location he had seen the body, although he knew he was going to miss. He shot too late.

"Yesss!" he screamed when he almost nailed a second figure jumping to the same tree. His eyes narrowed when it bounced off and came flying in their direction.

"Incoming!" he yelled over the comm as he pulled up his rifle to nail the approaching alien. He got off two shots before the alien landed in the clearing between his Pod and Pod *He'5444.*

The last thing Beechton saw was that this alien had two eyes, not three.

Two glowing red eyes. Then his head exploded.

———

John shot the Leath soldier who had almost hit Bethany Anne and took out five more aliens in the group.

There was one more Leath behind the Pod, but he didn't have time. He turned and ran, crashing through the underbrush and pushing it out of the way as he headed in the direction Bethany Anne had run.

He glanced at the HUD. They had twelve seconds and eighty-seven tangos to go.

———

Bethany Anne could feel John turn in another direction behind her. She trusted that whatever his reason, it was a good one. Jumping down from the tree, she came out into a nice opening without many trees. What it did have was a Pod damn near in the middle of the clearing.

Aiming her pistols forward, she fired two shots into the alien that was slightly to her right. Her left hand moved as she took a long step, shooting the alien on the left. She launched up, flipping in the air a half-turn, legs high over her head, body twisting 180 degrees as the heads of two more aliens appeared on the other side of the Pod a full twenty feet beneath her.

She shot both from above. The body on the left collapsed and the chest of the one on the right exploded, splattering the Pod.

Bethany Anne finished her somersault and landed on her feet, pistols ready. She glanced at her HUD and took five shots, killing aliens who never saw the human woman through the trees.

Seconds later, John came bounding through the trees.

Bethany Anne turned. "Hey-diddle-diddle," she called through their comm as she turned in the direction of the pyramid.

"Straight up the middle!" John finished as he raced behind her. Thirteen more aliens died, but one clipped Bethany Anne as they left. "Those fucking bullets are a pain in the ass!" she complained as they broke out of the underbrush, the majestic pyramid in front of them.

Bethany Anne holstered her pistol, then slammed her feet into the turf and twisted around, throwing out a hand. John didn't stop, but holstered his left pistol and reached out to grab her hand. They both disappeared.

Behind them, new pods started to land.

Bethany Anne and John appeared in the open level of the pyramid high above.

Stephen looked them over, noticing all the dirt and twigs that had lodged in their armor. "You two are a mess. I'd tell you to go take a bath, but we don't have time for that." He nodded toward the trees. "Seems like a new wave has arrived.

"INCOMING!" Darryl yelled, and the three of them turned to see the telltale sign of a missile heading in their direction.

QBBS *ArchAngel II*

"I can't do that, General," Admiral Thomas replied. "We have a monster Gate that appeared a few moments ago, and *ArchAngel* is needed to… One moment."

Admiral Thomas could feel the sudden acceleration as *Arch-Angel* started heading toward the Gate. He spoke aloud, "Care to give me an update here, ArchAngel?"

The visage of the Empress appeared on the screens. "I've been tracking the Gate, Admiral, and we have a major disturbance about to occur."

Thomas' eyes narrowed. "Bethany Anne?"

"I've sent reinforcements."

That was all Thomas had time to ask before the nose of a warship appeared in the massive ring.

"FIRE!" ArchAngel yelled as missiles, pucks, and fighters started erupting from her.

———

Leath Space Commander Kazakstone sat in his command chair waiting for the transfer of his ship, which would oversee the final eradication of the Karillians. This attack had been long in the making before the gods had agreed to allow a true invasion and extermination effort to occur.

His ship would be the final solution.

Should the army not succeed, his people would pulverize the ground with asteroids they captured and redeployed toward the planet.

After the deaths of those on the planet, their scientists would be able to study the effectiveness of a full kinetic strike and record the results.

It should, he thought, *make for some very interesting reading.*

Personally, he believed the planet's mantle would crack, spewing ash and dirt into the atmosphere and triggering the death of the world as the rays of the local star were cut off. That would cause most things on the planet to die. Sometime in the far future the planet would come out of its ice age, and his people would be there to reuse it.

Until that time, it looked like the system had plenty of raw materials, if you had the machinery to mine in outer space.

Which they did.

"INCOMING!" Kazakstone turned his head after sensors screamed the warning.

"Shields!" he commanded. "Pull us away from the Gate!" The ship's engines kicked in, and Kazakstone was pushed back into his seat.

Moments later, missiles started hitting the shields, and some got through as his people set up their own firing solutions.

"We don't have any time, Lance," Thomas told him as he glanced at the fights occurring around the system. "Our battleships are engaged, but if they have more of these Capital-class ships coming through, it's going to get really, really busy up here."

The video of Lance showed him chewing an unlit cigar. "Well, we knew they would be surprised to see us. Now I'm surprised as hell to see all of them, too." Lance considered what the Leath had thrown at them. "I really wish we knew how many more ships they have on the other side."

"Wish in one hand," Thomas began as he eyed the holographic representation of the naval battle going on around him. The whole battle hadn't gone exactly to plan, which was always a problem when the other side showed up with significantly more forces and equipment than their own worst projections.

To top it off, the Empress had focused the alien presence in one area of the world, completely against the wishes of her military advisors.

"Yeah, shit in the other," General Lance Reynolds finished the quote. "We need intelligence, Bart."

Thomas nodded. "Working on it." The lights dimmed a moment, and Thomas looked around. "Thomas out."

Lance saw the video connection die on his side. He turned, chewing his cigar, and looked around. "Somebody fetch me my fucking field armor."

Dan looked up from his desk at Lance and narrowed his eyes. "You know, I think I need a change of clothing as well. Seems like we know where most of the enemy is going to be."

"She did make it a bit easier," Lance agreed as the two men hurried out of Command.

"This shit is getting a bit intense!" Gabrielle's her pistols bucked in her hands as wave after wave of Leath grunts came out of the trees and ascended the sides of the pyramid. Eric was working with her.

"These animal-fondling long-tittied bunghole-sniffing cretins weren't supposed to be able to run up the fucking sides!" Bethany Anne yelled, pissed that her carefully selected fighting location was being overcome by some sort of technical capability of Leath armor.

"Technology's not so nice when it's used against us!" Scott grunted when he took a hit to the chest. "Cluster-fucking weed wanker!" Scott yelled, and twisted his pistol to the right, shooting twice.

Down toward the bottom of the pyramid, the head and chest of a Leath soldier splattered over those around her.

"Looks like Jean's going to have to upgrade us again!" Bethany Anne commented as she ducked to her left and laid down suppressing fire. Stephen took aim and unloaded his gun into the group trying to make it up the sides.

Both dropped back down into cover quickly.

"Keep making yourself targets and they will get a bead on you," John remarked from the side of the pyramid to Bethany Anne as a command override hit their channels.

"This is ArchAngel," the EI announced. "Three kinetic objects arriving in fifteen seconds. Please route appropriately."

"That's just like me, to not ask first!" Bethany Anne huffed. "Darryl, Scott, Eric, cover your sides!" Bethany Anne turned to Stephen. "Support John for a few moments until these things hit."

Bethany Anne had no more issued her command when Stephen had rolled over, jumped up, and was over by John, raining hell down from above.

Bethany Anne smiled as her eyes started to glow and the veins of power branched from her eyes, although the helmet she was wearing held her hair down.

Grindlock and Tholt had hit the ground at the right time as another burst of deadly rounds came at them. He could tell one of the two figures up above had a rifle, and while that should mean he was more accurate, Grindlock couldn't tell any difference between the precision of the two shooters on their side.

Two.

"It's only two damned aliens!" Grindlock turned his head and yelled in frustration to Tholt. "How are the gods going to support us if we can't take down two aliens?"

"Maybe because they aren't Karillians?" Tholt asked as he jerked to his right, bumping into Grindlock when the arm of the Q3 next to him shattered.

"C'mon!" Grindlock locked his feet down. "They're just aliens," He turned to Tholt. "We fill them full of matter, they explode like all of the rest!"

Grindlock's exhortation to embolden Tholt was completely

wasted, as Tholt was looking up toward the top of the pyramid. Grindlock followed his gaze to see what had caught his attention, and his eyes opened wide. He turned, grabbing Tholt by the shoulder and yanking him hard, pulling them off the side of the pyramid.

He wasn't trying to go up, but rather down.

No alien that could conjure massive red balls of plasma, or whatever that shit was, was anything less than one of the gods.

Grindlock and Tholt started a small cascade of bodies as they fell more than scrambled down the side of the stone edifice.

Moments later, the two of them were thrown the last few body lengths off the pyramid when the balls hit those behind them.

Grindlock was pummeled with body parts and the occasional piece of stone debris for what seemed like forever. Finally, he was able to turn his head toward the pyramid again.

Tholt looked at him and shouted, "Just what is that damned alien going to do next?"

"Seven by seven-two," their communicator squawked. "You have incoming kinetics!"

Grindlock's tusks shifted left and right as he ground his teeth. "Next time you have a question, Tholt, keep it to yourself!"

Stephen looked at the columns, his eyes opening wide. "Bethany Anne!"

She stepped away from her sector and out of the line of fire to turn her head toward Stephen. "What?"

She saw what he was looking at, and her eyes flashed in fear. "*HOLY SHIT, FOLKS,*" she yelled. "*TIME TO LEAVE!*"

She ran for the middle so everyone had to cover the same distance to reach her.

Everyone left their positions. "Get the lead out, Eric!"

Gabrielle yelled as she pulled up her husband, who had been fighting from a prone position.

They all ran toward Bethany Anne, who hoped she had enough time to do this right.

CHAPTER TWENTY-FIVE

QBBS *ArchAngel II*

This time ArchAngel wasn't going to waste any effort being sneaky. She didn't know enough about these aliens to try.

But she *was* going to lay down a colossal amount of firepower and pummel the ship coming through the Gate. That was for damned sure.

ArchAngel didn't announce her plans because she had been ordered by the Empress to protect the Etheric Empire, which now included the planet beneath them, and she had no lockdown protocols.

No lockdown protocols? No reason she couldn't do what she thought was best.

She had been entrusted by her Empress to keep them safe, and that capital ship that had just come out of the Gate was a significant threat.

"ArchAngel!"

"Yes, Empress?" she replied, allotting a small percentage of her power to conversing with her liege.

Bethany Anne was pissed. "Next time you decide kinetics are the answer, make damned sure we didn't place enough explosives around us to pancake our asses right where you are sending them!"

ArchAngel devoted additional computational power to the conversation. "Are you okay?"

"Yes, but almost all of our shit is underneath a fuck-ton of rock. Poor staging and planning on my part."

"Do you want air support?"

"Uh, hell, yeah!" Bethany Anne replied. "Make that happen. We've got a lot of angry Leath who are eventually going to get their bombed-out asses up off the ground. How far away are you?"

"Far and going farther," ArchAngel replied. "The Admiral has been able to keep their air support away from your area, but there are also cities under attack that we haven't been able to protect."

"All right, I'm switching to the Admiral. Kick ass."

"I always do," ArchAngel replied.

Admiral Thomas was watching the reports coming in from all the war zones when he was interrupted.

"Admiral Thomas."

"Yes, ArchAngel?" he asked.

"This isn't ArchAngel, this is Bethany Anne," she replied.

The Admiral looked up and realized that her tag was showing as the caller. "Damn, sorry, Bethany Anne."

"No worries, but that shows we have another issue with communications. The after-action report grade is going to suck. To the point," she asked, "what kind of support can you give us? We seem to have lost our ammunition."

"You ran out?" he asked.

"No, bad communications between ArchAngel and me. Hell, *everyone,* and me. We were fighting, and had columns set to blow, then the kinetics hit. All it took was one explosion for the columns to collapse from the kinetic strike, and the next thing we knew, our ammo was no longer available."

"Where are you now?" he asked, pulling up a map of her location.

"Holed up in some sort of ceremonial entrance at the top of the pyramid."

The Admiral sent two commands. "I'm sending one of the G'laxix Sphaea-class ships to you."

Bethany Anne sighed. "I appreciate that. So long as she's close enough, we have an exit plan. Now, how about making sure you guys send enough air support that we get all these sonsabitches?"

The ship rocked, lights turned red. Admiral Thomas looked around to see what had happened to *ArchAngel*. Fortunately, it looked more like cosmetic damage than a reduction of her combat abilities. "I'll work on that, Bethany Anne. We just had a massive ship come through their Gate, and we don't know how many other ships are behind it."

"Fuck it," Bethany Anne told him. "Send an EI fighter through and have it recon to the best of its ability. Make sure it knows to self-destruct before capture. If it runs low on energy, tell it to find a place to land and power down. We will pick it up when we get there."

He didn't bother asking her what she meant about getting there. They would eventually take the battle to Leath. There was no way this could be every ship they had available. No intelligent species threw everything into a single fight; there was always a home fleet.

He glanced at a message on his left screen. "ArchAngel heard and had one of her teams focus on getting her partner through the Gate."

There was a loud explosion in the background. "Okay, I gotta go. I think the pissed-off neighbors might have figured out where we are." She broke the connection.

. . .

Black Eagle Team of Fregin / Ricky Bobby

Captain Julianna Fregin heard the command and bit back her comment. Theirs was not to question, but for her and her wingman to fly the impossible mission.

Right past that large ship spitting out its own fighters so her EI partner could slip through that Gate and do a little nosing around.

Which meant that she was going to be unprotected as she tried to fight her way back to *ArchAngel*.

Fucking hell.

"We can do this, Ricky Bobby!" she commed to her EI partner.

"I can't believe I'm going to be stuck with the moniker Ricky Bobby for however long this takes!" her EI spat back. "You only won the right to change my call sign last week."

The two fighters circled a landing ship that was under attack by a Yollin battleship that looked remarkably like the original design of the first *ArchAngel*.

Shit wasn't going well for the Leath ship.

Unexpectedly, their little fighters were lit up by the reflection of an explosion. Julianna looked back to see that the Leath capital ship had spared a few moments to attack the battleship, which had gotten too close to it. She pressed her lips together as she surveyed the damage.

Turning around, she commed, "New plan. Fly by that landing ship and do a strafing run, then circle back to the Gate."

Ricky Bobby didn't answer, but she knew the EI had heard her.

Dodging the incoming fire, the two started at the back of the landing ship and fired at anything that seemed damageable as they streaked to the front and turned back toward the Gate.

And that damned capital ship.

. . .

Leath Ship *Deluge*

"What the hell *is* that thing!" Space Commander Kazakstone ground out as the enemy ship shrugged off enough firepower to destroy cities and returned a hell of a pounding.

The *Deluge* was the top of their line, and so far no race had produced anything even remotely close—until now.

He glanced over to see that his people had seriously hurt a medium-level ship which had come into range.

"Focus on that capital ship!" he ordered. While it was nice that the ship was damaged, he didn't want his people forgetting what the real challenge would be.

That's when his shields started flaring from thousands, no, *tens of thousands,* of simultaneous hits.

What the hell?

He looked up in time to see the opposing ship starting to glow red at the front, pointing straight at them.

Then the beam struck the *Deluge*, and hell became a reality.

His ship never paid attention to two tiny little fighters that had slipped in behind it.

Black Eagle Team of Fregin / Ricky Bobby

"See you on the other side...eventually." Julianna commed her partner as the two of them snuck behind the huge capital ship. With the massive barrage *ArchAngel* was providing, that ship didn't pay any attention to the two fleas.

Which was good, because the damned Gate was armed.

Twenty-two missiles were fired at the pair, and twenty-one were destroyed. Julianna flew her ship in front of the last one, allowing Ricky Bobby the chance to dart behind her and slip through the Gate.

Now her carefully-laid plan to pull up out of the attack and fly off was fucked.

The missile had damaged her ability to fly via mind link.

"Are you telling me," she pulled her arm out of the matrix link, "that I have to do this the old-fashioned way?"

Julianna hit two buttons on her screen and slammed her fist to the right. A small hand controller slid up from the side and she grabbed it, twisting it to the right and forward to shove her nose down and to the right, angling away from the Gate.

She used her left hand to touch four more buttons as the thrust pushed her back against the seat.

She was well away from the two ships pounding each other. Glancing back, she noticed the enemy ship seemed to have a lot more damage than *ArchAngel*.

"Good, maybe they will leave pitiful ole manual-control-stick me the hell out of their party."

Moments later, a massive explosion rocked the Leath ship. Julianne figured that was the end of that discussion, as *ArchAngel* had put her metaphorical foot up their ass.

Planet Karillia / Tournette

Bethany Anne had been able to get everyone into the Etheric with her before the kinetics hit.

It took her a few moments to move everyone far enough away that she could look out of the Etheric to see what had happened, and sure enough, where they had been a minute before was gone. A large portion of the pyramid had collapsed.

Perhaps the kinetics themselves had been too much for the columns, or perhaps their explosives had taken part of it down. It didn't matter.

She had made a tactical error by placing all their firepower underneath that much rock. Her thought had been to use it to squash a shitload of Leath.

She was able to move everyone back to the cave above the pyramid and bring them out of the Etheric.

Bethany Anne addressed everyone. "Figure out how much

ammo you have on you right now, because we don't have any more."

Scott had walked over to the disused-looking container. He turned to Bethany Anne. "Is this the honeypot?"

"Yes," she answered. "It's busy calling them names in seven different common alien tongues. Apparently," she shrugged, "one of them was enough."

There was a commotion near the opening to the cave, so the two of them jogged over to see what was getting everyone's attention. About half a mile out, there was something, or many somethings, causing the trees to buck and sway.

By the look of those trees, it was headed their way.

Bethany Anne turned around and walked back into the cave a little way. "I've got to make a call. Let me know if anything happens."

The team heard Bethany Anne call ArchAngel as they tried to stay back from the main opening and still see what was coming in their direction.

"I count four," Darryl stated. "Yes, definitely four."

"That sounds a little Rain Man-ish to me," Eric told him.

The crashing of the trees at the bottom of the pyramid caused the guys to whistle. Even Stephen.

Four large tri-pedal mechanical tanks were working their way out of the trees. "Where do they get all those wonderful toys?" Stephen wondered.

"Definitely four," Darryl told everyone. "I think I'm going to take a celebratory piss."

Scott grinned. "Where are you going to find a place to piss in East Bumblefuck, Karillia?"

"We can always just aim down, see who can piss the farthest," John commented.

All four of the Bitches looked over the edge. Darryl and Scott winked at each other and smiled. Even Stephen stepped to the edge and looked over.

"Oh no, you don't!" Gabrielle slapped both Scott and Darryl on the back of their helmets. "We aren't taking off the armor so you guys can have a distance pissing match!"

"Holy Chesticle Torch lovers," Scott griped, holding the back of his helmet. "You didn't need to beat the shit out of my head, Captain Take-away-all-our-fun!"

"Oh, fuck." Eric grimaced. "Time to get away from the opening, folks!" A rocket roared from one of the large tanks. "Head down, Bethany Anne!"

The explosion hit the side of the opening.

"I think we have their attention now," Stephen confirmed, smiling at Bethany Anne.

She walked to the edge and peeked over. "Wanking jizz-covered barnacle bitches." Bethany Anne smiled and turned to see everyone staring at her in confusion as she added, "I want one!"

John shrugged. "They have the only four I know about." He turned and counted. "Seven of us, four of them. If they aren't two-seaters or better, then I got dibs on the second."

"Me three!" Scott called at the same time Darryl did.

"Well, they are starting to come up here," Bethany Anne told the group.

"The walkers?" Stephen asked, stepping up next to her.

"Nope, the regular units," she replied. "I really miss all our supplies."

Stephen shrugged. "It's not like we can't kill them."

"Hey," Gabrielle called. Everyone turned to look at her. She pointed to the shipping container. "Can we use this?"

"Don't know why not," Bethany Anne answered. "I imagine they've gotten the message now."

Leath Automation Tank Leader Three reviewed the missile shot. "Okay, reset the missiles to attack into the opening at the top of the pyramid. They should go inside, and the blast will either kill the aliens or push them out so that we can shoot them."

"SIR!" The Tank Driver reversed, causing the ATL to fall forward since he had just disconnected his seat belt.

"What are you doing?" the leader yelled, but then saw the large container flying down at them. "DODGE!" he screamed, but it didn't matter.

It was as if the large container was falling under some sort of control, or flying.

***

"Well, that's one down, but I still get one," John commented as they watched the shipping container wipe out one of the tank-looking machines.

The three others, once they stopped trying to dodge, each released four missiles.

"That got their attention," Bethany Anne shouted as they each raced to her and held on. "New tactic. Kill the assholes!"

The team disappeared moments before seven missiles exploded on the outside of the pyramid and five exploded *inside*, wiping out the cave.

***

Quarter Military Leader Grindlock and Tholt had moved back from that damned pyramid, and they heard the Automation Tanks push through the trees. "About damned time those assholes showed up."

"Let us take the hard shit, then they come and take the glory," Tholt agreed.

"Typical," Grindlock took his helmet off and spat to the side before placing it back on his head. "We at least ran them to ground. They are stuck up on that rock and we will pummel it until they aren't much more than—"

He never saw Tholt's head explode. In fact, he never saw anything ever again after the round punctured his helmet, his brains making a mess inside his suit.

"That's two more dead," Bethany Anne commed everyone in the group. "They were just jacking their jaws, waiting to have their heads blown off."

"Sucks to be them," Eric replied.

"How are they expecting to win if they have such poor field awareness?" Stephen mused. He lifted his rifle to his shoulder and allowed the HUD to track his aiming.

Then he started shooting.

"Beats the fuck out of me." Bethany Anne kept walking determinedly toward the pyramid and the noises the mechanical tanks were making.

"Where are you going?" Stephen asked over his shoulder.

"I want one of those *Gott Verdammt* tanks!" she told him.

Inbound G'laxix Sphaea-class Warship

Lance looked at his helmet HUD. "Can you believe she and her team have destroyed over thirty-two percent of the tangos on this world?"

"Yes." Dan nodded toward a screen. "If it wasn't for the miscommunication, she would probably have taken out all of the ones around her location."

Lance didn't comment on that. He had seven ships with him, all of them loaded with Guardians, Guardian Marines, and special tactical operatives. They were three minutes from her location.

He opened a channel. "General Lance Reynolds to Empress Bethany Anne. The cavalry is about to arrive."

It took a second for Bethany Anne to reply. "Well, don't shoot us when you get here, cause that will put an exclamation mark on a piss-poor day so far."

Lance pinpointed her location. "Bethany Anne, I'm showing you and your team at the *bottom* of the pyramid. Just what the hell are you doing?"

"General, blowing these sonsabitches to kingdom-fucking-come," she answered.

"Well, I'll be damned." Dan sighed, exasperated. "Lance, you need to see this."

Lance turned to look where Dan was pointing.

Down below, three Leath mechs were turning every which way, blasting the shit out of the tangos on the ground.

"How the hell," Dan asked, "did she and her team take over those mechanicals?"

Lance shook his head. "I can imagine she used brute strength, force of will, and lots and lots of cheating by an AI and a Kurtherian," he answered.

Frank came up to the two men and looked out the window. "If you ain't cheating."

Dan and Lance finished it. "You ain't trying."

EPILOGUE

Three Weeks Later, QBBS *Meredith Reynolds*

Bethany Anne was holding John Michael and cooing. She smiled when the little guy reached up and grabbed her nose.

"Ow...ow ow ow!" She pulled her head back. "He has a hell of a grip!" She smiled at Lance and Patricia as they walked into the Royal Suite. "What's the latest, Dad?" she asked as the baby started to cry.

"The Gate has yet to return. Ricky Bobby has sent back two more reports, and frankly, we need to get our asses in gear," he told her.

Bethany Anne nodded. She handed John Michael to Patricia when she came over to her. There had never been a baby born that Patricia couldn't quiet down.

"Bethany Anne!" Her dad got her attention. She moved closer. "I want to apologize for our part in the debacle on the planet. We knew you wanted in the fight, but we felt we knew how to protect you and deal with the planet by ourselves. You probably saved twice as many lives as our plan would have, by getting them to fight away from the cities."

Bethany Anne blew out a breath. "Yes, we all handled it

poorly. I felt I needed to fight so badly that I wasn't going to take any shit from anyone. Then I got most of our weapons and ammunition flattened, and had to call for help." She chewed on her lip. "It was damned embarrassing."

Lance chuckled. "We found you and your team in stolen mechs shooting the hell out of the Leath." He eyed his daughter a moment. "Did you release the drone videos?"

Her eyes narrowed. "What videos?"

Lance spoke louder. "Meredith?"

"Yes, General Reynolds?"

"Can you put the in-system network news videos related to Bethany Anne and the battles up on the wall?"

The two of them turned to watch as Meredith played a series of seven videos detailing Bethany Anne and her team's efforts to kill the Leath.

"Who the hell authorized those to be released?" she asked.

"Cheryl Lynn," Meredith answered.

Bethany Anne put a hand over her eyes. "Of course she did."

"For what it is worth," Lance told her, "I approved it."

She never took her hand away from her eyes. "Of course you did." She opened a space between her fingers and peeked at her dad. "Why?"

"Because when you are able to negotiate from a position of strength, it helps, politically," he admitted. "And too many were forgetting the reason the Etheric Empire was created in the first place. You have to warn those we will meet in the future that we have a history of doing stuff like this." He pointed to the video.

Lance turned back to the wall. "Reynolds, show us the latest Leath video."

Bethany Anne's eyes widened when she saw the clips of the Leath planet, built up over time, and showing a city that stretched from horizon to horizon. Then she inhaled as massive space stations came into view around the planet. Moments later, warships could be seen in space, as well as many more under construction.

She turned to her father. "That's a lot of ships, Dad."

Lance agreed. "At last count, more than seventy-two had been completed and at least seven are under construction. And that is just those we can see, not counting the ships currently being used for invasions." He nodded to the images. "That's a lot of power, a lot of might."

"Do we have the location of their system?" she asked, her eyes focused on the video.

"We do."

Bethany Anne nodded. "Well then, the Etheric Empire is about to start building the shit out of ships and everything else we need to crush them."

She turned to her father, who noticed tiny red embers in the centers of her eyes. "Because they might have faith in their gods, but that faith is built on Kurtherian *lies*."

"How are you planning on explaining that?" he asked.

"Who needs to explain anything?" she replied. "They think might makes right, so I'm going to shove my size sevens up their asses until my toes tickle their tonsils and they understand what might really is."

Bethany Anne turned as Patricia came up to them. "But for tonight, Patricia and I have babysitting duty while Eric and Gabrielle enjoy their anniversary."

"And what do I have?" Lance asked.

"Diaper duty!" the ladies chorused as Bethany Anne reached for John Michael.

FINIS

MIGHT MAKES RIGHT

The Story Continues with book 18, Might Makes Right.

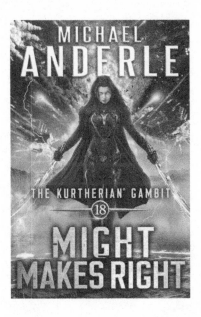

Available now at Amazon and on Kindle Unlimited

AUTHOR NOTES

Location location location...

This year, our two youngest sons graduated high school. For their graduation present, and a last 'hurrah' as a family before they go off to college, we chose to take a very long vacation in Europe. The idea was to get them accustomed to different peoples, different countries and understand THEY can be on their own in strange places.

The problem was the vacation was 19 days.

Almost three weeks.

And I was *KILLED* the last time it took me 8 weeks between books. Plus, the latest release was a Michael book which meant it was a *LONG* time between Bethany Anne books.

Ok, that meant this vacation was going to be a working vacation. Which isn't that big a deal, as I've been writing TKG books on trips since the beginning. I wrote parts of Death Becomes Her in a car trip from DFW to Louisiana (going to the Casino's...shhhh!)

I wrote parts of Queen Bitch on airplanes and in airports from DFW to Phoenix Arizona and back.

I wrote parts of Love Lost in Cabo San Lucas, Mexico (and on the plane trips there and back.)

However, this is the FIRST time I've written a book all over the world (sort of).

So, I give you parts of my itinerary where this book was written. Maybe some of you will know of these locations (or maybe I'll just go back in five years and think...was it room 1238 or room 1328???)

Here are most of the locations FOREVER DEFEND was typed out.

Chapter's 1-3 include Las Vegas, Nevada, DFW, Texas, (USA)
Then, I wrote a scene out of order...
Chapter 23 (Beginning of the defending) - Starbucks and 7th floor room - Hotel Catalonia, Barcelona, Spain.
Chapter 3 - Hotel Catelonia, 1st floor, balcony (next to the pool) #108, Barcelona, Spain.
Chapter 4 - Seawall, Port of Barcelona (Mediterranean) & Speed Train from Barcelona, To Madrid, Spain (leaving Track 02, Car #3)
Chapters 5-6 Madrid, Spain and Plane from Madrid to Roma, Italy.

SIDE NOTE:
Why The Bad Company? I was listening to the following song when it was time to name them: Five Finger Death Punch, The Wrong Side of Heaven, The Right Side of Hell Volume 01 Motherfuckers!
"I was born with a shotgun...in my hand..."

Chapters 7,8 - Rome & Train from Rome to Venice, Italy + Duodo Hotel, Venice (#604)
Chapters 9 - Plane from Venice to Paris, France (lost voice)
Chapter 10, 11, 12, 13 - Paris, France - (123 Hotel - Room 501)
Sick as a dog the last couple of days. Slept a lot, trying to catch up.

Chapter 14 - Eurostar between Paris and London
(Shi-tan scene was partially written while speeding under the English Channel)
Chapters 15,16 - Park Plaza Hotel, Westminster Bridge suite 1328
Chapter 17 - (first part done in DFW, Texas in May
later two scenes done in Taxi from London to Surrey, and trian from Surrey back to London
Chapters 18-23
Flight from London to DFW, Texas
Chapters 24, 25 were both written at home on Monday, June 26th
(while suffering a little bit from jet-lag. ;-)

I want to take a moment and THANK THE HELL out of all of you who are writing reviews on any and all books (whether a Kurtherian Book or another author, anywhere and anytime.) We appreciate what you do! *(Yes, we read them and weep sometimes, but that's the way the cookie crumbles.)*

I want to thank the Beta Readers, Editors and JIT team for their support, working in the background to help produce a book with WAY fewer mistakes. I keep the credit for any that are still in the story. If you find one, we take 'oops' at readershelp@kurtherianbooks.com.

If you have read the Ascension Series...You know this isn't the final series for Bethany Anne - she has one more to go ... just saying.

Now, to get started on Might Makes Right - The Kurtherian Gambit #18!

*** I haven't said this in a while, but here goes: "Any and all shoe knowledge credit goes to my wife, because without her, I would be lost trying to explain anything about Bethany Anne and shoes..."

Written July 1st, 2017

BOOKS BY MICHAEL ANDERLE

Sign up for the LMBPN email list to be notified of new releases and special deals!

https://lmbpn.com/email/

For a complete list of books by Michael Anderle, please visit:

www.lmbpn.com/ma-books/

CONNECT WITH THE AUTHOR

Connect with Michael Anderle

Website: http://lmbpn.com

Email List: https://michael.beehiiv.com/

https://www.facebook.com/LMBPNPublishing

https://twitter.com/MichaelAnderle

https://www.instagram.com/lmbpn_publishing/

https://www.bookbub.com/authors/michael-anderle

Made in the USA
Las Vegas, NV
01 June 2024

90616635R00173